REMINISCENCE: Lost Souls

By Rose Marie

ISBN-10 061553484

ISBN-13 978-0-615-53484-8

Reminiscence: Lost Souls

by Rose Marie Skinner

Published by:

Rose Marie Publishing

rndskinner@comcast.net

Self-Published

21 Burns Plaza

Palmyra, Virginia 22963

This book is dedicated to my three lovely children; they are my best work.

Gabriella Harley

Graceanne Skinner

Tristian Skinner

Thank You

When I started this book two years ago it was barely a glimmer of an idea, more of a strong thought. It came into my mind one fall evening. I can barely remember exactly how it all started, but I do remember thinking it was going to be easy. Little did I know that the effort and time involved would be tremendous.

Throughout this period, not only did I have lots of inspiration, but an overwhelming amount of support from a wide range of people. I'd like to take this time to specially thank some individuals who made a difference on my path to completion. After my two fabulous editors and cover artists, the names are in alphabetical order.

Becky Blanton, my primary editor and writing coach. We hammered out the hows and whys of dialogue and so much more over Subway sandwiches and pizza.

Sarah Smith, for capturing the cover art perfectly and making me feel like I could step into the cover photo and be on the beach in seconds. Incredible art!

Denice Thibodeau, my final editor and proofreader. Denice is not only a great Scrabble player, but an incredible comma chaser and detail-driven proofreader!

~

Daryl Hammond, information on military background and a look into what it takes to become a sniper in which helped me to create Sam's Character.

Tiffany Kelly, who took time to review the manuscript and give me such great feedback on my first rough drafts. I can't tell you how rewarding it is to have someone take time to read and offer honest feedback.

Howard Lagomarsino, a fire investigator for Fluvanna County here in Virginia. Howard is a true professional and a gifted investigator. He helped me with the realistic information I needed to describe the fire and arson scenes and to understand the mindset of the arsonist.

Jerry Shank, who was instrumental in helping me learn all I needed to know about the handling of a handgun, gun safety and how to teach someone to fire a handgun. Thanks to him, my gun-handling scenes rock!

David Skinner, my husband, my rock and support throughout my adventure in making my dream of writing my first book a reality. Thank you David for "Playing for Pizza" and the arrangements you made for the experience of learning how to fire a handgun. The time, effort and energy I spent through this entire process, and your help with it, I will never forget.

Greg Sluiter, for suggesting the subtitle to the book and for his expert background and knowledge about military training. His input also helped me create Sam's character.

Will Thomas, for his inspiring details and his passion for sailing, ship terminology and life on the open sea. Will, you made my sailboat feel like a home and not just a setting. You helped me capture the soul of the Franciska!

Patricia Zinnanti, a friend and a natural witch. Patricia brought to life the characteristics of a natural witch with descriptions and in depth discussions about what being a witch is, and isn't. Her candle making help and descriptions are displayed prominently in the chapter on Candles and More and her tips, help and suggestions made the shop where my character gets her fresh start come alive.

Last, but certainly not least or in alphabetical order, thank you **Facebook Fanpage fans** for your constant support and praise and your relentlessly hounding me with questions about, "When's it gonna be done, when's it gonna be done?" It's finally done, damnit. I hope you're happy!

Table of Contents

Foreword by Becky Blanton

I'm so happy to be part of this book and how it came about. I met Rose while doing business with her boss and continued to see her around the office and to talk to her from time to time. We were talking about books and publishing one day and she asked if I knew of anyone who edited books. I said, "I do. I'm a small publisher and writing coach."

Funny how the most obvious solutions are sometimes right under your nose. We began weekly meetings to talk about dialogue, story lines and plot. I'm a ghost writer, but this is all Rose's story. I mostly coached and gave her feedback and worked with Denice on editing, formatting and cover layout.

I didn't have to do much. Rose was determined, creative and figured out how to bring the realism she wanted to her story. It's been a joy working with her and waiting impatiently for the next chapter and the next because I got caught up in wanting to know "what happens next?" just like you're going to as you read it.

This is the first in what we both hope are a series of books about Effie, the psychically gifted, crime-solving lawyer. They're books about love, crime, mystery and relationships. I thoroughly enjoyed Reminiscence and I think you will too.

"Be more concerned with your character than your reputation,

because your character is what you really are,

while your reputation is merely what others think you are."

— John Wooden

PROLOGUE

The rat bastards just wouldn't let up. All four of them were shooting spit wads at the back of his head as he heard laughter bellow from the back of the bus. It was the same four boys, day after day. He hated the sixth grade already, and the added taunting didn't help.

"Why me?" he asked himself. He was quiet, did his work, stayed out of trouble and never said shit to those guys. He was a little shorter than most of the kids and a little rounder too. It didn't help that his mother always dressed him in the Kmart blue-light special clothing and "husky" jeans. What was she thinking? You think she would know better.

He looked out the window. She needed the money for her own clothes, for the men in her life who meant more than he did. He kept his mouth shut. He never told, just like she told him to do. They were rat bastards too, all of them. He didn't always keep his door closed, so he knew. He knew.

"Where's your momma? Bastard. Your momma's a whore! A whore!"

Embarrassment burned through him, ripping his heart open before plunging a knife deep into his core. He didn't move.

"Boys! Connor, Reggie, Alex, Andy! That's not nice. Now apologize!"

"But, Miss Thacker, his mother is a whore." The laughter was harsher than it had ever been.

"Apologize!"

"We're sorry you're so fat and your mother's a whore, fatboy," the group said.

Miss Thacker rolled her eyes and turned to the sullen boy behind her.

"Sweetie, I'm sorry. They don't mean it. Just ignore them," she said.

The bus hadn't come to a complete stop before he made his way from his seat to the front door. Miss Thacker stopped reassuring him and turned to scolding him, telling him to sit back down, but he kept moving. He didn't care anymore. He left the bus as quickly as he could, but knew deep down inside that getting home after school from now on was going to be a whole 'nother ball game. Everything, he said to himself, was going to be a whole other ball game.

Head bent over to his notebook, he stressed throughout the entire day of school and spent another lunch hour sitting at a table with a boy whose grease from his hair rolled into his food. He had decided to walk home from school today even if it would take him more than two hours to do so.

He waited after school until the buses rolled out and headed out on foot. He passed the house of Connor, asshole number one. Saw his fancy BMX bike in the front yard. He grabbed the knife from his backpack and shredded the BMX tires, seat and cut his brake lines.

An odd and newly satisfying warmth spread through him. He felt great. Vindicated. So much so that he went out of the way to visit Ronnie's house too. No one was home. He suspected everyone was at after school soccer practice.

There was nothing to cut apart in Ronnie's yard, so he broke the window to Ronnie's bedroom, climbed up on the flower box, into the house and into Ronnie's room and pissed all over his bed. He went down to the dining room and dropped his pants and took a crap on the dining room table, then used a kitchen mitt to spread it around the table and on the walls.

He was Superman now. The adrenaline rush had kicked him into overdrive. Lastly, Alex and Andy's house, assholes three and four. A knife across the throat of their dog took care of them as he stood and licked the blood off of the blade. Yep. This was going to be a whole new ballgame.

CHAPTER ONE

Remembrance

I didn't like his thick, soft hands, or his manicured nails. What real man gets his damn nails manicured and clear nail polish added to them? I didn't like his attitude and I sure as hell didn't like his assumption that I was the law firm's personal call girl.

"Richard, zip your pants up," I said. Richard Tattenbaum, CEO of Healy Motors, had come back from the men's room with his zipper up. As he sat down and edged closer to me on the circular bench the zipper came down.

"You've hurt my feelings, Francisca," he said with a frown.

"That's not all I'm going to hurt, Dick," I smiled coldly. I hadn't wanted to do bankruptcy law to begin with, but with each case I was learning more and more that money meant control, and not in a good way. With each bankruptcy case I won I noticed the rich got richer and the poor got screwed. I never thought I would ever hate law, but I was wrong. Seeing how the rich manipulated the system to just get richer made me sick. Having to tolerate not only their greed, but their leering and groping, while I worked on their cases made it worse.

Damn it. As an assistant attorney for Dillard & Bentley, the largest law firm handling corporate bankruptcies in Michigan, I didn't go to lunch with clients to have my ass grabbed and my clients flashing me. But what really ticked me off was having Derrick Bentley, the senior partner say, "Oh, come on Franciska. Couldn't you just lead him on a little bit? We really wanted that account. What's a little harmless flirting? Let the man grab your ass."

I probably should have given a month's notice, but Bentley's comments, captured for posterity with my cell phone's "record" feature, and then my cell phone photo of Richard's penis in his hand at one of the swankest restaurants in Michigan, plus my threat to post them both to my Facebook page, seemed to eradicate the need for a notice.

I no longer had a job, but I did have a hefty "early retirement" package and a very generous departure bonus in exchange for promising to deep six the photo and recording. I also had something I hadn't had in a while— my freedom. Now it was time to use them.

I slid the sunroof open on my black Lexus ES 350 and tossed my cell phone on the back seat. I let the sun hit my face and the cool Michigan air run through my long dark hair as I left Ann Arbor for the first and the last time. I felt no remorse for my quick and unexpected exit and yet I felt no glee for the new adventure that lay ahead of me. I felt nothing at all. Feeling this numb was not something that I was accustomed to.

I blamed my job and partially blamed myself for taking it. In the past, it was either a proposal (twice) or live-in (three times) that would cause me to take flight, but this time it was my job. My mom always said that it was the "Gypsy" in me that would never allow me to stay in one place, and she was probably right. But then again, I was also coming into myself, who I was, what I wanted. I was tired of taking crap from the rich and moneyed monsters I encountered on a daily basis at the law firm. I wanted something, or maybe someone, real. I wanted something I couldn't buy with money. I wanted freedom. I had learned from the best to go after what I wanted, no matter what it was. I learned from my mom.

My mom was a single mother and she moved a lot. Growing up in one place, staying around one town, one house, one school for very long just didn't happen. I had attended nine different schools and that was just the times I could remember. I never met my father. Mom said he left us before I was even born. My grandparents filled the gap and almost assumed the role of parents, so the fact that my father wasn't in my life didn't bother me much. I was always very close to them, partially because of that reason alone.

My grandfather was a tall, slim man, with a wiry build, a full head of wavy gray hair and a thin dark mustache. His name was Tiborc Varga. Tiborc is a Hungarian name, given to him by his father when he was born near the Tiber River. Everyone called him "Tiber" because it was just easier to say. He was kind of a nut, too. Telling jokes was something he was good at and laughter always filled our home. He had a way of taking an ugly situation and poking fun at it so it wasn't so bad. I can still hear Grandma saying, "Tiber, be serious for a change, would you?"

We would laugh when she would say that because her accent made it sound like she was calling him, "Tiger." Grandfather was, as they say, "old school." He kind of reminded me of old slapstick comedy with a touch of Benny Hill. Yes, his humor was slightly risqué, too. I really loved how he loved life.

I think one of my fondest memories of my grandfather, besides his love for his wife, was his ability to tell a great story. He would fill his glass with scotch, Johnny Walker Black, and ease himself into his favorite green Lazy Boy. He would take a long slow drink, lick his lips, skootch to the edge of the chair and lean forward as if to whisper a secret. Then he would say, "I have a story for you and it goes like this."

It was the only time I ever saw him so serious. He always captured my interest; every story was different and so alive, and told it like he had lived it personally. When I was young, they were just stories; but as I grew older, I began to question how much truth there was to them. How much truth, how much story, how much scotch, I wondered.

As a young man, he was a fisherman by day and a violinist at night. He married my grandmother when she was just fifteen. They belonged to a small nomadic group of people that traveled Eastern Europe and would entertain along the way. We know them as "Gypsies," or "Roma." My grandmother, Franciska—a Hungarian name that means "free"—read tarot cards to supplement their income.

Well, she did more than just read them. It was rumored that she really didn't read the cards but could read people's futures when she touched them. She was very spiritual and always had a bit of mystery to her. I was named Francisca after my grandmother, and my mother said I always took after her in other ways, too. They had both passed away several years ago and I was always sad that I never put their stories to paper. Out on the road there was time to think and thinking about family always brought back great memories.

"Thank you, Grandma. Thank you, Grandpa. Thank you, Richard Tattenbaum," I hollered at the top of my lungs, wind blowing through my hair. Thank goodness I was free again. Free at last. Now the numbness was finally beginning to wear off. I hoped by the end of the day it would be gone entirely.

I followed 23 south until I came to the Ohio Turnpike and then pulled over on the side of the road. I opened the wooden box my grandfather had carved for me when I was a little girl, and took out my tarot cards. The box was a deep red and he had burned a river onto the top of the lid. It was supposed to mean "free river," which was how he thought of himself with his soul mate, my grandmother.

I held my tarot deck to my heart and thought to myself, "When I come to the Queen of Wheels, I'll let that card determine my direction." I started with the top card and flipped them onto the seat beside me, one at a time.

"South, east, west, south, east, west" and kept going until I saw my card—south! I put the cards carefully back into the box and headed on my way. Somehow I already knew I was headed south, but I just had to make sure. I wanted to put as much distance between me and the law firm as I could, but I was also tired of the dark, dreary, long Michigan winters. I wanted sunshine no matter what the temperature.

Living in Michigan was nice, don't get me wrong. It's a state loaded with lakes and there's always some kind of activity to do, but I swear that out of the three hundred and sixty five days of the year only sixty contained sunshine. It was kind of fun letting the cards tell me what direction to take and since I had no clue as to where I was headed, I was game to listen.

I decided that at each major turning point in the road, I would simply let the cards decide which way I would go. It had been a long time since I had taken them out of the box, let alone used them. I used to read the cards for my friends all the time, but after a while I quit because someone either got scared, became angry or purposely tried to change their direction, just as I did when I took the job that I was now leaving behind.

I had done my time in college and then gone on to law school. I had sent fifteen resumes out and had interviewed with several firms. The one that really wanted me was a firm called Dillard & Bentley. They made me a nice offer, but I still wasn't sure, so I read my cards. The cards told me this was not the right path. The cards don't usually lie.

Like many others who do the opposite of what the cards say, I took the job anyhow. Bankruptcy and the greedy, self-serving rich who used it to deepen their own pockets at the expense of small businesses had definitely ended up not being, as my mother would say, my cup of tea. Dillard & Bentley always reminded me that the name poking fun at attorneys, "Dewey Cheetum and Howe," was based in reality.

After five years of fending off passes and horny old men, and watching rich people erase their debt and get richer with my help, I was done. Richard Tattenbaum was just the final nail in my employment coffin. I felt like I belonged on the proverbial bus going over the proverbial cliff with one empty seat. I did my job well, though.

That's what I was trained to do; it was in my blood. No matter what I chose to do in life, I always did it very, very well. I also chose to save money and to save enough money to run, which was something else I knew how to do well. The severance and bonus package made my flight even easier. I smiled at the memory of the obscene number of zeros on the bonus check. What goes around comes around, I thought. The rich had finally paid for their abuses.

I followed Interstate 75 south through Dayton and then Cincinnati, and stopped in a rest area about forty miles past Lexington, Kentucky. It was definitely warmer now and I was glad to have the cold March air behind me.

I opened the door and grabbed my lunch and my pack of cigarettes. Smoking was a habit I wanted to kick, but now was not the time. I sat at a picnic table overlooking a lush green valley loaded with wildflowers and tall pine trees in the distance. Taking a deep breath, I wondered if life could get any better than this—being free, single and on a new path.

I thought about stopping right there but I could feel that it wasn't the right place. I could feel it and now I was not only asking myself questions but was answering them, too. This would be the perfect time to call my mom and let her know all was okay. It would sure beat the hell out of talking to myself. Instead, I took out my cards and began to read them again.

I didn't even so much as get them laid out on the table when a young woman, maybe in her early 20s, asked me if I was reading tarot cards. She was about five and a half feet tall with a slim build and square shoulders, probably wore about a size three compared to my size ten. She had long, blond, wavy hair and was with her boyfriend, traveling to meet his parents in Louisville. He was slim, like her, but a couple of inches taller. He was wearing a baseball cap, but I could still make out his sandy brown hair; that and his blue eyes were a combination I had always liked.

"Yes," I said. The young woman introduced herself.

"My name is Kim. Would you have enough time to read mine? I will pay you, of course." She explained that she was very nervous about meeting her boyfriend's parents because they were very wealthy and her family was not. I thought to myself, this is my opportunity to save her from the evils of money. I could always lie and tell her this was not the direction for her. No, no I couldn't. I wasn't a person who could do that. Money, ugh, I hated almost everything about it.

"Have a seat, Kim; I'll do it for free."

The young man was very skeptical and I could tell he was making her uneasy, so I asked him, "Do you mind if we do this first set without you here?" He told Kim that he would grab them some sodas from the vending machine and hesitantly walked away.

I looked at Kim and asked, "What do you really want to know?" She was immediately taken aback.

"What do you mean?" Kim asked me.

"It's not just the money that bothers you; there's something more, and I feel it."

"Something more?"

"Yes, Kim, you have uneasy written all over you."

"It shows that much?"

"Maybe not to everyone else, but I can read your energy very well."

"When you sit with me to have your cards read, you have to be honest and open-minded."

Kim's eyes watered. "I have been with my boyfriend for two years and I want to know where our future is headed."

"Ahhhh, that's what I thought. Well then, let's begin."

I placed all the cards on the table and one of her rings in the middle of the cards. The ring would represent the querent, Kim. A querent is the person who is having their cards read and it is customary to have a token of the querent placed in the middle of the layout. This has always been the way I read the cards, just like my grandmother used to. I used a layout called Sevens. This is where I would place eleven cards in a row, each card being chosen by counting the seventh card from the top of the deck. Each seventh card would be placed next to the card prior until eleven cards in total were lined across the table. Each card represented a time line.

"First card," I said. "This tells about the forces in your past that you're no longer concerned with." It was the King of Knives. "An older man is in your past. He was a dominant person in your life. He was tall, with dark hair and dark eyes; a man of power and authority and intelligence."

Just then a breeze came through the picnic area and began to lift the cards. I threw my hands over them quickly to keep them from changing order. The thumb on my left hand touched the ring and I saw a flash in my head. It was a tall, dark-haired man with a heavy build standing over a tiny, blond-haired girl; she couldn't have been more than five years old. In his hand was an old, broken fishing pole with a cork handle, but no reel. Just then the image went away.

I looked up at Kim and said, "Did your father used to beat you with a broken fishing pole?" Kim gasped, horror filled her eyes and her skin went pale.

"It's been a long time," Kim said. "The horror lasted for about three years, from what I can remember, anyhow. One blessed night he drank too much, ran his car off the road and died. How did you know about him?"

"I got a vision and it's very hard for me to explain it to you."

"Did you see my mother?"

"No; has she passed too?"

"I really don't know what became of her. I have often wondered, though."

"I don't understand."

"After my dad died, she shut herself off from the whole world and me too. She dropped me off at a friend's house one day and never came back. From there I was thrown in 'the system,' but, lucky for me, I ended up in a really good foster home. They are wonderful people and they gave me a nice home."

"I'm so sorry to hear this about your parents, Kim. I'm glad, though, that you were well taken care of."

"One never forgets the pain," she said softly.

"Do you want me to go on?" I asked. She quietly gave me the okay with a short nod.

I went through the rest of the cards with ease now, confirming that her boyfriend, who was represented by the Page of Staves card, was taking her to meet his parents. The cards were right. When I came across the card signifying travel, which was located in the "forces at work now" placement in the layout, I could see there was more than just physical travel for Kim. She, too, was on a personal journey.

"There's some importance to this trip. I'm reading, or seeing signs of, something symbolic. There's something that represents family and fertility." I paused, wondering what this trip meant for her and how it might mirror my own flight south.

The next card was the Justice Card. With that, I thought for sure that marriage was in Kim's immediate future, along with the possibility of relocating or traveling near a large body of water following the wedding. I kept seeing San Diego in my head, but she was clueless as to why San Diego might be a destination. Maybe all of this was why her boyfriend didn't feel that this card reading would be a good idea. It wasn't skepticism, I realized. He was concerned that I might be able to see what was coming and spoil the surprise he had planned. I think it did. I asked Kim if she understood her reading.

"Does it feel right? Make sense?"

She smiled, "I think I understand what you're saying. I really needed this and it was fun. Thank you so much."

"Do you have any more questions?" I asked.

"No," she said again, looking happy about the reading.

Kim nodded at her boyfriend, who was leaning against a tree not far away. He was looking kind of funny as he feebly attempted to snatch bugs out of the air as he waited. Seeing we were finished, he walked over and asked, "How did it go?" Kim told him that she appreciated him staying a little longer and that the reading was uplifting.

She tried again to pay me, but I told her, "No, thank you; it was a pleasant break from many hours spent on the road." It was too. I hesitated, and then reached for my purse.

"Before you leave, let me give you my card. It's old—I don't work here anymore—but the cell number at the bottom is still good. You might have questions down the road and if you do, please feel free to give me a call. I know that sometimes I'll have a conversation with someone, then be thinking about them later and say, 'I wish I had said this,' or, 'I wish I had said that.' You know what I mean. If something comes to mind, or you want to talk about something from the reading coming to fruition, call me!"

"Thank you so much. I will."

"Take care and have a safe trip!"

I watched them walk away, hand–in–hand, and thought how nice it would be to find love again. Maybe this time I would try to stick around wherever I landed. I gathered my things and slowly walked to the car. It was time to head to Tennessee. That's where I would stay the night and get some rest. It was also where Interstate 40 meets Interstate 75, where I planned to let the cards guide me again.

As I drove, I replayed what just happened in my mind. I had never had a vision like that before. I always operated on intuition and reading someone's energy. It's hard to explain to people. I let the cards guide me and my mind closes the deal, but I'd never experienced anything like this. I grabbed my cigarettes and took out a Camel Menthol Light. A few drags would help. I inhaled deeply, letting my whole body fill with the clean minty tobacco, and exhaled with a feeling of contentment.

"It was her ring," I thought. I knew my grandmother could do this by touching the person. The only difference is that grandmother saw the future and I just saw the past. I was thinking about whether I'd ever have such a clear reading again, when the loud vibration of the rumble strips on the side of the road caught my immediate attention.

"No more daydreaming for me," I said to myself. But that was impossible; I was on the road to somewhere and nowhere. What else is there to do beside think? I thought of ways my life could be different. I thought about how much fun it was to give someone hope, and the feeling of complete satisfaction from doing so.

"I need to simplify," I said to myself. For the past ten years my life had been so fast-paced. I had schedules on top of schedules. I was always surrounded by high-powered people and their material possessions. Their stuff overwhelmed me and, worse, it seemed like it started to latch onto me. I hated it and I was done with it. No more superficial people and no more superficial things. Before I knew it, I was in Tennessee. I pulled into a Holiday Inn Express for the evening. I didn't need five-star accommodations, just a good bed and a good night's sleep.

The next morning I awoke with the same enthusiasm as the day before. I took a quick shower and checked out, but not without grabbing a hot cup of black coffee and a donut from the small complementary breakfast set up in the lobby. It was a cloudy day. I stood at the hood of my car, with my cards held next to my heart again, and said to myself, "When I come to the Eight of Cups card, this is the direction I will travel."

The Eight of Cups represents the leaving of material success for new roads. I quickly turned the cards: east, south, west, east, south, west, and east, and then, "South it is!" I continued on Interstate 75 until Knoxville was in my rearview mirror. It was a beautiful place, but I knew it wasn't the place for me. What was the place for me? I knew one thing: I was in search of the opposite of the life I had been living and grown accustomed to, one that had gone against everything I believed in. My mind began to drift again. What kind of person does it take to leave everything and everyone familiar to find something new, something fresh, and a make complete new start? It takes me, Franciska Marie Varga.

This thought reminded me of a night out on the town with some co-workers a few years back. We were sitting at the Gandy Dancer, sipping on cosmopolitans and discussing our futures. After hearing about all the superficial dreams, I blurted out, "I want to disappear someday." Not surprisingly, Clare burst out laughing. Clare had a one-track mind, which included mansions, yachts and trips to Paris.

"Why would anyone want to disappear, unless they disappeared into a rich man's life," she'd laughed.

It was my turn to laugh now, and I did. I thought, "Clare will never achieve her dream, although she plays the part and wants it badly enough." Clare was one of those that lacked the smarts and ambition to obtain it herself, and she didn't possess the looks to land that kind of a fish either. Did I have what it took to reach my dream of disappearing? I was about to find out.

As I neared Atlanta, another fast-paced, high-dollar city, the temperature outside rose. Although Atlanta was warmer, which was to my liking, it wasn't a small town by any stretch of the imagination. I had to make some decisions soon, before I ended up driving off of Key West. Being in Georgia was nice, though. It brought back some more memories. I swear this was a trip down memory lane, a trip of remembrance and longing.

Georgia was known for its peaches, and now I could practically smell the peach pies that were baked in my grandmother's kitchen. It had been my mother's favorite and mine. Grandma served it to us hot with a scoop of vanilla ice cream and cinnamon sprinkled on top. My grandmother loved to bake and peach pies were her favorite, but she could only do it when I was around.

Grandmother had a problem: she hated touching the fuzz on the peach. I understood, because I had my own pet peeves; peeves as annoying as the sound of someone running their fingernails across a blackboard.

So I would peel the peaches for Grandma. I was pretty good at it, too. By the time I was eight years old, we were baking ten pies a day to sell at the country farmers market. The memory was reassuring in some way, telling me I was on the right track.

I exited Interstate 75 near Juliette and pulled into a Shell station to get gas. After I finished filling the tank, I pulled my car into a small parking area. "Juliette, Georgia," I said to myself. I think that's where they filmed Fried Green Tomatoes. I'll have to look that up when I get some time to sit at my computer. Meanwhile, I pulled out my atlas to get a better idea about where I was. I liked Georgia right then, liked the warmth of the sun and liked the thought of making peach pies again.

I took a long look at the map and made my decision. It wasn't hard. I was one of those people that used word associations to help in making decisions like this. I grabbed my atlas and hurried into the car so fast that I shut my hair in the door. I laughed to myself and set myself free. "That settles it for sure," I giggled as I darted off to the highway.

Fourteen more miles to go, the sign read. I was getting excited, and I was somewhat relieved, too. It had been two long days. I was tired and excited all at the same time, if that made sense. I sipped my Frappuccino and took a deep breath. I could smell salty air now. I rolled down all my windows and took another long, deep breath. The air was warm but crisp. It was ocean air and that meant clean, refreshing and relaxing.

"Well, if I am going to start fresh, let's start with this," I thought. I grabbed my cigarettes off the passenger seat and dumped the remaining smokes in my hand. In one quick motion, my hand jetted up through the sunroof and they were airborne. That was littering and I felt bad about it, but not ashamed.

I had come to the final miles of my journey by car. The road in was long and there was marshy land on either side of me. It reminded me of the time I made a trip to the Florida Keys and drove through the Everglades; the only thing missing here, of course, were the alligators, and those I could definitely do without! I was nearing the bridge in to town. It was an awesome sight. The sun was beaming down and dancing off of the bridge cables. It was a picturesque sight, and most definitely an image to capture. I veered off the road and parked long enough to take a photograph and admire the view, burning it into my mind.

The top of the bridge tower looked as if it was forty stories tall and the cables streaming down reminded me of the pictures we used to make as kids, with nails in a board and thread strung around them to form an image. String Art! That's what we called it when I was in grade school. I always created the same picture of a sailboat. Maybe because it was easy and maybe because of other reasons, but this bridge was much like my picture.

It was called The Sidney Lanier Bridge. Going over it was just as much fun as seeing it for the first time. It arched upward for what seemed like a mile, but I knew it was much less, maybe half a mile. I was climbing quickly and before I knew it I had come to the top of the bridge and could see out over the harbor town.

I could see everything from fishing boats and sailboats to shrimp boats heading in with their catch. Soon I found myself chasing the sun's rays and the smell of a new day, a new town and hopes of a bright new start for me. There it was! The city limits sign. It was like a breath of fresh air. It was a breath of fresh air.

The sign read, "Welcome to Brunswick."

CHAPTER TWO

Meetings

Brunswick was the name of the company that my grandfather worked for when we lived in Lake Forest, Illinois. My mother had lost her job in Michigan when the company that she worked for moved to Mexico. She didn't have very many skills to start anew without financial help. My mom always talked about how rough the 1980s were, so we packed up and moved in with my grandparents.

It was only the two of us, so it wasn't that hard to do. My grandparents were doing quite well, residing in a very comfortable house in a quiet subdivision, and they actually seemed quite glad to have us.

The house was at the end of a cul-de-sac, with a large back yard and a tree house that my grandfather built for me when he learned that we were coming. There was also a clearing further back from my tree house, in the left rear corner of the yard.

He had set the corner aside as his future boat-building pad. My grandfather had been a fisherman once and, like all fishermen, fell in love with boats, all kinds of boats. He always loved wood sailboats the best, and worked for a boat-building company after he stopped working as a fisherman.

I was very small then, maybe six or seven, so I don't remember all the details. It was in the mid to late 1980s that he started working for Brunswick in the quality control department, but he missed being a boat builder. When I left for college, he began building a boat in the backyard. His dream was to sail into the sunset with his beloved. Only a year later, my grandmother passed away. After three long months of grieving for her, he followed her.

I think it was depression that took him, or the loneliness of being without his best friend. The boat was never finished. It sat in the backyard for the longest time, until Richard, one of his coworkers and a friend from his old fishing days, called my mother to see how he was coming along with the boat.

She ended up giving him the unfinished boat. He completed it in two years, sails and all. Richard named the boat Franciska and sent me a picture of her for Christmas of 2001; she was absolutely stunning. The memories and feelings washed over me again as I thought about.

So, here I was in Brunswick, Georgia. Everything inside of me was telling me this is where I'm supposed to be. My time has changed, I have changed and my time to follow my heart has begun.

I followed the signs to Brunswick Historical Downtown. It was beautiful. The city had obviously been working on restoring its buildings and roads for quite some time. The downtown area was small and quaint, and paved throughout with cobblestones. The buildings, mostly constructed of brick and block walls, were only two stories high.

The windows were tall and narrow, and each building had a green and white striped awning that covered about half of the sidewalk. The nose-in parking places slanted toward the front of each storefront. It was a small thing, but I liked it because I have never been a fan of parallel parking.

Planter boxes in the front of every store were filled with bright yellow, orange and red flowers. Palm trees lined the center of Newcastle Street, which was the main street. They were the only things that divided the two directions of traffic. I wish I could tell you what types of palm trees they were, but I didn't grow up around them.

That's okay, I told myself. I now have time to learn about all the different kinds of palm trees. The palms were tall and slim, reaching toward the downtown buildings' second story windows in height. They had a large bulb near the top of the palms, just below the fronds. The fronds didn't resemble the fan-type palm I was used to seeing, but were long and narrow with shorter and thinner leaves, maybe six to eight inches long. Familiar or not, they were pleasant to look at.

I parked my car in front of a small hardware store and decided to get out and walk around for a bit. There were two things that I needed tonight: a place to lay my head and somewhere to eat. One thing I learned very early in life was that word of mouth was always the best form of advertisement—and I liked to talk.

I didn't anticipate any problems finding either food or a safe and welcoming bed. I followed the sidewalk north until I came upon a small candle store. I stood there for a moment, noticing that the salty air was covered with another scent. I was now breathing the earthy scent of patchouli that was wafting out through the windows. I have always loved that smell, so I decided to go in.

The entrance was a large, heavy wooden door with an antique glass doorknob. It was a very rich mahogany color and looked like it weighed a ton. Near the top of the door was a small, thick-paned, round window with an etched design of different shaped squares in the center. Artsy I thought. The name of the shop was "Candles and More."

I opened the door and bells chimed like it was Christmas. Swinging from the backside of the door was a long brown leather strap with eight heavy brass jingle bells. My eyes lit up immediately. Patchouli may have caught my attention outside, but inside the scent of lilac incense and a hint of coconut oil filled the air. The shop was long and narrow, like an ally in an old Italian city. The floor was made of old, refinished wood planks.

On the high walls hung many oil paintings by an artist I wasn't familiar with. They were paintings of different cities from around the world. The lines weren't crisp, but blended so the paintings almost looked blurry, as if you were seeing the city's reflection in water.

There were shelves and shelves of candles. The shelves were made of glass and the cases had a mirrored backing, so depending on where you stood, it appeared that the candles disappeared into the wall and there were twice as many candles than you thought at first glance. All the candles were placed according to scent and size. The larger carved ones were on the lower shelves and the votives and tapers were on the top shelves. Each section was unique to scent.

Next to the candles were a variety of fresh potpourri, incense, bath and body oils, salts and other items containing the same scent as the candles in that section. In the center of the shop, reaching all the way to the rear of the building, were antique bookshelves, lined side-by-side and stuffed from edge to edge with books you wouldn't find in a normal public library. Every book was cultural to some degree. There were books on different foods, music, myths and fables, boats, the arts, magic and spells, religion and sex and even on how to read tarot cards. I stopped right there and stared in amazement at the entire section. That's when I heard a soft voice from behind the counter: "Can I help you find something?"

"No thank you," I replied. But all the reading material aroused my curiosity. This was definitely not your ordinary candle shop.

I approached the young lady sitting behind the counter. "Hello?" I peeked down to see that she was unwrapping some very unique crystal balls.

"Oh! I'm sorry. What can I help you with?"

"My name is Franciska and I just arrived here today. I am looking for a place to stay until I can find a job and an apartment or house to rent."

The woman stood up with a lovely smile on her face and held out her hand. She was about medium height and slim, with shoulder length, light sandy brown hair that had warm golden blonde streaks atop dark brown eyes. Her skin was very tanned and covered with sun-kissed freckles. I reached out to shake her hand and noticed her near-perfect French manicured fingernails and the several bracelets that hung from her wrist.

She said, "Welcome to our town! My name is Paisley, or Pea to my friends," she winked.

She shook my hand. The moment I touched her hand, flashes of light began to swirl in my head, stars and planets, along with charts and graphs at a drafting table. Pea was there, pencil in hand, counting days on the calendar, but not on an ordinary calendar. I dropped her hand quickly, almost as if I just touched a hot stove. There it was again—a look into someone's life

"Are you okay?" she asked me.

"Oh, I'm fine; just a little cramp from driving all day," I replied. She didn't seem convinced.

Maybe I just needed to change the subject.

"Pea? What an unusual nickname."

"Yeah, it's kind of a funny story. When I was a kid, I had a slight speech problem, so when I would ask for things, I would say Pea want this or Pea want that. From then on out, everyone referred to me as Pea."

I smiled, "That's cute, and I like it. Then you have to call me Effie; deal?"

"That will work just fine for me too."

With that said, I explained to Pea what I was looking for. I was hoping to find a small bed and breakfast in a quiet neighborhood close to town. Pea took out a small black box and began looking through some business cards. She pulled one out and handed it to me. The paper was stiff, the font old-fashioned, and showed a drawing of a very ornate Victorian house on the front. It read, "Peach Tree Manor, Bed and Breakfast, Owners: Liz and Ryan Stringer."

I set my purse on the counter to take out my cell phone and place a call to the Stringers, when my ring caught a tiny piece of loose fabric in the purse, pulling it off the counter and sending it tumbling to the floor. In one fell swoop, my life was scattered on the plank floor along with my lipstick and perfume.

Pea came around the counter to help me pick up some of my items that had fallen. She noticed the wooden box lying sideways, half open with three tarot cards edging out. I didn't notice whether she had seen them, but was almost immediately embarrassed.

I quickly threw everything back in my purse, grabbed my phone and stood up to make the call, squeezing out a quick "Thank you" in the midst of all the motion. I dialed the number on the card and Liz Stringer had answered the phone. The conversation was short and to the point. She had a room. I told her that I would see her in an hour and put my phone away.

"What kind of work do you do?" Pea asked.

"I'm a lawyer, but I'm looking to make a change in my life, wanting to do something different. I've spent too much of my life fighting for rich people who want to keep their wealth at the expense of the poor, and now I just want simplicity and quiet," I replied.

"How would you like to read people their cards?"

Ah, so she did see the tarot cards that fell from my purse. I was hoping to keep that part of my life a bit quiet. Then again, what was I thinking? I wanted a new start, a fresh start, and something very different.

"I have never done readings for money, only for fun and entertainment."

"I think that's what the customers come here for; many don't take the reading seriously. It's kind of a strange coincidence, don't you think?"

"What's that?" I asked.

"The fact that you showed up from nowhere and I'm looking for help."

"I suppose so." A part of me knew she was right too. But I would I listen?

"Can I show you the room the last gal worked out of?" Pea had interrupted my thoughts. "Come with me, I think you will like it." I followed her to the back of the store and she opened the last door on the right.

I walked in and couldn't believe my eyes. In the center of the room lay a large square rug with a zebra-like pattern and a small round table with a brown leather top in the center of the rug. There were also two matching leather chairs, one on each side. Each corner of the room had a white crackled stone pillar that reached the ceiling.

The ceiling had a very intricate grid system made of steel cables, which held a lush jungle of dark green ivy in place. Their ropey vines had stretched up from base of the pillars to wind throughout the ceiling. There was a small, quaint fireplace to the right, made of large round river rocks. Candles filled every shelf that surrounded the room. On the opposite side of the room, water trickled down into a very small square stone pool from a tall, narrow black stone wall that resembled a washboard.

"This room is incredible!" I said. Someone had obviously gone to great lengths to decorate it very carefully. I kept looking around. Each time my eyes swept the room, I noticed additional details that I missed the first time. Fringed red drapes softened the bare walls in the rear. Various crystals hung down from the ivy covered ceiling along with a chandelier with no obvious light bulbs.

Pea caught the direction of my eyes and said, "In the morning when the sun comes up, beams of light bounce all around the room, kind of like shooting stars from crystal to crystal," she smiled. Beams of light, I thought to myself as I remembered shaking Pea's hand just moments ago.

"What happened to the gal who used to work out of this room?" I asked.

The smile on Pea's face vanished. Melancholy replaced her joy. "She disappeared," Pea answered.

"What do you mean, she disappeared?"

"Well, one day she didn't come to work and no one has seen her since."

"Could she just have run away, like I kind of did?"

"She just wasn't like that and honestly I feel like something bad has happened to her; I just can't put my finger on it."

"Oh, I'm sorry, what was her name?"

"Helena."

"Pretty name. Can I think about this for a day?" I asked.

Pea nodded, "Take all the time you need, but I have this strange feeling you won't need long. I'll see you soon."

I made my way to the front door and tucked the directions to the bed and breakfast that Pea had given me into my purse. As I was opening the door, I turned back and asked, "You don't happen to practice astronomy by any chance, do you?"

Pea gasped, "How did you know?"

"Let's just call it intuition and leave it at that for now." I smiled and gently closed the door, and headed back down the street to my car.

I sat in my car for a moment, doing a once-over of my directions, before I headed south on Newcastle until it came to a T at Hanover Square. So far, the drive had been delightful and picturesque. I followed Hanover Square to the right until it reached back around to Newcastle again; it kind of reminded me of a very large traffic circle.

I made a left on Prince Street and then a right on Union Street, going one more block up. Suddenly I was there. It was a beautiful two-story house with a wrap-around porch, kind of your typical A-frame in a way. Three large windows were directly above the porch, with a single window above them. The single window I pictured as a typical attic window, small, but large enough to let in light and a cool evening breeze.

The siding was white and all the trim green, a color combination that I have always liked. A white fence surrounded the yard. There was a quaint arbor at the entrance and meandering paths lined with aromatic, brightly colored gardens. I shut the engine off and got out of the car. I followed the walkway to the house and Liz was already there to meet me on the porch.

"Franciska? Hello," she said, "My name is Liz; I am very pleased to meet you. Pea called and told me that you were on your way."

I reached out to shake her hand and there was nothing! No lights, flickers or snapshots of her life. "I am very pleased to meet you too; your house and yard is stunning."

"Thank you," Liz replied. "Where are you from?"

"A little here and a little there, but mostly from Ann Arbor, Michigan"

"Brrrrrrr, you're a ways from Michigan, definitely warmer here. How did you end up in Brunswick?"

"Now that's a story for down the road, but for now let's just say, warmth, sunlight, the salt air, the ocean and peace and quiet."

"How long do you need the room for?" Liz asked.

"I'm actually looking for an apartment or house to rent and I'm not sure how long that will take. I know this may be an absurd question, but you don't happen to have a room for about a month do you?"

Liz smiled, "You're in luck. We just finished remodeling our attic. It's the newest addition to our bed and breakfast; you would be our first guest."

"How much a night is the room?" I started to ask, but Liz was already heading toward the front door to show me the room.

Liz was tall, taller than me, with a medium build. You could tell that fitness was an important part of her life. She had long brown hair with a hint of auburn and brown eyes. Her skin was nicely tanned like Pea's, and I was already dreaming of my skin turning the same lovely shade. I must look like a ghost to them, I laughed to myself.

I passed the main sitting room, which was absolutely one of the most beautiful rooms I had ever seen. Ornate, deep red Victorian wallpaper dropped down to meet the white chair rail and kissed the bottom of the matching white dentil molding along the ceiling. A small, red velvet loveseat rested just in front of a wall, with two small oval mahogany pedestal tables on each end. It was the flower arrangement on the coffee table that really caught my eye.

The clear crystal vase was sleek and tall, maybe eighteen inches high, with a wide mouth at the top and a heavy, thick base. The arrangement itself was of simple wildflowers, gold, orange and red. Scattered throughout the flowers were towering cattails and pussy willows. I followed Liz up the stairs.

Once at the top of the stairs, Liz stopped just to the right of the landing and unlocked a door that led us up the second set of stairs. The top step spilled out in the middle of the attic loft, separating both sides of the room. It was hard to believe that the room I was standing in was once an attic.

There were three half-walls of spindles, all hand carved and stained in a rich chocolate color, surrounding the stairwell. It is almost like the stairwell had always separated the sitting area from the sleeping area in a very unique way.

A small coffee table and love seat, along with two end tables holding antique lamps delicately on top, were to my right. Above the couch along the far right wall were two stained glass windows, rich with colors and well-crafted, faceted designs.

The lower window was a basic square and just above it was the half-moon shaped window. The sunlight was beaming through and bouncing off the walls. A chandelier hung just above the center of the stairwell and contained lights that resembled candles enclosed in an octagonal-shaped glass casing.

To my left, in the far right corner, was a private bath. A Victorian-looking queen size bed was snugged up just against the wall, just short of the door to the bath. You could tell that the bathroom had been added later, but it was done so carefully that both rooms fit together perfectly. A tall, nine-drawer dresser with a mirror was placed against the wall on the left, across from the bed and bathroom. I walked over to the bed and sat down.

"How much does this room run a night?" I asked Liz.

"It's eighty-five Monday through Thursday and a hundred a night on weekends."

"Will you take twenty four hundred for the month, paid in advance of course?" I offered.

"Not a problem," Liz agreed quickly.

I went back out to my car and grabbed some of my things, the whole time thinking that at least this was one less thing to worry about for a while. I met Liz on the porch and gave her the money. She handed me the key to the door at the bottom of the second set of stairs and a small card with the code for the side door entrance. I was almost all set. Now my tummy began to grumble.

"I'm going to take my things to my room and then grab a bite to eat, and maybe get a drink. Is there somewhere that you can recommend?"

Liz just about did a dance right in front of me. "Oh, you have to go to the Seaside Grill; it's just a block up from Pea's shop. Tell Damon that Liz and Ryan said hello. He'll take good care of you at the bar and you won't feel so alone," promised Liz.

"At the bar?" I questioned.

"It's not like that. It's a very upscale place with really good food. It actually won the Georgia Award three years in a row. It's not a pick-up joint, if that's what you thought. I just meant the bar is very cozy and comfortable, since you'll be by yourself."

Liz gave me the directions to the Seaside Grill and I got back into my car and headed out for a little dinner. I backtracked the same way that I had come to the bed and breakfast and found the restaurant without any problem, since it was only a block away from Candles & More.

I parked almost in the same spot I'd been in before, and got out of the car. I had to do a quick stretch; it seemed like I had been in the car all day long. While I was standing there, I stared at my car. I had almost forgotten that my car symbolized 'corporate slave' to me and might to others as well.

"Tomorrow I will have to get something a bit more reasonable, something carefree and casual and maybe a little more fun." I said to myself. After all, I was tired of being stuffy. Getting a new car would be first on my list in the morning.

The Seaside Grill looked very nice. It was a three-story building with a stucco exterior that was painted a creamy cappuccino color. The windows on the top two stories were tall and slim and each one had a slight arc on the top. The framing around all the windows was a dark, milk chocolate color.

The entrance had double doors with two sets of large square windows on each side that nearly reached the bottom of the second floor. The trim was the same color as the others. A string of small twinkling lights surrounded each window on the lower level and white drapes hung from each window to the opposite corners.

Once again, there was a tall palm tree in front. This one was a bit different from the others I had seen earlier that day. It had fan-like clusters of shorter leaves and looked almost perfectly manicured into a ball shape. There was one table on each side of the door, each with a white canvas umbrella and white linen tablecloth. I thought to myself that, so far, everything looked very nice and I entered the restaurant.

The inside was half full and it wasn't too loud, which I liked. There were square tables throughout with the same white tablecloths. The floors were all a rich colored, well-worn but well preserved hardwood. The walls were constructed of the original brick, and vintage-framed photos of ships and boats were hung between lighted wall sconces. According to a plaque by the front door, Brunswick was one of the first shipping ports authorized by George Washington when the colonies were formed.

The hostess came and greeted me. She was cute and a bit younger than me, I was guessing still in her late 20s. She had a short, dark, sassy haircut and make-up beautifully done. She wore a simple diamond on the right side of her nose and one in each ear, matching the heart-shaped cluster of diamonds that hung from a chain around her neck. With her black skirt and white shirt she looked very classy. "Hello, my name is Dona. Will someone be joining you this evening?"

I replied quietly, "I'm actually by myself; would it be okay to sit at the bar? Oh, and I am supposed to give a special hello to a man named Damon from a Liz and Ryan."

Dona said, "No problem to both of those. You can help yourself to the bar area and Damon is the bartender this evening."

I made my way toward the bar and took a seat in the middle. It was simple and quaint, all dark wood, and had tall mission-style stools with a burnt orange cushion to sit on. Bottles and glasses were stacked in tiered sections in front of large mirrored glass.

The sweet smell of a cigarette burning a few chairs down had reminded me of my recent departure from smoking. The day had gone by at such a fast pace that I had forgotten my once bad habit.

The air was filled with a reminder now and I could feel the smoke entering my lungs. I was aching for a cigarette and even contemplating asking for one in mere desperation. I leaned down to set my purse on the foot rail in front of my toes and raised my head slowly as a cocktail napkin was dropped in front of me. The most mesmerizing man's voice said, "What can I get the lady at the bar to drink this evening?"

The voice practically sang to me, and when my eyes met his, the voices in the restaurant muted, my angst for a smoke subsided and the world as I knew it just stopped.

CHAPTER THREE

First Sight

"Can you make a mojito?" I stuttered.

"I make the best mojitos in town," he answered, and then turned his back to begin the special regimen of muddling mint and lime. I could still see his face in the mirrored glass and couldn't help but stare; he was absolutely gorgeous. I told myself it was time to take a deep breath. I sure as hell didn't want to look like some neighborhood dog in heat. I couldn't help but watch him, though.

He was nearly six feet tall with a medium build. He had dark hair, almost black, with a slight wave to it; although it was short, he had just enough length on top to wear it messy. It wasn't shaved in the back, but cut short and neat, just hitting the collar of his shirt. It was tousled a bit and looked wet, like he'd just walked out of the ocean.

His facial hair appeared to be kept trimmed at a two- or three-day growth, just enough to give him a shadow along his crisp jaw line. His full red lips looked like they had just touched a glass of red wine.

His nose was slim and masculine, but nothing too big. Just below his dark, full, sharply arched eyebrows his seductive green eyes were warm enough to melt any woman's heart. I watched him as he muddled the lime and mint in the glass. His white shirtsleeves were rolled up to just below the elbow and his hands were strong.

With every move, I could see the veins rise and the striations of his muscles appear more vividly. He had broad shoulders and was physically fit. I drifted off for a moment picturing him lying on a beach with his awesome body and the abs to die for. He turned to give me my drink; his smile and teeth were as perfect as the rest of him.

"Tell me what you think," he asked. I wasn't sure if he really wanted to know. Did he want to know what I thought of him or what I thought of the drink? The drink, of course, silly, I chuckled to myself. I lifted the glass to my lips and took a small sip through the straw.

"It is perfect," I told him. "You wouldn't happen to be Damon by any chance?"

"Yes; how did you know?"

"I just came from Liz and Ryan's home and I was supposed to pass along a special hello."

"Are you staying there? Where are you from?"

I told him a bit about myself while leaving out a few things, like my line of work. It was a very basic background and I wasn't about to make myself sound more interesting than I was, especially since, well, since he's a bartender.

There were two types of "won't date" men in this world for me: a pilot and a bartender, both of whom are around women all the time and neither of whom I could ever trust.

He sure was nice to look at though, I thought to myself. I got the distinct feeling he was looking at me, too.

Damon suggested the crab cakes and they arrived shortly after. They were probably the best crab cakes I ever had, and it was just enough to make me feel whole again. By time I had my third mojito, the dinner crowd was slowing down.

Damon wandered over and leaned on the bar, looking straight at me. One arm rested on the bar in front of him while his other arm was bent to allow his chin to rest lightly in his hand.

"What's your name?" he asked. "I can't believe I haven't even asked for your name."

At this point I nearly fell off my seat. Think fast, I kept telling myself. I was actually trying to think of a fake name to give him. I was in no mood for any connections, relationships or even one-nighters. But he was so damn hot, and instead I just blurted out, "Effie."

"Effie?" He asked.

"Yes, that's my nickname; my real name is Franciska. I was named after my grandmother, who was Hungarian. The name means 'free.' Effie is just kind of a shorter version of Franciska. Don't ask me how, though."

"I like that, I like that a lot. Does my name have any meaning?"

"What is your family background?" I asked.

"I'm Italian and I'm assuming that my name is too."

I thought for a moment. This name was a little harder for me. I was used to giving the meanings of more traditional names. Now he's going to think I'm a nut for knowing the background of names. I thought to myself, "What do I care?" The new deal was to be myself.

"I think it means 'one who tames,'" I said, thinking what an odd combination the meanings of our names were.

At that moment, he said almost exactly what I was thinking: "How interesting to have two people at the bar talking, one who is free and the other one who tames."

If he couldn't see me blush he must have been blind, because my face suddenly felt one hundred and four degrees hot. He excused himself to do some things that needed to get done in the back room and drifted away. I was relieved; I needed time to cool off and regain a little composure.

"You're a fool to think he would be anything meaningful," a voice snarled from behind me. One of the waitresses thought she would offer her opinion to the new girl in town.

"Excuse me?" I responded sharply.

"I'm just trying to warn you before you get too hooked. Damon is a womanizer. He will woo you with his voice and eyes, but at the end of the day, he will move on to the next; he's only after one thing."

"Sounds to me like you're jealous, rather than giving me a heart-felt warning."

"Of what?" She asked snottily. "Paaallease!"

"Hey if it walks like a duck ..."

Then she left, but not before I caught the name on her cheesy gold chain: Cali. "Way to go Effie," I said to myself. I haven't even been here for twenty-four hours and I have already made an enemy, without even stepping one foot into a courtroom. However, she did get me to thinking.

Rule number one on my dating scene is no pilots and no bartenders. I just wasn't sure that I wanted to follow the rules anymore. That was the whole point of turning a new leaf. I still couldn't help but think how incredibly attractive Damon was. That's the type of guy that really can get just about any girl; why would he want me? I'm kind of plain. My skin is pale and my hair is long and unremarkable. I have been in the car all day and the makeup that I applied this morning has now nearly faded. Who was I kidding; Cali was probably right. I was ready to break my rules, though, and go for someone normal, someone without money, and I had to snap myself out of that. Just then Damon interrupted my thoughts.

"Is everything okay?" he asked.

"Yah, I guess."

"Well then, good. The bar is closed and since you're new here I thought I would offer you a tour of the restaurant."

I stepped down from the stool, grabbed my purse and followed Damon. He showed me the wine cellar, the kitchen and then took me upstairs to the private dining room. This is where they did dinners for twenty-five to fifty people. They had a few waiters and one waitress cleaning up from a rehearsal dinner earlier that night. I noticed Cali right away and she glared at us. She really made me feel quite uneasy.

"What's with that waitress?"

Damon laughed, "She's so unhappy with her life that she insists on making everyone else around her miserable. I saw her talk to you earlier. She didn't say anything unsettling to you, did she?"

"No, I'm a big girl; I can handle myself pretty well," I replied.

Damon laughed again, "I bet you can."

I walked around the room once and looked out the window. I thought to myself, it's such a pretty night and such a pretty place; I hope this works out for me. Brunswick was already growing on me. I yawned, "Damon, I think I'm going to go. It has been a very long day for me and I definitely need my beauty sleep."

We walked back downstairs, passing the kitchen and the bar. I thanked Damon for the tour and keeping me company for dinner.

"Liz told me I'd be well taken care of," I said.

"Was she right?" Damon smiled, tilting his head to one side, looking sincerely interested in my answer.

"Oh, definitely." I said. I wasn't lying. So far, I'd met a lot of very kind people here. Being from Michigan, that was a very new thing. It must have been the cold temperatures and lack of sunshine that kept people there so grumpy all the time. I definitely wasn't used to all this "Southern Hospitality" but I could quickly learn to love it.

"I'd be happy to show you around town as well," Damon said.

"You're so generous," I said, not ready to commit, but not ready to blow him off either.

He handed me a card from the restaurant with his number on it. I accepted it graciously and stuffed it into my purse, but at this time had no plans on calling him, no matter how drop-dead gorgeous he was.

"Thanks again," I said and walked out the door.

I unlocked my car and sank into the cool leather seat. While setting my purse on the floor of the passenger side, I looked back through the open door of the restaurant and noticed Damon talking to the hostess, Dona. It looked like the conversation was serious, and at that point I thought back to Cali's comments, wondering it really was the truth she was telling me. I had no visions or feelings other than the normal about Damon. Then again, I never touched him, not even a shake of his hand. Well, it's a small town and I'm sure I'll see him again, I thought. Next time I'll touch him and see if I can get a vision. I started my car and headed back to the bed and breakfast.

The house was dark when I arrived and I walked around to the side entrance, used my code, and entered. A small hallway light came on when I entered the door; it must have been set on a motion sensor. It was a comforting touch. I unlocked the private door to my attic room and climbed the last set of stairs.

"Finally," I said, as I sat on my bed, tossing my shoes halfway across the room. I removed all my clothes and slid between the sheets and the down-filled comforter. I closed my eyes just for a moment and I was out.

I awoke in the morning to the smell of pancakes and hot maple syrup. I opened my eyes to see the wonder of sunbeams dancing and shifting into the room through the stained glass window. As I slipped on my clothes from the day before, I knew it was time to carry up my suitcases and bags from the car.

When I left Michigan, I didn't bring much. I packed my trunk and part of my back seat, and sold half of my furniture. All the rest was sitting in a ten-by-ten storage unit in Ann Arbor. I refused to move any more of my things until I felt secure in a place.

I brushed my teeth, threw my hair up into a quick ponytail and headed downstairs for breakfast. I entered the dining room, which contained antique lamps, pictures, a buffet and a china cabinet. I sat at a table that was large enough to hold twelve people and Liz brought me a cup of coffee.

"Good morning," Liz said. "How was your dinner last night?"

"Good morning. Dinner was very good; it was a great place and the atmosphere is very nice there. Thank you for suggesting it."

"Did you see Damon?" Liz asked.

"Who could miss him? He is absolutely dreamy. Kind of mysterious, too."

I went on to recount the evening to Liz as I sipped at my coffee. I told her about the tour of the restaurant, the bitch waitress and how Damon had offered to show me around Brunswick. Liz sat down with her cup of tea and filled me in on a few things. She told me about Cali and how she slept with every man she could get her hands on, including married ones.

Liz summed Cali up: "She's the village whore; just avoid her if you can." Liz went on and told me about how Dona had a special relationship with Damon, but that it was more of a friendship than anything else.

"It's kind of strange when they're together because I always get the feeling that they are keeping secrets," Liz said. "I know that must sound funny, but, believe me, there is nothing going on in the romance department with those two. You should take Damon up on his offer."

"I'll think about it," I replied hesitantly.

Liz brought me some pancakes and a bowl of fresh fruit, which I ate right away. I then hurried to my car and took up the first load of bags, and returned for three more trips until the car was empty. My once darling room now looked like a closet gone mad. I didn't care. Organizing this place was just going to have to wait.

I jumped in the shower and washed my hair. It sure did feel good to be clean again. An entire day in the car would make anyone feel filthy. I threw on a pair of black shorts and a white baby-doll top with spaghetti straps. I quickly combed out my hair and threw it in a ponytail again. "This time I am putting some make up on before I head out," I said to myself. After another fifteen minutes I was good to go. I went downstairs and peeked around the corner into the dining room.

"Liz," I called. A moment later she appeared around the corner.

"Are you heading out for a while?"

"Yes, I'm looking for a used car dealership. Do you know of any somewhat reputable ones?" I snickered.

"Go down to Newcastle and Third; there is a smaller and more upscale dealership called Hartford Motors. So, what you want to do is head back out to Newcastle and instead of heading north, you want to go south until you come to Third, and then hang a right; it will be there on your right hand side. Ask for Joe and tell him that we sent you."

"Thanks again," I replied, "When do I get to meet your other half?"

Liz answered joyfully, "He'll be back this evening."

Yup, I was on the road again. "This is getting old real fast," I said to myself. I followed the directions Liz gave me and in a few minutes arrived at the dealership. I got out of the car as carefully as I could, to try to look around first without getting caught. The last time I had done this, I hit a bunch of dealerships in a row on a Sunday when they were closed so I wouldn't be bothered.

It didn't take long at all and I saw what I wanted. It was a white 2005 Jeep Wrangler 4X4 with all the bells and whistles I wanted on a Jeep, including new tires. The best part was the six-speed manual transmission. Now that's me! I loved everything about it. I love my vehicles. I owned a Jeep six years ago and had missed it ever since I sold it.

"Can I help you?" said a low voice with a heavy southern drawl.

"Ummm, yes, I think you can," I answered. "Liz Stringer told me that I needed to talk to Joe; are you Joe?"

"You got him."

"Well then, Joe, I have a deal for you!"

I leaned against the Jeep and gave Joe a little of my background, and then pointed to my car.

"It's paid for and I'll trade you even up for this Jeep. I know you don't make a dime this minute. However, you can sell my car for well under retail and make more money than you would make on this Jeep."

Joe knew I was right and quickly agreed. I followed him into his office to sign all the paperwork.

One hour later I pulled out driving my Jeep. As I shifted each gear, my natural euphoria grew and grew. I backtracked and made my way to Newcastle Street, except instead of turning to go to the Stringers', I went straight. I was headed to Candles and More, Pea's store. It had only been three days since I left Michigan, and I just could not believe how much I had already done. Even though I wanted a little time off, I decided to go talk to Pea more about her job offer.

On the way there, I thought about my birthday, which was just around the corner, April eighth to be exact. It was probably going to be pretty uneventful this year, but I had to admit the stress that I once felt was gone and my body actually felt better, even after all the time spent in my car. It goes to show you that stress affects the body worse than a two-day trip in the car headed to who knows where.

I would be thirty-three two weeks from today and for some reason I felt like I accomplished nothing in my thirty-three years of existence. I knew that wasn't true, but there was this emptiness that I was yearning to have go away. It's almost like when you sit and wonder, "What is that one thing in life that I'm supposed to do?" And for me, it felt like I hadn't done that one thing yet.

I pulled into a parking place at Candles and More, locked my Jeep and went into the store. "I love the sound of those jingle bells," I said when I entered the store.

I stood there for a moment, getting a good second look at the store, and heard Pea call out, "I'll be right there." A moment later she appeared from the back and I could not believe my eyes when Damon appeared right behind her. We all said our brief hellos.

"This is a small town," I laughed.

Damon said, "I agree. Do you still have my card? I am still offering."

"I still have it, and I am still thinking."

"Think harder!" Damon winked.

He gave us a quick goodbye as he headed out the door, but not without a slight turn of his head and another small wink. Shit, I was blushing again.

"It appears that he likes you," Pea said.

"Maybe," I responded carefully.

"So, are you here for the job?" Pea asked.

"I am, but I have some questions." I took a deep breath.

"I want to know how you will pay me and what my hours will be. I also want to know if I can have contact with clients outside of work, and if someone wants to come and see me unexpectedly, can I meet them here even if it's not during regular business hours?

"I also would like it if the clients can see me discretely, if they like. How will advertising work? And the biggest question I have is, how religious is this community? I have had people say and do things to me in the past because they didn't believe in what I was doing. I do this mostly for fun, but every now and then if someone wants a serious, more extended reading. I would like to offer those customers a different rate."

The questions just poured out of me, not giving Pea time to answer even if she was trying to. It surprised me how strongly I wanted to do this, no matter what Pea's answers were.

When I paused to take a breath Pea grabbed her chance to interrupt me.

"Let me save you some breath. You set it up how you would like to and I will follow your guidelines. This means the hours you want to keep and what you would like to charge, too. I handle the ads, with your input, of course. All money can come through up here at the front. The way we did it in the past was to create a service receipt and the customer would bring it up when they were done.

"I would collect all the money and then give you sixty percent and I would keep forty percent. I will pay you daily or weekly. As far as the conservativeness of the community goes, it is quite a mix; we have never had any problems here before. I don't see why any would start now. I'm very easy-going and I like you already, and don't even know you. I hope I answered them all."

I was nodding as she talked. I didn't need to think.

"This sounds good," I answered. "Can I have until Monday to get organized? I really need a break, anyhow."

"No problem and welcome to Candles and More."

"I would like to spend a little time in the room, if you don't mind?"

Pea led me back to the room, unlocked it and then handed me the key, "Take as long as you like; it's all yours now," she said.

I entered the room and set my purse down on the round leather table in the middle of the room. I walked around the room, examining every inch. This would be a really nice place to spend some of my days.

I felt myself feeling calmer with each passing minute. I think the combination of green ivy everywhere and the trickling water was all it took. I was at peace. I took a seat in one of the leather chairs and thought that maybe I might like to add a little love seat to the room. After all, it was plenty big enough. I was sizing up the back wall and trying to figure out the best way to add it when Pea walked into the room holding a white cardboard box.

She held it out to me and said, "There's stuff inside that you might be able to use. Helena left these items behind, so I put them in this box for safe keeping in case she came back."

I took the box from her, set it down on the table and thanked her. She disappeared down the hallway before I could say any more. I lifted off the lid and peeked inside. Helena had left some rocks and gems, basic office supplies, a large crystal ball and its three-pronged pewter stand, tarot cards and a Rolodex.

I glanced through the Rolodex and saw several names, addresses and phone numbers, so it appeared to be her client list. This would definitely help me get started. I never had a crystal ball before, although I loved them. I reached into the box with both hands and carefully pulled out the ball while sitting back in the chair. It was slightly heavy, but beautiful.

All of sudden I saw visions again—not in the crystal ball, but from holding it. I saw a short, fairly stocky woman with shoulder-length blonde hair. She was lying in a marsh, wrapped in scarves. I almost dropped the ball. I stood up quickly, catching my hip on the edge of the table and sending the rest of the contents of the box and my purse flying to the floor.

Pea appeared and asked, "Are you okay?" She continued, "You look like you've seen a ghost."

I looked up and replied, "I think I have."

Pea left to get me a glass of water and when she returned, I drank it quickly. It took me a while to calm myself, but I knew I had to explain.

"Thank you so much," I said. "Pea, can you please describe Helena to me?"

"I need to know what Helena looks like?" I begged.

"She's kind of short, about five-foot-four maybe. She has naturally curly, blonde hair and blue eyes. Her skin is paler than most people that live around here and she's a bit overweight. She is very bubbly and everyone liked her."

"I saw her," I mumbled.

"What do you mean, you saw her?"

"I get visions ... well, more like flashes. I sometimes get them when I touch someone, or from things that belong to people."

"Helena had something like that too. Please tell me more."

"My grandmother had the ability to see future events, but I can only see the past or the present. I haven't quite learned how to control it or channel it yet. It is still very new to me."

"What did you touch?" Pea asked me.

I lifted up the crystal ball, which I was holding on my lap. Pea looked at me and was quiet for a moment. Then she asked the big question.

"What did you see?"

I left out the part about the marsh, just describing what she looked like and how scarves surrounded her. Pea chuckled, "That's Helena all right, and she loved her scarves. She wore them in her hair, as belts, around her neck and sometimes wore the bigger ones as a top. She even had a few that were big enough to wear as a wrap dress."

"Yeah, she's cute."

"Is that all you saw?" Pea asked.

"Yeah, pretty much. Like I said, I am still new at this. I just get this feeling that something has drawn me here. I don't want to scare you, but I almost feel like Helena is talking to me."

"Not much scares me; there is still a lot you don't know about me. But what scares me is, if it is Helena, it would mean she is in her spiritual form."

"Let's not get too carried away just yet." I quickly changed the subject, not wanting to discuss Helena any longer. I was almost sick to my stomach and didn't want to look like some crazy quack. So, for now, I decided, I'm keeping my mouth shut about it.

"When I saw Damon earlier, he wasn't leaving with a purchase. How do you know him?" I slyly inquired.

"He actually buys a lot of candles from me. He likes the scent of amber, eucalyptus and vanilla, of course. What man doesn't like the scent of vanilla? He stops by from time to time to just say hello. Today was one of those days."

"Oh," I answered.

"He seems to like you," Pea said. "You should take him up on his offer; he's really a fun guy to be around."

I smiled, but quickly wiped it off my face. "I have two rules that I don't like to break: don't date a pilot and don't date a bartender. I actually have a third one now: don't date men with money."

At this point, Pea was giggling and said, "Well at least rule three doesn't apply, so you wouldn't be completely going back on your dating guidelines." She was really laughing when she added, "So, just be friends. That's usually a good place to start anyhow."

I finished cleaning up the mess that I made in the room and got all my things together. I placed Helena's box in the Jeep and took that with me, too. I thought it would be safer in my attic. I interrupted my own conversation. I have to find another name for where I am staying right now.

I think I shall call it the penthouse, I thought, and chuckled to myself. I said my goodbyes to Pea and told her that I would see her Monday morning and headed for my ... penthouse. I stopped. I really didn't like that word. Penthouse sounded so snobby, so ... rich.

On the way back to the Stringers' I was playing with words in my head. Loft, flat, sky parlor, bird's nest, nest; but none of seemed to click, and then it came to me. I'm going to call it the suite.

I finished acting silly by the time I reached the house and pulled into the side parking area. Liz came running out of the house as if it was on fire. Her hands were both up waving in the air and she was bouncing all around. I jumped out of the car immediately! It happened so fast it must have looked like I was stung in the ass by a bee. We sure must have been some sight!

I yelled out, "What's wrong?"

"Nothing, nothing, nothing. I love your new wheels! I have always wanted a Jeep. Take me for a ride, please, please."

"Sure, no problem, but can you not be quite so excited? You nearly gave me a heart attack!"

Liz jumped in the passenger seat and said, "Let's go!"

"Liz, we will leave as soon as you take the towel off your head and change out of your bathrobe." Now Liz was blushing.

She ran back in the house and in minutes came out wearing flip-flops, a pair of shorts and a tank top. Her hair was still wet from just washing it, and she had a comb and cute pink baseball hat in her hand. "Okay, I'm ready now," Liz said in a calmer voice.

We took a short drive along the shoreline. It was late in the day, so the sun was just getting ready to start its descent. The breeze and smell of salt air was almost indescribable, serene maybe. We stopped at a video store on the way back, where I opened an account and rented two movies for the night.

Liz was quiet most of the way, just enjoying the drive and telling me where to turn. We arrived back at the house an hour later. She thanked me for the drive and I headed to my suite.

I ordered a small barbeque pizza and took a bottle of chardonnay out of the small refrigerator hidden inside an antique cabinet next to the bed. I poured myself a glass to sip on while I waited for the pizza to be delivered and set up my laptop to watch the first movie. I sat back and laughed to myself, remembering how funny and excited Liz looked when I pulled up. This was definitely a good way to end this day, even though thoughts of Helena were still unsettling to me.

Halfway through the movie, I fell asleep, pizza barely touched.

CHAPTER FOUR

A Taste of Italy

I awoke the next morning on the floor, with the empty bottle of wine and almost-full pizza box not far from me. My head was pounding and my entire body ached, so I took a few aspirin and stepped into the shower, which helped me feel better quickly. I wrapped my hair into a towel, wiped the steam off the mirror with a washcloth and took a long look at my face.

My eyes looked tired and I could see mouth creases starting, the creases a friend of mine referred to as smile lines. My neck was still slim and my jaw line still crisp. Thank God I have no gray hairs, I thought to myself when I pulled the towel off my hair. The hair fell down and nestled around both my breasts, just covering the nipples.

I rolled my shoulders back and sucked my stomach in slightly. I wasn't quite as lucky as girls with board-flat stomachs. Mine has a slight curve to it. My breasts still looked good: full and firm, with no sign of sagging yet. I posed in the mirror for a few minutes and my mind drifted. I was missing the feeling of being with a man. I could feel it in my breasts, in my legs and throughout my entire body.

Just then a knock came from the door at the bottom of my stairs. "Just a minute," I called, as I threw on a robe and went down to open the door. It was Liz.

"I was just checking on you because you didn't come down for breakfast."

"I'm sorry; I slept in a bit," I reassured her.

Liz was quiet for a moment, and I had to ask her, "Is everything all right?"

"Yah," she said. "I was just hoping to hear a man's voice up there," she giggled.

"Hmmm, that makes two of us," I wished loudly.

I wondered if Liz was looking for anyone in particular for me. It seemed to me that she would be the type to enjoy match-making. Not that I minded that, but I was just not looking for anything serious, so any match for me right now would be a short-term gig. Maybe I should just tell her I'm only interested in sex, I thought to myself. Nah, I don't want to burst her bubble.

"Do you have any fruit left over?" I changed the subject.

"Oh, yes. Come on down when you're ready; I'll make you a fruit plate. And it looks like you could use a cup of coffee." Liz said.

"That's awesome. Let me get dressed and I'll be right down."

I threw on a new summer dress that has thin straps and a wide elastic band that lay just beneath my breasts, accentuating their size. It was light blue cotton with a few embroidered daisies on it. I slipped into my flip-flops and let my hair down. "Coffee, here I come," I thought to myself as I entered the dining room.

Liz peeked around the corner, "Do you mind eating in the kitchen today? I know it's informal, but I have some cleaning up to do and would like to talk with you for a while, if you don't mind."

"Sure," I replied, and followed her into the kitchen.

The kitchen was large and combined a very modern, commercial look with some antique touches. The white cabinets, glass inserts on the upper cabinet doors and white granite counters gave it a sort of 1800s feel, but the island and appliances were all very twenty-first century.

I sat at the island, where Liz had placed a plate of fruit with a scoop of low fat cottage cheese and a cup of coffee.

"Did I tell you thanks, for taking me for a drive last night?" Liz asked.

"Yes, a hundred times," I sighed. "You really need to get out more," I said, and laughed loudly.

The fruit was very good. She had arranged ripe slices of fresh peaches alongside fresh blueberries, raspberries and blackberries. She lingered, obviously wanting to say something, but not quite sure how to begin.

"What would you like to talk about, Liz?"

"There are a lot of things to do in this area and so many wonderful beaches. I think you need to see a few of the little neighboring islands, too. I think that it's sad to have such a fun ride and not be going anywhere."

"Would you like to go somewhere today?" I interrupted her.

"I'll gladly take a rain check; I have a lot to do today, but I know a great tour guide."

"Okay, okay, I'll call," I said. "Is that what you were trying to get me to do? Is this our big conversation?"

Liz grinned a very evil grin. I took out my cell phone and looked at Liz. "The number please?" I asked, knowing full well that she had it on the tip of her tongue.

Damon answered, "Hello!"

"Hello, Damon," I said. "This is Effie. Is the invitation still open for that tour?" Liz listened to my side of the conversation with a funny look on her face.

"You can relax; he'll be here in an hour," I said.

"Effie?" she asked, "Who the heck is Effie?"

"Ohhh," I snickered. "That's my nickname, Liz; you can call me Effie, too, if you like."

I finished my fruit plate and took a second cup of coffee up to my room so I could get ready.

I parted my hair on the left side and threw a little mousse in it, leaving it wavy for the day. I applied some make-up and did something else I haven't done in a few days ... I added perfume. A short time later I heard a horn, grabbed my purse and headed down the stairs. Damon met me on the front porch. I took one look at him and nearly came undone.

His face alone was enough to make any girl forget about keeping her virginity. A tight green short-sleeve shirt hugged his biceps and his long khaki shorts weren't so long as to hide his equally tanned and toned legs. His sunglasses were pushed up on his head and his eyes were even brighter and more piercing in the sunlight. He told Liz to not expect us for a while because he packed a lunch and was going to show me some of the beaches. I followed Damon to his car, well broken-in International Scout.

"How nice, Damon; you definitely don't see these in Michigan," I said.

He laughed. "Just imagine ... it was made in Fort Wayne, Indiana, and everything on it is original except for the interior, which was reupholstered a couple of years back."

The Scout was orange with a tan leather interior. It was old and rugged, just the way I liked my cars. Character, was what I was thinking to myself. It had character.

Damon had removed the hardtop, which made the Scout even more exciting. He opened the door and held out his left hand to me. I grabbed his hand to get into the vehicle and had my first vision. This one was a bit different than the others.

There were flashes of red, yellow and blue, continuously rotating and then they were gone, but I was still holding his hand, which felt very warm to me now. He had wide palms and his hand nearly engulfed mine. I really didn't want to let go, but I did. He shut the door and I got comfortable. Damon got in, shut the door behind him and said, "Ready to go?" I was more than ready and we were soon on our way.

Damon drove me through several parts of Brunswick, pointing out different stores, restaurants and points of interest. Then we headed south on Highway 17 along the bay and crossed over on Downing Musgrove Causeway, going east toward the Atlantic Ocean. Today he was taking me to Jekyll Island, one of three small islands he said people from Brunswick like to visit.

Our first stop was the Island History Center. Although it was small, we spent an hour there, looking at artifacts and reading about the island's history. When we left the History Center, we spent an hour at the Georgia Sea Turtle center and then drove through three 18-hole championship golf courses to get a better look at the grounds. We had an in-depth conversation about golf and found that we both liked the sport.

From there we hit the Horton House which, I have to admit, was very interesting. Built in 1746 by Major William Horton, an aide to General James Edward Oglethorpe, the house was now a two-story ruin. It was a Tabby structure, meaning the primary material used to build it came from oyster shells. On the grounds was also Georgia's first brewery. Damon and I talked very little while we toured these places, which I didn't really mind that much.

When we finished touring the ruins, Damon drove us to Clam Creek, which was a popular picnic area with a covered fishing pier. He parked the Scout and extracted a picnic basket from the back seat. Believe it or not, it was a traditional woven wooden basket with wooden handles and a red and white checkered lining. We walked to a picnic table near a beautiful palm tree, and he laid out a checkered tablecloth, tying the corners down underneath the table. He then set out plates, napkins, silverware, two wineglasses and a bottle of Soave wine.

"I hope you enjoy this wine, it's one of my favorites."

"I've never had that kind; is it sweet or dry?" I asked.

"It's a dry wine. It's a wine from the Veneto region in Italy, which is close to the city of Verona," Damon explained.

"Soave is a flowery and delicate aroma with a soft full taste to it. It's a fruity wine with pear and lemon flavors and a slight almond aftertaste."

My mouth was watering already.

"Do you have anything else in that basket of yours?" Without missing a beat, he pulled out a bouquet of wildflowers and handed them to me. I was blushing again. Then he set out the best part of the picnic: a silver tray with kale garnish and an amazing variety of meats, cheeses and fruits.

He started at the left of the tray, explaining each food to me. He pointed to the first item and said, "This is sliced mozzarella with tomato, a bit of olive oil and a sprinkle of basil. In this dish, olive tapenade, a wonderful spread on top of Melba toast. You can also use the bruschetta in this bowl. To the right of the bruschetta is prosciutto cotto, which is an Italian ham that has been cooked. I am partial to the prosciutto crudo, a raw Italian ham that has been cured for one to two years, but I thought it might be too much for you on a first date. Then over here I have Gorgonzola, which is much like a blue cheese but a creamier version. I like to eat this type of cheese with pears and grapes."

He pointed to a separate container filled with pears and grapes. I was in such awe over the spread that Damon provided I almost missed the part where he referred to this outing as a first date.

He poured the wine in both our glasses and then placed a little bit of each food on a round glass plate for me. He raised his glass and said, "I'd like to propose a toast. To Effie, for adorning our city with her beauty."

I smiled and took a sip of wine. It was absolutely wonderful and just like he had described. I took another sip just to make sure. I set my glass down on the table and started with the mozzarella and tomato. It was a nice round slice of mozzarella, maybe a half of an inch thick, topped with a thick slice of a fresh tomato.

I cut a small piece and placed it into my mouth. It was a perfect combination with the olive oil and basil. My mouth watered and wanted more. I had never eaten mozzarella this way. I enjoyed the olive spread and bruschetta with the crackers. The ham was simply divine and the Gorgonzola with a slice of pear was a perfect compliment and almost required a taste of wine to follow.

As I was enjoying all this food I asked, "Damon, where are you from?"

After a slight pause, he replied, "A little from everywhere, but my family is from Verona, Italy. I have one sister and I have not seen my parents in a very long time." Then he asked the same.

"The same," I smiled. "A little from everywhere, although my family is from Hungary. I have no siblings or a father. It has been my mother and me for a very long time. We have traveled a lot." I quickly changed the subject. "I wondered how you knew so much about the wine. It was a description that most people would not be able to provide."

Damon laughed at that, and then I did too.

We finished the food—all of it, and it wasn't hard to do. Then Damon packed up the dirty plates and empty glasses, placed the basket back in the Scout and returned to the table with a small green blanket.

"Let's take a walk," he said and held out his hand. I clasped his hand and attempted to get up when all those colors started spinning through my head again, red, yellow and blue. Some were thick and swirled and some were thin and straight. They were gone as quickly as they came to me.

"Are you okay?" Damon asked.

"I'm just fine, maybe a little light headed," I replied.

I sure wasn't going to volunteer any unnecessary information at this time. He didn't need to know that I was having these strange and unexplainable visions; that would be the perfect mood killer.

We followed a small footbridge for about two hundred yards and over a slight berm to dump us out on the beach. It was eighty-two degrees and the ocean breeze made that temperature near perfect. The smell of salty air filled my lungs and it felt so clean that I couldn't imagine how anyone could leave the coast; I certainly was in no hurry to.

We walked south on the beach, close enough to the water that when the waves washed up on the sand, the water lightly covered our feet. It was cool and refreshing, yet very stimulating.

Damon reached out and grasped my right hand. "Do you mind?" he asked me. I didn't say a word; I just smiled. We walked for about a mile and I talked about the places I had lived and some of the things I had done. I told him about law school, saying that I didn't enjoy it and was really looking to find something that I did like.

Damon stopped and laid the green blanket down in the sand. "Please sit," he said. I was almost was afraid to, and not for the reasons that most people would think. I was about to break my rules, to change my life, to get involved with a bartender. I sat. Damon sat down next to me and I just stared at the ocean. It was so beautiful and the sun was just starting to set. Reds and oranges began to fill the sky.

I looked at Damon and said, "Thank you for the wonderful day."

"It was all my pleasure," he said with a sense of accomplishment and satisfaction. Somehow I knew he meant it too.

I lay back staring at the sky for a while and slowly closed my eyes. Everything was so perfect, I thought to myself. Then I felt Damon's lips fall onto mine. They were soft, moist and still tasted of wine. He lightly kissed my lower lip and then my upper lip, and then embraced both my lips with his. I opened my mouth slightly to allow him inside. I tasted him fully now.

His tongue caressed mine and his fingers fondled my hair. I pulled him on top of me so I could feel his full weight. The desire from deep within my body boiled to the top as he grasped my sides. I reached up and tangled my fingers in his hair, pulling his face closer to mine. My breathing was heavier now and my heart raced faster, as I could hear each breath he took in my ear. The once soft kisses had turned to deep passionate kisses.

His mouth moved slowly down my neck, exploring each inch and circled my collarbones, biting them slightly. I wanted his lips touching mine again, but my body was craving his mouth too. I gave a small push, rolling him onto his back and into the sand, and now I was on top of him. My lips collapsed onto his and I was in control of what I wanted. My tongue encircled his, tasting and devouring every part of his mouth.

I pressed my groin firmly to his as my breasts pressed against my dress; they were longing to be kissed and caressed too. A loud thud hit the sand, startling me so much I fell off and landed in the sand next to Damon. A man with long gangly legs appeared out of nowhere.

"My apologies to the both of you. My son has a very strong arm and my legs are not what they used to be," he said to us. Damon sat up and tossed the football back to the stranger.

"No worries," Damon said. I looked at Damon, still blushing.

"On that note, we should probably head back; but I would say that this afternoon has proven to be a first date after all." I smiled.

Damon grinned feverishly in reply and nodded.

We made our way back to his Scout and he drove me to the Stringers' in a comfortable silence. I leaned my head back, letting the breeze run through my long, black hair, using my fingers to detangle a few of the knots from our earlier tussle in the sand. I closed my eyes, and recaptured the excitement for a short moment as he pulled in the drive.

He shut the car off and walked around to open the door for me. I had beaten him to it, but he did jump in and offer his hand to me. I reached up, grabbing his hand and holding it as he walked me to the front porch to say his goodbyes. Liz met us at the door, of course, and giggled when she opened it.

"What's so funny?" I asked her.

She began to stutter, "Well ... uh ... um ... you're both covered in sand."

Damon laughed now, "We were just standing there on the pier and this dust devil came from out of nowhere and engulfed us," he explained.

Now Liz was really laughing, "Wrong state, silly, but nice try." She winked at me.

When she turned to go back into the house, she whispered, "I expect a detailed summary when you come in, Effie."

I looked at Damon and smiled. "I haven't been here that long, but I sometimes get the feeling that Liz is living vicariously through me."

Damon sighed, "That's not such a bad thing, is it?"

"Oh, no, I actually think its kind of cute. I like Liz a lot, and she always has me laughing and feeling good about myself; she is very trusting though, almost too trusting," I responded.

Damon turned toward me now and said, "I want to see you again. Can I call you tomorrow?"

"I look forward to it," I answered.

He then took my chin in the tips of his thumb and index finger and raised it toward his face, and ever so softly and lightly kissed my lips. Then he slid his thumb across them as if to seal his kiss. "Good night."

He returned to his car and I stood on the porch for a few moments longer, watching his tail lights slowly trail off down the road. As I turned to go inside, I was thinking that it was going to be a long night.

I looked at the door for a few minutes and then thought that I would just try to sneak in. I pressed the thumb lever down on the handle and very slowly opened the door a few inches. I couldn't hear anything, so I stuck my head in to get a quick look around. I turned sideways, edging myself through the door with just enough to squeeze inside. I was in!

I turned back around and, as slowly as I could, I closed the door behind me. Boy, does this bring back memories, I thought to myself. As a senior in high school, I had mastered sneaking in and out of every door in my house. I knew where all the squeaks were. My skills weren't quite good enough. Suddenly Liz was there, hands on her hips, staring at me as I turned around. We looked at each other for a long silent minute and then both burst out laughing.

"We must be a sight for sore eyes," I said to Liz. She was laughing so hard now, her eyes began to water.

She got control of herself and asked me, "Would you like to have a glass of wine?"

"Do you happen to have a Bolla?"

"But of course I do."

I followed her to the kitchen, where the inquisition would soon start.

Liz opened the bottle, poured two glasses and set the bottle in a bucket of ice. She looked at me and told me how, not so long ago, Damon came to Brunswick, much the same way I did; and that he had also stayed with them for a short while.

"We were always quite fond of Damon and thought that he was a little lonely. We have been friends ever since and, with the restaurant he works at, I come by all these great wines."

I must have looked as surprised as I felt.

"I knew you'd ask. I just wanted to tell you first," she said, taking a sip of wine.

After hearing about how she knew Damon, and just happened to have the same wine I tasted earlier, I decided to tell her a little of our night, but not all of it. There are always some things that can be safely omitted without losing the whole picture. So I told her about all the places I saw, the history I learned and the fabulous picnic that

Damon had prepared for me. While I was describing the picnic, I jumped off the stool and ran out to the porch. I returned with a bouquet of flowers.

"You don't happen to have a vase I could borrow?" I asked.

Liz opened the cupboard doors beneath her sink and pulled out a vase.

"We own a bed and breakfast; we have just about anything that you would need." Liz winked.

"I should have known."

Liz was a class act and did nothing half-assed; she was five stars all the way. I finished the story, talking about our walk and how we sat in the sand and kissed once. I knew Liz didn't believe all that. After all, it looked like we took a bath in the sand. But it was good for now. A few moments later, Liz's husband, Ryan, came home.

He was tall, with dark eyes surrounded by wire-rimmed glasses and dark hair styled in a typical male cut, very professional looking. After a quick introduction and some chitchat, all three of us were soon drinking Bolla and laughing. Ryan had the best stories about previous guests and certain goings-on.

"When are you going to light up that nice outdoor fireplace of yours, the one on the side patio?" I asked.

"We haven't done that in quite a while," Liz said.

"How does tomorrow night sound?" Ryan offered.

It was final then. I imagined sitting there with long sticks and roasting marshmallows, pulling them off and smashing them between graham crackers and Hershey's chocolate. Liz offered to get all the ingredients needed for Smores, and my mouth was watering just thinking about it.

"Do you mind if I invite Pea over tomorrow?" Liz asked.

"Why would I mind? I think that would be great."

"I could invite Damon, too." Liz teased.

"Now you're pushing it," I said.

"I thought you liked him."

"I do, but I want to take it slow; I almost lost control earlier today."

I took a last sip of wine from my glass while Liz called and talked to Pea. After a brief conversation, Liz hung up the phone and gave me a nod to confirm that Pea would be coming tomorrow.

"Pea loves a good fire," Liz said. "She will have a lot of good stories to tell, too."

"Is she a good storyteller?" I questioned.

Liz hesitated for a moment, then told me a little about Pea, including how she follows the moons and the stars and does charts for people based on their astrological signs.

"I already knew that."

"She is somewhat like a natural healer, too, but I will let Pea fill you in more tomorrow."

"On that note, I'm headed to bed. Goodnight, all."

Morning came too soon, but I was up and out and ready to see something new today. This time, I met the others guests at breakfast. There was a couple from California; a single, older man with sparse gray hair, in town visiting his elderly mother; and two gentlemen who struck me as being a gay couple. It was quite a variety of people, although none of them seemed like anyone I wanted to sit down and discuss details of my miserable life with.

Liz cooked up another five-star breakfast—Belgium waffles stuffed with a cream cheese filling and topped with hot maple syrup and fresh fruit. She had a side of maple-flavored bacon, orange juice and a sampler plate of nuts. The morning coffee had Frangellico in it, and was absolutely wonderful. After everyone had left the table, I gathered a few dishes and brought them in to Liz. As I handed her the dishes, I inquired about shopping.

"I thought that I might like to do a little shopping today, so I was wondering if there was somewhere small, like a boutique, but with reasonable prices."

"There's the Dream Catcher, which is in the 1600 block of Newcastle," Liz offered. "I'm sure you'll like it. What are you looking for?"

"I know this may sound silly, but something nice for my birthday, even though I have nowhere to go."

"When is your birthday?"

"It's Wednesday."

"Can we plan something for you?"

"I would rather you didn't; I don't really like birthdays"

"Why not?"

"Just never really had any good ones."

"Okay, then," Liz said. "Is there a breakfast food that you like the best?"

"Eggs Benedict is my favorite"

"Done deal."

It was about lunchtime when I arrived at the store. It was a cute little boutique, just the kind I like. Every dress in the store was very unique, unlike the racks of mass-produced clothing you see in the malls. I thumbed my way through the racks and heard a familiar voice behind me.

"Can I help you find something?" Dona asked.

"I know you from the restaurant; you were hostess the other night. Must be hard to have free time when you're working two jobs," I said, feeling surprised and curious.

"This is actually my full-time job," Dona said. "I just help out at the restaurant part time— well, barely even that; just when they need me." Dona went on to explain that she managed the boutique for an older lady who spent most of her year in Brazil, her home country.

"I took the job because I liked the concept of the store. It's also nice to be paid well to run it. I have plans to buy her out in the future." Dona added.

The store was special. Every item of clothing was designed and made for that store. Some of the designers were high-dollar and some were just starting out. Fame didn't matter; I just liked the idea of putting something on and not seeing it on anyone else.

"So, what can I help you find and what is the occasion?" She asked.

I sighed. "Every birthday I buy a new dress, so that's what I'm here for."

"Ohhh. When is your birthday?" Dona asked.

"It's Wednesday; I have nothing special planned, just here for a new dress."

Dona tugged at my arm and led me to a rack in the back room. Apparently these items were just out of the box and waiting to be steamed, and she had one that she wanted me to see. It was a white linen dress that consisted of three pieces. The skirt was long, with embroidered flowers around the bottom hem.

The top was a halter that had a thin sheer white piece of material that went around the neck and stopped just below the collarbone. The bottom part of the halter was constructed the same way, with the sheer material running along the bottom just above the navel and tying in the back. There was a long extra piece of linen that could be worn as a scarf, hair band or a sash.

"I love it." I told Dona. "I don't usually wear white, or at least I never did in the past, but I'm going to start now."

"How much do you want for it?" I asked.

"Two hundred and ten dollars."

"Sold."

"Don't you want to try it on?"

"Nah, this will be fine; but if you could steam it for me and hold on to it, I'll pay for it now and pick it up on Monday."

"No problem."

I pulled the cash out of my purse and completed the transaction painlessly. "I'll see you Monday," I chirped.

I left the store, happy about my purchase, and decided to drive a round a bit. I grabbed a box of buttery popcorn. Last night's craving for sweet s'more was now gone; today I was more wanted salt rather than sweets. It definitely was proving to be a different kind of day for me. I grabbed a burger from McDonald's and headed back home for a quick nap.

Nightfall came quickly. When I woke, I could hear voices outside coming from my window. I must have been tired, I thought to myself. I grabbed my popcorn and headed downstairs. Ryan was making a beautiful fire and Pea was already enjoying a glass of wine.

"Hello there, sleepy-head," Liz said cheerfully.

"Hello all. I'm so sorry that I didn't come down sooner, I was exhausted."

"Don't worry about it; you're here now." Ryan said

"And well-rested too," Liz interrupted

Liz handed me a glass of Bolla, and I took a seat at the table in a comfortable chair that not only swiveled but rocked, too. Candles where everywhere, the night was clear and the stars were in the sky. The temperature was a very pleasant sixty-eight degrees. The mood was very relaxing, but different somehow.

"This almost reminds me of a séance," I said out loud, without thinking.

Pea giggled, "Its funny you said that. I used to play with Ouija boards all the time when I was a kid."

"So, what changed that?"

"Let's just say one bad incident."

"I was always told that nothing good ever comes from that board."

"It doesn't even have to be that particular board," Pea told me.

"What do you mean?" I asked.

And then the stories began. Pea told us about all the incidents that occurred from that board when she was a teen. There was the story about the release of ladybugs and how they infested her bedroom. There was the story about the dog that went crazy after a spirit entered his body. There was the story about burning the board and how the flames rose up and spelled h-e-l-l across the sky.

The last story was about how she made her own board from a piece of scrap wood and used a glass ashtray to travel across the letters to spell words. I don't think that any of these were simply stories though. I could tell there was something different about her. It wasn't anything bad. I felt that Pea was really a good person, but she was definitely different.

As the flames grew brighter, my body grew more relaxed. Heat rolled off the bright red and orange flames. Sparks and embers danced in the night and my eyes were mesmerized by the glow. I had to admit that I loved the feel of the heat and was glad to be sitting here. Pea caught my attention for the last time that evening.

"I didn't want to say anything before," she said slowly. "But, I'm a witch."

I wasn't shocked at that statement. It was the one that followed that really got me.

"I think you're one, too," she said with a smile.

CHAPTER FIVE

Visions

Before I knew it, Monday had arrived. It was April 6 and a beautiful sixty-nine degrees, as I stood outside of Candles and More with my morning coffee. Pea wasn't late; I was early. My phone was ringing now and I was fidgeting through my purse to find it.

"Hello." It was Damon. He had called to wish me luck on my first day of work. After a very short conversation I agreed to call him at the end of the day. It was actually kind of nice, hearing his voice again. I was immediately daydreaming of his lips touching mine again.

"Good morning" Pea said. "Are you deep in thought?"

"Not really," I answered. "I was just reminiscing."

"From the look on your face, I would say it was more of a daydream—about a man."

I blushed and followed her in the store.

Pea showed me around the whole store, introducing me to light switches and such. I especially liked the small kitchen where she made all her candles; I was very eager to learn how to make candles, too. Pea handed me a ring full of keys, explaining where each key went before showing me to the small office.

"This is where you can put together your letters or postcards to the old clients," Pea offered. I was excited to get started.

"I'd like to get those out first thing this morning, if you don't mind." I put my purse away and pulled out my laptop from my small attaché case. I began typing up a small letter with my background on it, offering my services. By noon I had finished my rough draft and I was hungry.

"Hungry?" Pea said as she peeked in the doorway.

"I think you read my mind!" and Pea laughed with me.

We walked up New Castle a couple of blocks and came to a cute deli. We both ordered Cobb salads with white French dressing and enjoyed a cup of black bean soup with a dollop of sour cream. I showed Pea my letter.

"What do you think?" I asked nervously.

"This is great and very professional, but I didn't expect anything less from you."

"I'll run them off when we get back."

"The top right drawer where you were working has two rolls of stamps and the box of envelopes is in the closet."

"Two rolls of stamps? How many clients did she have?"

"Just under one hundred and fifty."

"One hundred and fifty! Holy shit!" I said, rolling my eyes. "She was a popular woman."

"She was good, too." Pea added.

"I guess I have large shoes to fill."

"No worries, you'll be fine ... I can feel it."

We discussed the ad that she was going to run for me and a few scheduling issues. I knew it was going to be a slow start and so did she, so we were busy planning a week full of different things to do to get me familiar with the shop and the area. Today Pea was going to teach me the basics on candle making. She said she also thought it would be neat to give each other a reading. I agreed, and in a short time we were back at the store.

Standing at the small stove, Pea laid out all the ingredients and told me that she was going to show me a very basic way to make candles at home first, and then move me up after I mastered that. She took out a heavy cast iron pot and a tin can that appeared to be an old vegetable tin with the paper removed. She filled the pot with water and set the can inside the pot.

"I'll show you how to use the kitchen kettles next week, but for now you must remember to use a form of the double boiler method to properly melt wax." She then took out the wax and explained that they use a blended candle wax, a premium wax that let her add the scents she likes to use.

The stove slowly warmed up to the point where the wax began to melt in the tin can. Pea then warned me, "You have to be careful of the temperature because wax has a flashpoint and can burst into flames." When the wax had melted, Pea grabbed a box of crayons and told me to pick a color. I chose a melon color and was amazed to watch her add it to the wax after she peeled the paper off of it.

"It's a little trick for quick color," she added. "The proper way is to use dyes, but I'm showing you the simple home version and it's just as nice—and fun, too." Pea then pulled out her tray of oils, which were one hundred percent pure, and asked me to pick one. I chose amber and she added only a half of an ounce because the amount of wax was so small. Then, she poured the wax into a wooden frame; it sat on wax paper to keep the wax from running out of control. We waited for it to cool.

When it cooled enough, she cut the square wax form in half and sprinkled rock salt and glitter on the two halves. Pea then placed one half directly on the other, after setting the wick at the very beginning of the stacked mold. She described the different kinds of wicks involved in candle making and agreed to teach me that at a later date, too. She began to roll it all up, beginning at the end with the wick until it was almost a perfect cylinder shape' she then smoothed the seam shut.

"Pretty soon we'll light it," she told me.

I was absolutely amazed at how easy it was. I did realize that there was more to it, because the candles she sold at the store were made from forms and carved when the wax was still pliable. That type of candle-making I would definitely like to learn. But for now, this was interesting and kind of fun. I thought it would be neat to have workshops to teach people the basics, but wiped that thought away as quickly as it came. If customers could make their own candles, Pea would be out of business.

We took the candle we'd just made and headed to my room for some one-on-one readings. After lighting the candle, Pea decided to do her reading for me first. She was very excited about it. We sat at the table in the middle of the room and she placed the wooden board in the center with the bag of runes. Pea's preferred method of readings were runes in lieu of tarot cards. Runes are very interesting in that they not only look historical, but rune readings date back to the ninth century.

They are oval-shaped stones with simple markings on one side and blank on the other. I mixed the runes in the bag and dumped all twenty-four of them out on the board. I flipped over the stones that had the markings facing up and spread them around the board. I looked over at Pea to see an expression on her face like none other that I have seen before. It was definitely an expression of suspense, almost like she was sitting on pins and needles.

The candle was burning brightly now and I was mesmerized watching it melt. The rock salt looked like crystals in the wax; and as the flickers of fire bounced off of them, I was transfixed. Pea interrupted my gaze.

"I'd like you to place your hand, palm down, just over the stones and move it ever so slightly over the stones until you feel heat from one of them."

I looked at her, almost in disbelief, but followed her instructions.

Pea added, "You might not feel the heat; only a small percentage of people do."

I did not feel it right away and stopped for a moment. I took a deep breath and switched to my left palm. I slowly went over the runes and, to my amazement, one of the stones produced heat that I felt in the palm of my hand near the thumb. I just about jumped off the chair, and so did Pea. A very slight satisfied grin appeared on her face now, one of accomplishment and success. I picked that stone out of the bunch and set it aside. I continued on until I had six stones picked out.

Pea now set each stone in place and flipped them over.

"Let the reading begin," she boasted. The first stone in the foundation placement on the board was a Wunjo stone, also called the glory stone.

"Ah," she said, "you view your foundation as successful and you recognize all your achievements. You have met all your goals that you set out to accomplish and found reward from doing so," She smiled.

The next stone was in the placement of the past. This stone had a marking of an arrow pointed down; she referred to it as the Warrior Reversed.

"This stone represents duty, discipline, responsibility, self sacrifice and strength. In your past, you had many conflicts that required great strength and responsibility to meet and overcome."

Pea hesitated.

"You had the insight to realize the situations that were set forth in front of you and, out of duty, you understood what needed to be done and accomplished the goals as a warrior does on the path to conquer and learn."

The next placement on the board was the present, or the now. The stone that was placed there was the Property stone. The related words with this stone were property, land, inheritance, home, permanence, legacy and a sense of belonging.

"You have been on an adventure through travels; at times you felt like they may have been pointless, but those explorations have led you home. This stone is the 'there's no place like home,' stone." I started to feel very warm and I knew exactly where she was going. I was happy here and this place was starting to feel like home. For the first time in my life, I felt a sense of belonging and the possibility of this place being permanent for me. Not only was I thinking all this, but the words were coming out of Pea's mouth at the same time were the same.

The next stone was in the placement of the future. I could almost see a glow coming from Pea.

"This is so good," she whispered, almost to herself.

"The energy of this rune is raw, powerful and distinctly masculine in the sense that it is pure, elemental fire. The words associated with this stone are energy, passion, vitality, wildness and sexuality, irrationality, the unconscious and the rite of passage." Pea looked up, tilted her head slightly to one side and smiled softly.

"There's an increase in sexual potency and energy in your future," she said.

"The symbol on this rune is representative of the hunt." Pea sat back in the chair and folded her arms in front of her, with that same grin on her face again. I wanted to glower at her but instead found myself blushing.

"Let's move on," I said, more loudly than necessary.

The next placement on the board was the challenge placement, which I'd like to avoid all together. The words associated with this rune are sudden loss, ordeal, destruction, disaster, clearance, testing, karmic lesson and drastic change. Pea's once giddy mood changed.

"This rune represents the destruction of old, being necessary to the growth of something new. It's also meant to give you a caution that when things are going good, we tend to let our guard down and something abrupt can happen to counteract the momentum."

She squirmed a little in her chair, like she was uncomfortable with what she had to say.

"Effie, this is kind of like a wake up call. There's no easy way to put this. Things are going to be going real good and then all of a sudden you're going to hit a wall, and hit it hard. However, you will learn and grow from this incident."

"What kind of wall?" I thought to myself. This concerned me a bit and I hated to admit it. To me, this sounded like an emotional conflict, but it could also be a physical hurdle. I hated to ask and didn't want to appear worried. I know how things go for me, and this was not a prediction I wanted to hear. It couldn't be the destruction of old, because I just did that; but sudden loss, disaster and drastic change could very well happen. "What does this mean," I thought to myself again?

"I can see this bothers you; would you like a reading just on this one stone?" Pea asked.

"No, at least not right now; let me ponder this for a while."

"You want to move on?"

"Oh yes, let's get it all out!"

"The last rune on the board is in the placement of new situation. The symbol is almost that of a lightening strike and is referred as the Sun rune. The words that surround this rune are success, positive energy, and an increase of power, activity, fertility, health and healing. The sun symbolizes life and growth, and motion and energy. Here is where you will become whole again. You will reach the end of your journey and become fully aware of the changing and transient nature of the universe. Once you have come to this point in your life, you will leave the 'safe' position that you have created and chose to continue on your journey."

I sighed. "I see the light. There is a light at the end of the tunnel for me and it's not me crossing over."

Pea laughed. "You're exactly right."

"Increase of power, too? Hell, yeah! Bring it!"

Pea laughed again. "That was a very powerful reading, I have to admit. I am not sure on the time span of this reading, but it didn't seem to me like this was going to be a long road. I received more of an impression that the now and the future were all going to happen pretty fast and abruptly.

"I only got this from the positioning of your runes. It also seems like you'll be thrown off course for only a short while and end up right back on it again. My only advice to you is that you keep your head up and be aware of everything around you."

"I just liked the powerful sexuality part," I piped in quickly. "Can I wallow in that for a bit before all the destruction begins?"

"Okay, wallow in it as long as you like; but just remember what else I said, too."

"Oh, my goodness!" I said, looking at the wall clock.

"Do you have some place to be?"

"Yes, I promised to pick up my dress before Dream Catcher closed."

"What's the dress for?"

"I buy a dress every year on my birthday; it's my gift to myself."

"That's right, Wednesday is your birthday! Are you sure you don't want the day off?"

"Nah, I would really rather be here."

"Okay then."

"How about I read your cards tomorrow?

"Sounds good."

Pea left the room and I started to get things cleaned up, thinking to myself how fast the day had gone. Maybe because it was a day filled with a lot of new things that had come into my life very quickly.

I grabbed the Rolodex to take back to the office. As I grabbed it, I felt like a current of electricity just ran from my fingertips down to my toes and I could not let it go. My eyes remained open, but everything went black. Then, just ahead of me, was a clearing and a light that started out as a small hole and slowly got bigger until I could see the entire picture.

It almost reminded me of how a scene faded out in a movie, only in my eyes it was in the opposite direction. There she laid, Helena in a shallow, murky body of water. Her golden blond hair had not only lost its curl but was now a muddy brown.

Her whole body was still wrapped in scarves as if she was mummified. She had one scarf in particular, a black one, wrapped around her neck. All the other scarves were colored. Tall saw grass was all around her, and I could see a low-lying bridge in the background.

All of a sudden, I couldn't breathe. It was as if someone had blocked my airway. I gasped and dropped everything I was holding. Pea came running from the front of the store, grabbed me by the shoulders and kind of gave me a shake.

"Are you okay?" she asked. "What's wrong, you're scaring me!"

I gasped and took in a deep breath of air. "Helena was killed," I cried out.

Pea dropped her hands off my shoulders and stared at me for what seemed like an hour. I sat down right there in the hallway and told her of my visions.

"She was strangled," I said. Pea went to get me a glass of water and returned very quickly. She handed me the water and gave me a tiny pill.

"This will relax you a bit. Don't worry; its nothing dangerous, it's herbal." After a half hour, I was feeling better. I stood up and gathered all my things.

"I need to leave, I'm late," I said.

Pea looked at me with concern.

"Are you sure you're ready to go? I think we need to talk to someone about this."

"Can we talk to someone tomorrow?" I asked.

"I need a little time to think—and prepare to be looked at like some crazy poser." Pea agreed and let me go.

I got down to my Jeep, jumped in and headed to the Dream Catcher. I was five minutes late but Dona was still there doing paperwork. I rapped lightly on the door and she let me in.

"What happened to you?" Dona asked. "You look like you saw a ghost."

"Oh, I'm fine." I said. "I was just worried that I wouldn't make it in time and didn't want to hold you up from going home." Dona laughed.

"The only thing you're holding me up from home is happy hour. Would you like to join me?" She walked to a rack next to the register where my dress hung nicely in a black garment bag. She bundled the paperwork together and shoved it under the desk, grabbed her purse and keys and handed me the garment bag.

"That settles it then; come with me, you don't want a drink—you need a drink." Dona chuckled. We left the store and Dona locked up.

"Where are we going?" I asked.

"To the Seaside Grille."

"Maybe that's not such a great idea for me"

"Why not?"

"Is Damon working?" I asked.

"Probably, but that's what you need anyhow; look at yourself."

Dona was definitely right. I was quite pasty and maybe I did require the company of something nice to look at after what I had just seen.

"I'll meet you there," I said.

It wasn't far, just a couple of blocks. Everything I needed seemed to be in a two-to-four-block radius. It was rather nice for a change: no traffic jams to tie up five miles of expressway for forty minutes. This meant I would always have extra time for myself.

I arrived at the Seaside Grille and Dona was waiting for me at the door. She opened the door for me and followed me in. I waited until she was through the door before I took another step.

"What're you waiting for?" She joked. I smiled and followed her to the bar. We took our seats and waited a bit; not too long, though. Before long, I heard a familiar voice and then saw a familiar face. The mere sight of Damon's green eyes and olive skin was as soothing as any drink could be.

"Well, hello there," he said. He reached out and grabbed my right hand, only to kiss it ever so softly.

"To what do I owe this pleasure?"

"I'm here, too." Dona interrupted.

"I'm sorry," Damon said very sympathetically. "What can I get the two of you to drink?"

"I'll have a glass of Chianti," Dona said, with her lips looking like they haven't seen water in two weeks.

"I'm going to have a Jack and coke, and can you make that a double, please?"

One eyebrow rose ever so slightly above Damon's left eye.

"It's only five-thirty. You have all night; are you sure you want to start with a double?"

"Absolutely!" I said as if I just answered the million-dollar question with certainty. Damon had turned to make our drinks and I looked at Dona, only to receive the same look that I just received from Damon.

"What are you looking at, and why are you looking at me in that way?" I insisted. "Can't a girl have a little fun at five in the afternoon?"

"I may not know you that well, Effie, but I know enough to tell that something didn't go right today."

I tried to laugh, but the noise that came out sounded more like a sick seal. It didn't matter. For now at least I was keeping the details to myself.

Damon brought us our drinks. The bar wasn't very busy. Mondays are pretty slow and the Seaside Grille tries to push happy hours on Mondays and Tuesdays. I looked at my drink—or should I say drinks—and asked, "Why the shot glass on the side?"

"In the state of Georgia, you can't put a double shot in a drink, so I have to give you your drink with a shot of Jack on the side." Now my eyebrow was raised. Well, if this is the law, I thought to myself, then I will follow the law. I grabbed the shot glass and raised it to my lips. Without even blinking an eye, the shot was gone and I was chasing it down with my second drink.

Up until this point, surprise covered Damon's face. Then, ever so slightly, the corners of his mouth started to curl upwards. He was enjoying seeing the other side of Effie, and I was dreaming about seeing the other side of Damon, the side that would stand before me with him wearing only beams of moonlight.

"Could I have a lime, please, and another Jack and coke?"

About five Jack and cokes later, I was absolutely worthless. Damon left the bar to get me a cup of coffee and some food, and Dona was talking to another couple at the end of the bar, when my least favorite waitress in the place approached me.

"Don't forget what I told you the other day about Damon." Cali said. I turned my chair ever so slightly and leaned my head to sit in my left hand with my elbow supporting it on the bar.

"You know what your problem is, Cali? You're the town whore who couldn't land Damon. So now that your life is miserable, you want to make everyone else around you miserable. If I were you, I'd take your little advice and go fuck yourself with it!"

Shock came across that bitch's face as if no one had ever told her where to go. That was all it took and she was gone. I looked down at the end of the bar and could see Dona gleaming with pride. She walked over and whispered in my ear, "I have wanted to say that for a year now. You haven't been here even a week and let her have it; I envy you."

I interrupted, "It wasn't me talking, it was Jack. He gets like that once in a while."

"Well then, my hat's off to Jack." Dona laughed.

"Courage in a bottle, I tell ya!"

"I am going to take you and Jack home as soon as you eat. Damon will pick me up at Liz's and bring me back to my car."

An hour later I had filled my stomach with some wonderful bread and light pasta. Dona had driven me home and Liz met us at the front porch. Liz escorted me up to my room and laid me down on my bed; seconds later I was out.

I woke in the morning to my cell phone. It was Damon. I wondered how much of Jack Effie he had seen. Apparently he'd seen all of him, judging by the nonstop laughter that was coming from the other end.

"All right, all right. Thanks for calling to check on me, but I have to head off to work now."

I said my goodbyes and jumped out of bed to get ready for the day. It was raining out, which I hadn't seen in a while. It smelled good. I grabbed my things and headed downstairs to grab a cup of coffee and a bagel. I wasn't good for much of anything else this morning. Liz had gone out to run some errands, which was probably a good thing. She had a friend filling in for her, helping with the guests. I introduced myself as I poured a cup of coffee, buttered a bagel and headed for my car.

Fifteen minutes later I was standing in front of the one door that I didn't want to open today—the door of Candles and More. Pea solved my dilemma. She opened the door for me, from the inside. She had been there an hour already trying to figure out the best way to handle our situation. I have never been one for covering shit up, but today I really would have liked to have done just that. Today, I would also have really liked to have had my cigarettes.

"What happened to you?" Pea asked.

"Nothing much, a little bit of spirits last night is all." I said.

"I called Sam; he'll be here in a few minutes."

"Who's Sam??"

"He's a friend. A good friend from school." Pea led the way back to the small kitchen where a coffee pot and assorted herbal teas were piled high in a wicker basket.

"He used to be a police officer, but now he's working as a private detective or something I think."

"You think?" I asked. "Is he a cop or a detective?"

"Well, he's working on some sort of investigation and he's not a cop," she shrugged.

"He's a little more open-minded and I thought that it would be better if we ran it by him first, before we actually went to the police."

Although she was usually a tea drinker, Pea made a strong pot of coffee and we were both enjoying a cup of it when Sam entered the store. He was a good-looking man, not like the short squatty private dick type I had always imagined or associated with private eyes. He was tall—about six foot two, with light blond hair cut very short in a military-type buzz, almost shaved. He had blue eyes and thick, full soft lips; the kissable kind.

He smiled, showing off his bright white, straight teeth. His skin was a very light tan and he was sporting a five o'clock shadow. He wasn't just good looking, he was built, too. He had broad shoulders, thick biceps and a small waistline. If I weren't attracted to dark-haired men, he would be next on my list of local men to get to know, I thought to myself.

Sam gave Pea a hug and kiss on the cheek, and they swapped the basic small talk that people have when they haven't seen one another for a long time. He turned to me and held out his hand.

"Hi, I'm Sam." I shook his hand. He had rough, wide palms; definitely a man that worked with his hands. He also had just recently been surfing. I experienced flashes of waves, a large orange surfboard and a feeling of being boiled by the heat and turmoil of the ocean.

I smiled and said, "Nice to meet you, Sam. My name is Franciscka."

"Is there somewhere we can sit, where it is somewhat private?" Sam asked. The three of us went back to my new room, where Pea and Sam took a seat on the small couch. Sam began to talk and we listened. He had taken the small bit of the information that Pea had given him over the phone and done a little digging on his own. It was true that Helena's family had not heard from her in a while. That wasn't necessarily a good thing, though.

What made it a problem was the fact that Helena often left her family in the dark, sometimes for months at a time. However, Sam still felt like pursuing the matter at hand. He had gone to the place where she was living and done a bit of "exploring," he said.

He admitted he had to be very careful because, after all, it was breaking and entering. But Sam knew how to get in and get out without disturbing a thing in sight. He had experience in this, he assured me, making me feel both comforted and nervous. Sam then leaned in toward me and very softly said, "Now, tell me your story."

Hesitantly, I told him everything. For some strange reason, I felt safe and secure when talking to him. It was almost as if I had known him my whole life. In some sort of way he dazzled me slightly, too. I was almost embarrassed to tell him the things that I saw, the things that I knew. It was difficult enough for me to understand, let alone for me to explain it all to some man I barely knew.

He seemed to be a critical thinker, someone who saw things as black and white with no shades of grey in between. Most people would see me as some kind of a quack, nut job, fruitcake; however you describe it, it all meant the same thing. I wasn't your average girl next door. Sam was surprisingly open about it, though, and gave me no indication that I was any of these things.

After hearing about my vision and my story of feeling choked, Sam sat there for a minute just staring at the ceiling. He was completely speechless. I wasn't sure if he was wondering what he should say or if what I said was true. I watched him curiously, trying to size him up. I couldn't take my eyes off of the blueness of his eyes.

The color had reminded me of the water in Key Largo. A lot of it had to do with the reflection from his shirt, but I was happier thinking that my "Dick Tracy" had an extra special aspect to his demeanor. My daydreaming was interrupted by Sam asking me the question I had been dreading.

"How do you know all of this?"

I smiled nervously, biting my lower lip, and responded, "The same way that I knew that you recently went surfing with an orange long board. As a matter of fact, you're a new surfer. The waves owned you this last time out. You were tossed, slammed and thrown to the ocean floor several times."

Sam gasped. "That is absolutely amazing. I'm not even sure what to say to that. Forgive me, but I have to know how you do that without calling you a witch."

I laughed.

"Being called a witch is not that bad nowadays. As long as you don't want to burn me at the stake, I'm okay with being a witch." He smiled, and I felt encouraged to continue.

"There are actually several different classifications to being a witch, including being kind of a psychic. Witchcraft is the practice of any of the arts of a witch, or the religion of a witch, and is the fastest growing religion in the United States and Great Britain, soon to surpass Judaism, which is the third most populous religion in the U.S." I stopped my rush of facts and bit my lip.

"Shit, sorry about that; I didn't mean to sound like a Google search."

Sam nodded and Pea stifled a smile, trying to remain serious.

"Let me take a step back and answer your question. When I shook your hand, and I don't really know how to explain further than that, I tapped into your energy or memories. I don't know how to explain it, but I get visions when I touch certain things, but I don't get them all the time. I have yet to learn how to control it; actually, I have yet to learn whether I even can control it."

Sam sat there silently for a moment, which seemed like an eternity to me. None of us said anything until the bells from the front door broke the awkward silence. Pea rose to her feet to go help the customer who entered the store, leaving Sam and I alone. He handed me a card and told me to call the man whose name was on it when I felt ready to tell the story again. He urged me not to tell anyone else in the department, knowing that many others wouldn't believe me.

The card was from the Georgia State Police and the name written on the front was Detective Mark Sawyer. I stared at the card for a minute. It felt cold. I got no visions or feelings from it, so I tucked it in my back pocket as I rose to my feet.

As we started to walk out, Sam said, "One more thing— when you do go talk to him, don't go in reeking of alcohol!" I blushed and tried to explain.

"No need for explanations," he assured me. "I think I would have been doing the same thing, too, if I saw the things you did."

On the way to the front of the store, Sam complimented me and told me how intriguing he thought I was.

"I really enjoyed our conversation," he said. I blushed again, not knowing how to take yet another compliment. Sam turned to me and held my hand, "I'll keep poking around. This isn't the kind of work that I'm used to doing, but there's something about all this that I just can't shake."

Then I heard a familiar voice. It was Damon. Sam left with a goodbye to Pea and a brief "Damon" and stiff nod of acknowledgment to Damon.

I thought that was a bit strange; it was almost as if they didn't like each other, but were attempting to be cordial.

"How is my little fish?" Damon chuckled.

"I'm doing a lot better this morning, thanks for asking. You didn't come all this way for that, did you?"

"I came over here for a couple of reasons."

"Oh, what are those couple of reasons?" I pried.

"The first reason was, of course, to see how you are."

"And the second?" I asked.

"I heard from a little birdie that your birthday is tomorrow and I'd like to take you to dinner."

"Hmm … I think that would be okay, but you could have just called."

"I know, but I wanted to see you, my morning sunshine."

"You are too sweet."

"Can you wear that new white dress that I heard all about? That same little birdie told me how stunning you looked in it."

"I think that could be done."

"On that note, I'll let you get back to work. By the way, is everything okay? Sam usually doesn't check in on people unless there's something wrong."

"Maybe Sam saw me from afar and thought I was cute," I winked. I immediately knew it was the wrong thing to say. Damon got quiet very quickly. I could tell that he didn't really appreciate my comment and it made him uneasy, although he attempted to laugh it off. I reached out and squeezed his hand and told him I looked forward to seeing him for dinner tomorrow. He left smiling, giving me one of his winks in return.

I turned to Pea with confusion and questions. I wasn't the only psychic. Before I had gotten the words out of my mouth, she had already begun to answer my questions.

"Sam and Damon used to be friends a couple of years back. Sam had a girlfriend named Jillian that he dated for almost a year, and things were starting to fade between the two of them. I think Sam was into her more than he let show, and that was part of the problem.

"They tried to make it work, but I think it was too little too late; one night she turned to Damon for comfort. Things went too far, one thing led to another; I guess you can figure out the rest. Jillian left and things were never the same. Damon has been trying to make up for it ever since."

There was a small piece of me that was disheartened by this new insight into some of Damon's past loves. I wouldn't judge him for it, though, because we all make mistakes. He who is without sin, cast the first stone, I thought to myself. I'd certainly made my share of mistakes in the past.

"I have some good news for you," Pea said, interrupting my thoughts.

"Some good news would be very much welcomed right about now."

"I made some appointments for you tomorrow."

"That is good news," I said excitedly.

"Do you want to do a practice run and read my cards?"

"That sounds like a very good plan."

Pea and I walked to the back of the store, where my room was waiting for me. The walk back seemed to take forever with all these new thoughts swirling around in my head. For the first time, I felt as if I was supposed to be here. I felt like this place had called for me to be here. For what reason I was as yet unsure, but I was confident that I would soon find out.

I carefully unfolded my black velvet cloth and gently laid it across the table. I sprinkled my sage across the top of it and began the set-up for Pea's reading. Pea shuffled the deck each time the seventh card was counted and laid it face down. She did this until all eleven cards were lined across the cloth.

I started with the set-up in front of me and began to read her cards, beginning with the first card, which signified what was behind her, what she was no longer worried about and that held no concern to her. This card was a foundation card. It showed that her home, health and stability was of no concern and that in the present day she was satisfied with where she was in those aspects of her life.

The next area of the reading dealt with Pea's hopes. The card that was flipped over was the fertility and family card, which needed very little explaining. It was quite evident that Pea had not reached this time in her life, but looked toward the future and acquiring it. I then flipped the card that represented her fears.

It was rather interesting. The card represented a fork in the road and the inability to make a decision. That card led into the card that represented the forces at work now in Pea's life, which was the balance card. Usually when this card is drawn, a person either has a perfect balance; if it's upside down, it reflects an inability to balance.

All cards are relatable, one way or another. Pea took a sip of her tea and remained very quiet. She had no questions for me, so I knew the cards were hitting home. The unfortunate thing was that I couldn't get any additional insight to add to the cards.

No lights, flashes or colors—nothing. I went through the four past cards, all of which represented travel, wealth and a good foundation, so the cards were flowing really well, but I wondered about the card of a young woman in her past. It was a priestess card.

Thoughts of Helena popped in my head as I turned the card. The last three cards were future cards. One of the cards represented disillusionment and the card next to it was a warning card with the description of a person on it.

The person was an older man with dark hair, possibly graying. He was a man of authority and power. The last card was the death card. Contrary to what people think, the death card doesn't mean death literally. I like to call this card the closing of a chapter in one's life and the opening of a new one. It can also mean a conclusion to something.

"That was a good reading," Pea said to me.

"I agree, but you seem to be a bit distant now."

"It's nothing; I just have a lot on my mind lately."

"I understand exactly what you're saying; I have been a bit speechless myself." We were both silent for a moment contemplating our readings and the future. Then we shifted back to the present.

"The clients coming tomorrow are regulars; you'll like them!" Pea said excitedly.

"I'm sure I will," I said, mirroring her energy. With that said, I packed up my things and made my way to the kitchen to make a few candles. Work was becoming a relaxing ritual for me now. I still couldn't help but feel like I was supposed to be doing so much more.

I rearranged my room a bit so everything would be ready to go when my first client came. Then I found myself exploring the antique bookshelves, grabbing Dracula and beginning to read. There is nothing like diving into the lives of a few vampires to take one's mind off of things!

Before I knew it, the day had come to an end and I was headed home for some much needed rest.

CHAPTER SIX

The Natural Witch

It was very quiet as I sat on my bed, deep in thought. I knew I was different; Pea's thoughts of me being a witch didn't spook me, but did make me curious. My laptop rested on my thighs and I could feel the heat generating from the underside.

I thought about checking in on my social networking page, but wiped that idea out as quickly as it popped in my head. Instead I found my way to the Google bar and typed in N-a-t-u-r-a-l W-i-t-c-h. I hated to admit it, but I had wanted to do this for a while.

It wasn't that I was scared at what I might find, because I already knew I was a little different. I just wanted to find some answers or something to help me understand my visions. Pea had merely reignited my interest when she brought up the whole witch idea. By no means did I think I was a witch. Yet, I pushed forward with my search.

Taking a deep breath, I started to read.

"One is born a natural witch and it is usually hereditary. Witchcraft is the fastest growing belief system in U.S. and the second largest religion in the United States." Yes, that's right; I read it myself—religion. Witchcraft passed Buddhism in 2005, Hinduism in 2007, Islam in 2008 and

Judaism in 2009. Witches are closely related to the earth and are known as the Defenders of Nature and Mother Earth.

"Witchcraft is the oldest known religion," the website stated. There is archaeological evidence that dates witchcraft back 106,000 years, with fragments of whalebone found depicting forms of calendar making containing moon phases and the tracking of the woman's menstrual cycle. Historians suggest that this is how witchcraft had begun—examining the mysteries of the woman's body, from menstruation to pregnancy.

Spells and magick rituals were nothing more than natural remedies with herbs and oils and prayers to the gods.

"One of the earliest known remedies came from the center, or hip, of a rose, which contains a very high concentration of iron and vitamin C. Rose hip was given in a tea form to a woman who was having her period to make up for the loss of blood."

It also said that there "were other trace ingredients that help with the mood swings. Today you can find rose hip tea in just about any natural food store."

That information about the tea made my head spin. I sat for a moment and thought back as far as I could. I was maybe thirteen when my grandmother had given me her special tea. She never referred to it as rose hip, but she always told me that it was floral and good for me when I was menstruating. I had to admit I remembered it helping. This memory now sparked my interest even more. Sitting there wondering, I pushed myself to search for more.

I quickly clicked on another link that caught my attention, "Natural Witch Characteristics." The natural witch can see things happen or make predictions; they also have strong senses and feelings of others. The natural witch will be drawn to the energies given off by runes, tarot or astrology, in which the practice of any of these methods will be very natural. The natural witch ability will run in the family, but it may not be direct; it is known to skip a generation.

The natural witch is affected by the moon cycle, becoming either more restless or more excitable. The natural witch is also drawn to the sea and finds comfort there. It's a sense of feeling at home and one with nature.

She will also have closeness with a particular animal, almost like a sharing of energy. Some witches will choose a name that reflects traits of this animal. Natural witches also channel their healing energy by soothing or comforting others with a single touch.

All right, there were clearly a lot of characteristics that described me, I thought to myself. I was starting to feel that maybe Pea was thinking in the right direction, but was still uneasy about calling myself a witch. Society has done a pretty good job of painting witches as evil and ugly. I scrolled down the page a bit and came across a link titled, "Psychic Abilities," and clicked on that. That page brought up many subtopics and I began to click on them, one at a time.

Clairvoyance, aka sixth sense, caught my attention first. I read through it quickly and saw that it can be triggered by a near-death experience. That took my breath away as I thought back about a year when I was mugged at knifepoint in Detroit.

I was lucky and only suffered a concussion, but I remember flashes of my life rolling before my eyes. I shook my head and read further, coming across "Clairaudience," which was hearing voices and felt elated that I didn't have that. Then there was clairsentience, the ability to pick up feelings from touching an object or person. That was enough to convince me there might be something to more to my abilities.

The sense that really caught my eye was "Clairalience," which is the psychic gift of smell. The more I read, the more I realized that I possessed these characteristics as well, and didn't even know it.

I laid back and stared at the ceiling. I felt warm, almost sweaty and a bit nervous. Closing my eyes now and concentrating, I remembered the smell as I entered the room of a college classmate many years ago. It smelled like a hospital room. I had asked her if she was doing some serious cleaning and she laughed at me. Apparently she didn't clean much. I never mentioned a word about the smell, but do remember her dad passing away a month later from pancreatic cancer. There are other times that I have smelled out-of-place scents, too, but none as noteworthy.

I closed my laptop and promised myself to do more research later, as I was getting a bit tired and I was little overwhelmed by all the information. I'm not sure how I feel about possessing all these characteristics. If this is a true gift, I thought to myself, I need to do something good with it. I had to admit, I was a bit scared, and being scared was not part of my normal personality.

CHAPTER SEVEN

The Birthday Wish

I woke early on my birthday morning, with one of my favorite scents drifting up from the kitchen ... Hollandaise sauce. I quickly jumped into the shower, got dressed, threw on a small amount of makeup and stormed down the stairs. It was like a queen's feast in front of my eyes. A small vase with a single red rose was in front of my plate. My plate also had a silver plated dome-like cover on it, so I couldn't see the food, but I knew what it was. Next to the plate was my normal cup of coffee, just the way I like it, and a glass of mimosa. I sat down and lifted the cover.

The plate was empty except for a small card folded in half that simply read, "Happy Birthday." Liz and Ryan came from the kitchen carrying a larger plate, almost like a platter, singing Happy Birthday. It was almost embarrassing. Liz carefully and proudly set the large plate in front of me. It held eggs Benedict, hash browns, and a side of bacon, a bowl of fresh strawberries and a glorious blueberry muffin with a lit candle in the center. I made a wish and blew out the candle.

"I hope your wish comes true," Liz said in excitement.

"So do I," I answered hopefully. "So do I."

After the wonderful breakfast and an enjoyable conversation with Liz and Ryan, I had arrived at work feeling pretty good. Pea was there before me again, wearing an ear-to-ear grin and holding a box.

"Happy Birthday," she said with barely contained excitement. It was obvious she was near busting with joy about the gift she held.

"I give up; what do you have in that box for me?" I asked hesitantly. A second later, I told her, "Never mind. I'll wait till the end of the day." Since gifts were not my thing, and Pea was excited enough for the both of us, I figured that it would be even more fun for me to wait.

I walked back to my room and began to get things set up. This was different for me and I have to admit I was a bit nervous, almost like a young girl being kissed for the first time. I needed to relax, so I sat in the middle of the floor with legs crossed and began taking some deep breaths, in and out. My goal was to try to clear my mind completely. I began to perform my usual meditation.

I closed my eyes and took a deep breath in, while imagining a light from the mid-section of my body expelling out of the pores of my skin and surrounding me like a sphere. I held my breath until the sphere was all I could see in my mind.

As I let my breath out, I imagined me inside this magical sphere, drifting to the uppermost atmosphere of the earth and now surrounding the earth. I took in another breath and held it. The sphere now left the atmosphere and was one with the universe.

I held it there for as long as I could and released it. The way I used my mind to convert my body into a form of light and energy was my personal way to relax. I was now ready.

The morning actually went pretty well. I had four customers and, for the most part, they completely accepted me. The last one was skeptical until I mentioned her mom's diamond-faced watch, which she wore to school one day without her mom knowing, and then lost it. Let's just say I made a believer out of her quickly.

Pea took me to lunch at the same deli we went to earlier in the week. She carried that stupid box all the way there; I still refused to open it and made her carry it all the way back. I could see her frustration growing and decided I was definitely having a lot of fun with this.

I only had a couple of clients in the afternoon and they came together. Believe it or not, there was a birthday coming up for one of them, Jan, and the reading was the friend's gift to her. They actually were a lot of fun and we spent a little while discussing our astrological signs. I convinced the birthday girl to ask Pea to do a chart for her. Jan's birthday was the coming Sunday.

After they left, all was quiet. I cleaned up my room and gathered my things. I figured since I didn't have any more bookings, I would leave just a little earlier so I could have some extra time to get ready for my dinner date. I told Pea that I was going to head home a little early and she was just fine with that.

"Can you open this now?" she asked as he held up the box.

"I just don't know ..." I responded. I could see the energy leaving Pea's body and figured she'd had enough.

"Well, I suppose I can." I said slowly. I saw the energy surge back into her body and she became very giddy once again. She kind of reminded me of the movie "Doctor Dolittle," where the dog is jumping up and down, yelping at the doctor every few seconds to "Throw the ball! Throw the ball!"

I chuckled to myself at the image and grabbed the box.

It was perfectly square and reminded me of a crock-pot box. Maybe that's what it is. I thought; she knows that I don't have a place of my own yet, and it's certainly heavy enough. It was wrapped in silver paper adorned with tiny rhinestones. The large bow on the top was a combination of white and silver. The edges of the box were covered with white lace ribbon. I swear, I thought the wrapping was more elaborate than the contents could possibly be. I carefully removed everything until the box was naked ... yes, naked. That's the only word I had for it at this point.

As I cut the taped sides with my fingernails, I was trying to imagine what could possibly be that heavy. I set the box down on the reception desk, lifted the flaps and pulled out the tissue. I was speechless. It was the most beautiful crystal ball I'd ever seen, and it was my own. I almost cried as I begged her to take it back, because I know how expensive they are.

"I'm not taking it back," Pea said.

"But this is too much."

"No, it's not. How about we call this work equipment for your job and a birthday gift combined?"

"No one has ever given me something like this before."

"I find it very hard to believe that a girl as pretty and talented as you has never received nice gifts," Pea said in surprise.

"It's not the gift itself, it's the thought behind it," I said. "You heard me say that I always wanted one of these and remembered."

I gave Pea a big hug and thanked her for the wonderful gift. She kindly reminded me that I would have to purchase the stand to put it on. She was going to do that, too, she said, until she remembered that sometimes the stand is very personal and she wanted to leave that for me. I understood exactly what she meant and promised that I would look for a special one tomorrow.

"Have a great time tonight," Pea said, and then followed it with a wink.

"I will definitely try. I don't think anything could screw this day for me. It has been wonderful thus far."

I grabbed my beautiful gift and drove back to my room. When I got to the house, I asked Liz for a short, sturdy drinking glass to keep in my room for a couple of days. She handed it to me and made me promise that I would stop down and talk to her before I left. I promised and took the glass to my room.

I set the glass on the table and removed a black silk scarf from one of my drawers and laid it across the top. I then gently set the crystal ball in the center of the glass. I sat and looked at it for at least ten minutes, just admiring the beauty of it. Then it was time to get ready for my date.

Half an hour later, the doorbell rang; I grabbed my purse and went to meet Damon. Liz had already let him in and was sharing small talk with him when I came down the stairs. He was as absolutely beautiful as ever.

Damon left Liz in mid-sentence and dashed for the stairwell with his hand held out. I grabbed his hand as I took the remaining four steps. Damon lifted my hand and kissed it so softly that my entire arm tingled and the tiniest hairs sprang up to leap and dance.

"You are the most stunning thing I have ever laid my eyes on," Damon whispered to me.

"Thank you; you don't look half bad yourself," I giggled. Liz said her goodbyes and smiled devilishly as we left.

It wasn't long at all before we were at the restaurant. Damon parked the Scout and raced around the front to open the door for me. We walked to the door together with his hand resting lightly on the small of my back and the door opened for us.

Dona was there to greet us, and let Damon know that everything was ready to go as he had requested. I have to admit, I was beginning to get just a bit nervous at this point. I was wondering exactly what he had planned for me, and the nerves were mixed with a feeling of excitement.

Damon grabbed my hand and led me up the stairs to the banquet room. I took two steps in and was awestruck. He had managed to take my breath away. In the center of the room was a table for two draped with a white embroidered tablecloth, and topped with two tall, lit candles and a dozen long-stemmed white roses. A bottle of champagne was chilling in a pewter stand.

Surrounding the table were four lime trees adorned with strings of white lights. The only lights in the room were the candles and the four trees. Sprinkled all over the floor were tiny white flowers, which appeared to be baby's-breath. As Damon led me to the table and slid the chair out for me, I could hear soft jazz throughout the room. I recognized the big band sound. It was Najee playing. I took my seat and Damon sat across from me. His beautiful eyes were gleaming.

Damon grabbed the bottle of champagne, labeled "Dom Perignon Rose, 1985," from the bucket and slowly let the cork out. He filled both of our glasses with the blush-colored bubbles and placed the bottle back in the ice.

The waiter arrived at the table, someone I hadn't noticed before, and gave us each a menu. The menu was rolled up in a scroll and when unrolled, dinner choices were revealed.

Damon said, "Order anything you like." We placed our orders and Damon lifted his glass.

"To a stunning woman; may this night be a night for you to treasure always." The champagne touched my lips and the dryness mingled with the tiniest hint of fruit. This had to be the most wonderful thing I ever drank.

"It's even better when you follow it with a strawberry." Damon slid the bowl toward me. We enjoyed light conversation about food and wine while we enjoyed our bubbly and oysters. By the time the lobster arrived, we were on bottle number two and I was having the most wonderful time that I had ever had with a man. Even if you took everything else away and left us in the middle of this empty room with just each other to enjoy, it would be just as grand.

We finished our dinner. Shortly after the plates were cleared, a Black Forest torte with a single candle in the middle arrived. I made my wish and blew out the candle, but couldn't take another bite; instead, I asked to take it home and enjoy it with my friends later. The waiter removed everything from the table except for the champagne and strawberries, and Damon and I enjoyed some more conversation.

It was quiet for a moment and the music became a little more noticeable. Damon stood in front of me with his hand out and asked if I would like to dance. My face felt warm and my hands grew moist. My heart must have been beating twice as fast now, so much so that I could practically feel it trying to jump out of my chest. I wiped my hands on the bottom of my dress, took a deep breath and stood up to take Damon's hand.

Off to the side was a small dance floor, which he led me to. His right hand rested low on my hip as I took his left hand in my right. We moved slowly, in steps so short it was more like a lovers sway.

The music was familiar to me and I was trying to place it, but it finally came to me. It was from the final scene in the movie Twilight; I think it was called "American Mouth." I chuckled to myself because that's what I was to him. I didn't need to fantasize about Damon being a vampire; but then again, I wouldn't turn down a little nibble on my neck. Then he pulled me close, so close that I could feel every contoured inch of his body.

Our movement became even slower and I rested my head on his shoulder. I could hear him inhale the scent of my hair and felt the heat of his breath at my ear. His lips were moist and soft as they found the path from my ear lobe to the base of my neck using small rhythmic taps.

Shivers of delight and nervousness streamed through my entire body, as if I was a schoolgirl being kissed for the first time on the playground. His mouth found its way to the underside of my chin, traveled up to the tip of the chin and was now resting on my lips, just barely touching them.

"What is he waiting for?" I thought to myself. I couldn't take the anticipation any longer and found my way to his mouth, tasting and caressing it entirely. We were intertwined like thunder and lightning and whatever music had been playing in the background now disappeared. Both of his hands were nestled low on my hips, then edged their way toward my backside. Damon then grabbed me and pulled me even closer into him.

It had been a long time since I had felt this tingling sensation and my body wasn't turning away this time. Damon's hands slid up my skirt, touching and massaging the bare skin on my lower back in slow but firm movements. He then picked me up off the floor and my legs wrapped around his waist as he carried me to the table and laid me down, still holding me with one hand and moving the champagne flutes with the other.

He untied my halter then pushing both halves to my sides. His hands were now resting on my breasts, cupping them so quickly I didn't have enough time to feel the chill of the air. I reached up and slowly unbuttoned Damon's shirt and pushed it back off his shoulders. His strong, tan chest was now exposed to mine. I ran both my hands across it, feeling the tightness and admiring the sight.

He lay down on top of me, and his mouth made its way to mine. I could taste the champagne from his lips and the excitement was pouring out of my skin. I no longer knew where I was, nor did I care. My dainty stringed panties were removed with the slightest effort and he slid his way inside of me. Slow, wavelike motions took over as my hips moved with his.

The full weight of his body was on top of mine and I was begging for every inch of him. My hands found their way to his muscular ass, pulling him into me even deeper now. The heat from our bodies was almost more than I could handle, as I tasted the salt from his skin. His breathing increased, as did mine.

Our bodies moved wildly now and I was at the verge of losing all control. My heart pounded feverishly as my body stiffened, unleashing spasms of delight as Damon's warmth filled me. He collapsed on top of me. My eyes closed and I didn't move, nor did I want to. I wanted this moment to last a little longer.

Then the unthinkable occurred. Damon whispered in my ear, "I think I'm falling in love with you."

By the time we left it was late and, thank God, we were the last two people in the restaurant. Damon locked up, led me to his Scout and helped me in. He started the engine, but just sat there quietly staring into space. He looked as if he was a million miles away.

"Have I thanked you for the wonderful time yet?" I asked.

"Yes, you did that before we ever left." He chuckled. "It was kind of cute."

"I am embarrassed to say that I got that from the movie 'Pretty Woman.'"

"It's even cuter now that you told me that."

I placed my hand in his and took a deep breath.

"I think I feel the same about you, too, Damon. Matter of fact, I know I do. I never had this type of a connection before and I guess I'm a bit scared, to be perfectly honest with you. A lot of strange things have been happening to me and a lot of new feelings have filled me so quickly that, well, I just want to be a bit cautious."

Damon took my face in both of his hands and stared into my eyes, and then he kissed me ever so softly on the forehead. He drove me to the beach, where we walked barefooted and talked throughout the night. We later sat in the sand, arm in arm, watching the sunrise. What a beautiful sight it was.

The night had come to a close and it was time for me to head back home to get ready for work. Damon let me drive his Scout to the house, which was almost more fun than anything else that night. I did say 'almost.' I quietly got out of the truck and gave Damon a kiss on the cheek as we crossed in front of the Scout. I quickly snuck in the house and to my room like a teenager sneaking home after a night of sneaking out.

CHAPTER EIGHT

Trouble Finds Me Everywhere

I arrived for work a little late that morning and was feeling like a whole new person. Yet, when I arrived at the door, my newly-found feeling had sunk into the pit of my stomach. Sam was standing there and although he was very handsome, he had this look about him. He smiled at first and then kind of looked at the ground. His hands were shoved deep into his pockets and he was looking everywhere around him completely, avoiding eye contact with me.

His mannerism was clearly telling me that something wasn't right. Thoughts started to rush through my head and I quickly began to prepare myself for the worst. My hands started to get warm and I was sure my once slightly tan complexion had just turned to eggshell. Sam gave it his best shot, though, and attempted to force a smile out, the kind of smile you get from someone who doesn't care for you, but is trying to appear pleasant.

"Hello, Sam."

"Hi, Effie."

"Is everything okay?" I asked.

"Not really; I came here to talk to you before the news broke. It's not going to be easy after it does."

"Let's talk inside."

I fumbled around in my large black purse, nervously searching for the key to the front door. All kinds of thoughts were racing through my head, but I had a feeling that I knew what was coming. I found the key and struggled with the lock almost as badly as I had just struggled with my purse.

I hung my sweater up on the coat tree and tucked my purse under the front desk. I didn't turn on the lights, though. Pea wasn't scheduled to come in for another twenty minutes, so I didn't want anyone to think we were open.

I asked Sam to follow me to the back. I wanted to hear this in my space, the space I met with clients. The room felt cool as we entered and I wasn't sure if that was the temperature or my nerves. We took a seat on the small couch I had recently purchased. We were quiet for a long moment.

"Do you want me to make you some coffee?"

"No, thank you; I'm good. I've had enough to last me for a week already."

"Sam, just come out and say it." I blurted out.

"Last night, two fishermen found the body of a young woman, just as you described, with the large bridge in the background. Yes, she was wrapped in scarves, and strangled with the one black one. Authorities suspect that it's the body of the young woman that was missing from here just before you arrived. The bad part of all this is that they are going to have a lot of questions for you."

The room, or was it me, went from cold to hot. This was not the way that I wanted to nurture my newfound gift. What will they want to know? Will they lock me up and throw away the key, or just place me in a padded room with a nonstop supply of tranquilizers? So many thoughts began to rush around in my head that I became dizzy and confused.

Then his hand touched mine. Sam's palms were wide and strong, practically swallowing my entire hand. The warmth and moisture in his hand was enough to comfort me. "Effie, I'm here to help you, no matter what it takes," Sam said to me in almost a whisper.

My eyes locked onto his and I could see the sincerity. I felt a little better, but was still unsure of what was yet to come. I looked up at Sam and said, "Tell me how this is going to go down."

Sam was definitely one of those guys anyone would want on their side. He was no stranger to the inside workings and politics of the government agencies. In between all her storytelling the night we sat around the fire at Liz and Ryan's Pea had filled me in a little on Sam's background, Apparently Sam had been around the block a few times over.

When Sam was twenty, he enlisted in the army. He went to boot camp and Advanced Infantry Training in Fort Benning, Georgia: home of the infantry. He was in the 29th Infantry Division. He went to the National Training Center and then to California, where he trained for deployment to Iraq. He spent time on the front line as a Cav Scout; where his job, basically, was to shoot everything that moved.

There was little talk of that time he spent in Iraq. He was asked to consider Army Sniper School, which he ended up completing back at Fort Benning. He passed every test in Army Sniper School, top of his class, and had spent a short time in England, training the King's Own Royal Border Regiment. No one really knew what Sam did for the next couple of years, let alone where he was.

All anyone knew is that he just showed up one day, working as a detective for the state of Georgia. Sam works for himself too, Pea said, but it is rumored that he has some high-powered federal government clients. I really didn't care; I just wanted him on my side. There was definitely a little aura of mystery around him and I kind of like that.

Sam interrupted my thoughts. "A man is on his way to see you. His name is Detective Ronald Fischer and he's with the Georgia State Police. He is not a very personable man, so I want to warn you ahead of time.

"Matter of fact, I find him to be a little on the cold side. He is also not one of those individuals that's going to warm up to your abilities. I only know this because I have collaborated with him on a couple of cases. He has a one-track mind and is hard to shake once he has his mind set in one direction."

"Shouldn't I have an attorney or ask for one?" I interrupted.

"No, I really don't see the need for that; he just has some questions for you."

"But."

"I know you are familiar with the law and used to be an attorney, so it might make you look guilty if you ask for one."

"I guess I see what you're saying; I just think this looks very bad for me."

"How so?" Sam questioned.

"Well, I'm new in town; I rolled in here, dumped my car and then directed people to a body."

"Look, I'm not disagreeing with you, but I would find you more to be a person of interest rather than a suspect."

"There's a fine line with that one, Sam."

There was no response after that, just a long moment of uncomfortable silence. Then I broke the silence. "When is he coming?"

Sam's words were more uncomfortable than his presence, "Soon!" he replied.

"Well then, let me walk you out." I sighed quietly.

We both stood up and left the room. I'm not sure why I was acting as if I didn't know what was about to happen because I definitely was well versed in law. Granted, it had been years since I studied criminal procedures, but a lot of it was still fresh in my head. I was beginning to realize that I just liked listening to Sam talk.

He almost came across as the great protector; maybe not so big in the romance department, but I'm sure he knew what to do when the time came. I immediately wiped that thought from my head as Pea came into view, standing behind the front counter. An immediate crease in her forehead and slight curl of the mouth came across her face as she greeted Sam. Pea didn't know about Helena yet, but I think she just figured it out. I felt like I was floating in space, watching from afar as the events came to light.

I watched Sam as he hugged Pea and whispered in her ear. They stood there for a moment, still in a silent embrace and then released each another. Pea was quiet and her face was impassive. Not one tear, I thought to myself. I always admired those who didn't cry when I knew I would. Pea went back to the front desk and I said goodbye to Sam. Just then, the jingle bells rang.

Pea looked up from behind the desk and I heard her say, "Good morning, Reggie."

The short, stocky man returned the greeting and then glared at Sam. You couldn't cut that tension with one of those whatchamacallit knives that you see on TV. You know—the ones that cut through tin cans and then finely slice a tomato.

The detective growled harshly at Sam, "You just couldn't stay out of it, could you?" Sam said nothing and left the store.

The short man waved his badge in the air and said, "I am Detective Fischer from the Georgia State Police and I have some questions for Franciska; would that be you?"

I looked at him for a long moment; oddly, all I could think about was the short, dark-haired man on the television drama CSI, and how much this detective looked like him. The only difference was that the man in front of me was clearly an ass; he displayed all the characteristics of "little man syndrome."

"Excuse me, miss, are you hard of hearing?"

"I'm sorry; you just looked familiar to me. What can I do for you?"

"You can answer a few questions for me, for starters."

"Do I need an attorney?"

"I don't know; are you guilty of something?"

Pea interrupted, "Reggie, why don't the two of you go to the back room to talk. I'll bring you some coffee and maybe you can lighten up a bit; after all, she is not one of your local crack dealers."

I walked to the back room and could feel this man breathing down my neck the whole way. I took a seat on the small couch, thinking that I am at least going to be comfortable for this. I was really bothered by this man, though. He took a seat in the chair next to the couch, obviously determined to keep his distance.

I spoke up. "Look, Detective Fischer, you are right in your way of thinking. We can either do this the hard way or the easy way. I am here to help in any way that I can, but you WILL treat me with a little respect. Otherwise, I can sit here with my mouth shut and make things more difficult for you. It wasn't that long ago that I worked as an attorney for a large firm in Michigan, you know."

There was no response whatsoever. Pea interrupted the silence when she brought us both some coffee. I watched her and the detective as they exchanged small talk. I wondered how it was that she knew such a snotty and disrespectful little man. I couldn't wait for our little interview to be over for two reasons now. One was because I could do without the situation itself. Two was because I was ready to pick Pea's brain. In listening to the two of them talk; it appeared as if he knew Helena.

And then the ugly little man growled at Pea, "Don't forget about client confidentiality!" It almost sounded like a threat, and really blew my mind. Pea left the room and the questioning began.

"How did you know Helena?" He asked loudly.

"I didn't know her. I never met her."

"How did you know about her murder?"

"I didn't know about that either."

"Then how did you know where to look for her?" he rattled back at me.

"I didn't know that either. I just experienced some visions one day when I was going through her things." I hesitantly offered.

"What things?"

"The things she used for work and left behind. Pea thought that they might help me with getting set up."

143

"Did you find anything else?" He inquired strangely, and then quickly interjected a new question.

"When did you arrive here and where did you come from?"

"Really? I think you already know. Matter of fact, I'm sure you knew quite a bit about me before you even entered that front door."

"Well then, explain to me how you ended up here."

"It's nothing more than your typical job burn-out story," I responded. "I was sick of law, tired of white-collar wheeling and dealing to get ahead in ways that ride the line of the law. I just simply left and was looking for a place to call my own. Oh, and I was also looking for a place with more sun and warmth."

"So, let me ask again. How did you end up here? Did you just point to a map and say, 'there?'" he asked as he stuck his short, stubby finger in the air, pretending to point to a spot on a map.

"Something like that. I let the cards and my intuition guide me," I answered quickly.

"Hardly typical," the detective said as he stood up to leave. He handed me his card. "If anything else comes to mind that might help, call the number on the card. Oh, and don't go anywhere. After all, this is your new home, right?"

I didn't even say goodbye. I was pissed at this point. I stood there holding his card and hesitantly glanced down at it. "Reggie." I said to myself. "Acts like a Reggie too!"

Only his card didn't read Reginald Fischer, it read Detective Ronald Fischer, but before I could think about that, I was interrupted by one of my visions again. I concentrated hard this time, probably the hardest I have ever thought about anything.

I just couldn't quite make out the scene; it looked like a clothesline in the middle of a field, with sheets clamped to the line as they blew fiercely in the wind. Some were white, there were a few colored ones and one sheet was black.

I thought about the sheets and what they could possibly mean, but soon was very discouraged. I put the card down and decided to try again later. Right now, I had to find some other answers.

I walked to the front of the store and entered the candle-making room. Pea was busy carving some candles of a recent molding. There was definitely an art to that whole process, and I hated to interrupt, so I stood by quietly until she set her tool down.

"Why did you call that man 'Reggie?'" I quietly asked.

"That's the name that I know him as."

"Well then, how exactly do you know him?"

"He has been a customer here at the store."

"Was he a client of Helena's?" I asked.

"You know I really can't tell you that, Effie." Pea said hesitantly.

"Helena is dead."

"Yes, I know. But I'm not."

I turned away slowly in disappointment and began to walk away. Pea didn't even look at me as she interjected one last thing.

"If you still have the box of Helena's things, you might find the answers that you're looking for in that box."

"Thanks, Pea." I turned around. "Hey, do we need to be concerned about this detective? I'm not afraid to say that there is something off about him, and I can't quite put my finger on it. I get visions from his card but can't really make them out. My gut is telling me that he is not a good man."

Pea turned to face me and she looked pale. "I think there is something to your gut." She said. "Let's talk later, though. I just found out that my friend really is dead."

I quickly walked to the front counter, grabbed my keys and headed for my car. Before I knew it, I was at home sitting in the middle of my floor with a large brown box marked "Helena." I started going through each item carefully and stopped when I saw my answer.

The Rolodex was staring right at me. I picked it out of the box and begun turning it. I looked under "F" for Fischer, but found nothing. I looked under the "R" for Ronald, but found nothing. I knew the answer was here somewhere. Reggie! I scanned the "Rs" closely. Everything was alphabetical. There was no Reggie.

I couldn't believe it. I just knew the answer was here; Pea had practically thrown it in front of my face. So, I looked again. There it was. Between Razello and Remington was the spot where Reggie's card should have been. All that remained was a tiny corner of a Rolodex card still attached to the roller. The card was obviously had been torn out. But when? And why? And more importantly, now what?

Reggie, or Detective Fischer, was more involved than he let on. It might be something and it might be nothing at all. In Michigan, I was surrounded by criminals that looked like normal hard-working people. I learned quickly that criminals come in all shapes and colors.

Find me a crayon box and I'll color you a rainbow. I found myself talking to myself again, almost as if I was in a heated debate. I contemplated telling Pea what I was thinking, but decided to give her some time before I threw this new information at her.

My phone interrupted the wide array of opening statements that I was already practicing out loud. After all, criminal law was my first choice and it was comforting to fall back on it as I tried to sort things out.

"Hi, Mom" I said excitedly. "How are you?" I enjoyed about twenty good minutes of catching up and was delivered the blow of more bad news. This week is looking like a real, live roller coaster and I was ready for the ride to end!

CHAPTER NINE

It's Bigger Than a Breadbox

I spent the next hour laying on my bed and staring at the ceiling, just trying to process my entire day. I was sad to hear about the passing of an old friend, my grandfather's friend Richard to be exact. It wasn't exactly the news I wanted to hear at the end of a very tiring day.

Then again, I guess there is never a right time to receive that kind of news. I had asked my mother if she needed me to come back home, but apparently he had passed away more than two weeks ago. She didn't want to tell me then because I was still getting used to the new changes in my life. It wasn't his death that had me staring at the ceiling, though.

Richard was an older man and I had known for quite some time that his health was failing. What kept me thinking about him was the news that he left something for me in his will. It was an unexpected gift, and an inheritance of sorts. I just couldn't figure out what I was going to do with it, and I didn't have much time to debate the answers. What he'd left me had to be moved in the next ten days.

I jumped off the bed, reached for a photo box from the top shelf of my closet and sat back down on the bed with it. I now found myself searching fiercely for one picture that I hid away years ago. "Some day," I keep telling myself, "I'll scan my pictures in the computer and keep them in one of those photo databases like Shutterfly."

Finally! There it was. The picture of my gift, a gift that originated with my grandfather's own hands and, yes, as my mother said, "It's bigger than a breadbox." It was the thirty-four foot sailboat named Franciska! Where was I going to put that?

After the shock of the gift wore off, I picked up my phone and called Damon. He was close to leaving work about this time. Hell, I wanted to hear his voice anyhow. The conversation was short and, before I knew it, he was at my door. As I looked at him coming up the stairs, it occurred to me that he had never even seen where I lived. Normally I was very careful on who I let come into my space. It was very important to me to keep any negative energy from getting into my home, no matter how temporary it was.

We embraced briefly and I grabbed his hand to lead to him to my bed. Damon started to laugh.

"Are we going to be wearing all these photos, or taking our own?" he asked, waving his hand at the photos that were still scattered across the bedspread.

"No, silly, I have something to show you. I've been given a rather large gift and I'm not quite sure what to do with it. I was hoping you could help me find a place for it."

I pushed a pile of pictures aside and he sat at the foot of the bed. He looked so delicious that I actually was thinking of what it would be like for both of us to be covered in those photos. I had to shake the thought from my head quickly. Damon sat quietly as I rummaged through the pile to pull out the one picture that I had of my newfound love. I slowly slid the picture in his hand and asked, "Any ideas?"

"Wow, that's one hell of a boat." He said to me. "I can see your dilemma, but have you forgotten where you live now?"

"Damon! I know where I live! I just want to keep it in the best and safest place. It has a lot of meaning to me."

"What do you mean?"

"This was the boat that my grandfather started, but died before he finished it."

"Who finished it?"

"The man was my grandfathers very best friend; he named it after me."

"And how is it coming to you?"

"I'm not even sure yet, but he passed away a little while ago and left it to me in his will."

"Do you know how to sail?"

"Not a clue. Do you?"

Damon grinned from ear to ear; I knew that was a big, fat yes. With that, excitement began to grow inside of me. I was ready for a new adventure already. Damon's next words popped that growing bubble, though.

"What are you doing over there?" He asked, pointing to Helena's box. At this point I wasn't sure what to say, but knew I had to have some kind of an answer. Matter of fact, I thought it might be better to tell him everything, just in case things got worse than they already were.

"As you know, I took Helena's place at Candles and More when I arrived in town. Pea let me go through some of her things, thinking it would help me to get started in the business. As I was going through several of the items, I would get visions of her, lying dead in shallow waters, all wrapped in scarves. That's how Sam got involved. He poked around a bit trying to find some answers. She was just found and the hammering from Detective Fischer began today. Except I think he had something to do with Helena's death."

Damon listened to my story with concern on his face. His eyes looked very worried, but he never said a word. It felt good to finally talk about everything and get it out. After all, it was a lot better than talking to myself.

The room felt cold and everything was quiet now; I began to second-guess my decision to tell him. Then he took both of my hands in his and said, "I want you to tell me everything that happens from here on out. I don't care if I am at work or asleep at four in the morning. Please be very careful; Brunswick may be small, but it's not all that quiet."

He paused and took a deep breath, as if to emphasize his next warning.

"Lastly, be very careful of Detective Fischer; rumor has it that he doesn't play nice in the sandbox." I agreed, and it worried me that Damon knew more than what he was letting on.

Then he asked, "What do you see when you touch me?"

"Colors!" I told him.

"They wind in circles and occur in straight lines, too. I only see the colors red, yellow and blue, though. To be completely honest, I don't try to think about it. What I mean is, I don't really concentrate on it because I don't want to see the visions when I touch you. I don't see them all the time, though, if that's what you're wondering. Last night when we were together, I saw only you. It was as if I forced any visions of you out of my head. I haven't learned how to control them yet, but I am learning how to ignore them. For example, if someone touches me and I see a vision, I know now how to prevent it from showing in my face. It's a good thing, too, because of the visions I received when I took Detective Fischer's card."

"What do you mean? What did you see when you saw Fischer's card?"

I hesitated.

"I saw a clothesline on the top of a hill, with sheets blowing in the wind. I can't explain it."

He listened, but didn't react. I could see him thinking about what he wanted to say, but then deciding not to say it; at least for now.

"When was your first vision?"

"I think I have had them all along but never really knew it. On my trip down here, I made several stops. I stopped at a rest area to read my cards and a young girl asked me if I would read her cards. When I did the layout, she placed a piece of jewelry in the center as the token representing her.

"When the wind blew, I threw my arms over the cards to keep them from flying off the table and touched her token. I saw visions of her dad beating her. That was the real first time for me. I think that specific incident was what told me that I was on the right path. Right now, everything seems to fall into place if I just let it. I'm learning to go with it, although I could definitely do without all the madness! I can't see the future, though. At least, not yet," I quickly added.

"Would you like to read my cards?" Damon asked.

"Not especially. I don't always like to read the cards of people who are close to me. Maybe someday I will; ask me again when things settle around here."

Damon then leaned over and whispered in my ear, "Grab your things, we're going for a ride. I am going to show you a nice place for your boat."

Suddenly I wasn't so tired anymore. The ride was a nice escape from the day and being with Damon reenergized me. He held my hand as he drove and the salt air danced through my hair. Not one word was spoken, but at this point no words were necessary.

It was late, so I couldn't really see much; I just knew this was a new direction and a new road—one I hadn't been down before. I noticed the sign for St. Simons Island shortly before we passed a small airport. I thought about how much fun it would be to go skydiving here and thought I might add that to my list of things to do in my new home.

I have to admit, I was becoming more curious about where I could possibly store a boat as we got closer to the ocean. We were in a residential neighborhood along the coast now, and the homes here were a sight for sore eyes, but I hadn't seen any signs for a marina. I could hear the waves crashing along the shore and dreamed of them putting me to sleep. We turned down Eleventh Street and followed it to the end, where Damon pulled in a driveway. The Mediterranean-style home was quite large and had clay roof tiles, which I love. It also had a circular drive.

"This is fabulous! But where are we?"

"St. Simons Island, known for its golden beaches and ocean access, "Damon said, grabbing my hand. He walked me around the side of the house until we were walking down a very narrow path leading to the shore. It was difficult to get a good view of the house through the tall green, hedges that lined the property. I wondered if we might be trespassing.

I laughed, "I know that, dummy. I mean whose house is this?" Damon didn't answer. Instead he pulled me along a little faster, over a berm, and into a clearing, where he stopped and pointed. There in the moonlight was a long, empty beach, a wide-open ocean and a very large dock with a fishing platform at the end.

"There's the new home for your new boat."

I looked at him with surprise.

"Go on, then. Go out on the dock and see how it feels. I'll wait here," he smiled.

I stepped up onto the dock and walked out to the end. I stood there and just stared out onto the open waters in amazement. Flecks of moonlight danced off the waves and sounds of the nearby seagulls sang to me.

This was so beautiful and so peaceful. I turned slowly and walked back to the shore where Damon stood at the first section of the dock. Why did all this seem so strange, I wondered. It didn't feel like this was bad or wrong, things just seemed strange. I reached the sand and asked Damon, "Why can I keep my boat here?"

"Because I live here."

I couldn't quite catch my breath and Damon interjected, "It's not my house; I just stay here and take care of it for the owner. He's a wealthy family friend and my rent is free as long as I maintain the house and the grounds. I actually live in the pool house, which is as big as most houses, if you can believe it. Would you like to see it?"

I followed Damon to a wrought iron gate and watched him enter a code in a small black box partially hidden by the hedge. The gate unlocked and I followed him into the courtyard.

"What an amazing house!" I thought to myself. The courtyard was large and inlaid entirely in cobblestone. I felt like I was walking down the alleyway of an old European city.

The main house was off to the right, near the entrance to the pool, which was located in the very center of the property. It was a long, rectangular saltwater swimming pool with a hot tub at the very end in the shape of a half moon. Just off to the left of the pool was the pool house and, yes, it looked just like a regular house.

The covered terrace had four pillars in front and just beyond them, shy of the sliding door, was a large outdoor sitting and eating area, with three large outdoor fans hanging from the ceiling. The exterior was quite square, with white stucco on the walls and the same red clay roofing tiles as the main house. Large palm trees loosely surrounded both the main house and the pool house.

Damon grabbed my hand and led me around the pool to the pool house. He unlocked the French doors and turned on the lights. I stepped inside as if I was walking on eggshells. Everything inside was very white and almost sterile looking. The main room had an open floor plan, with the kitchen and bar area was off to the right and the living area was directly in front of me, adorned with a large fireplace. Just off to my left, and beyond a stained glass door, was an oversized bathroom and dressing room; beyond that was the equipment room.

"Where do you sleep?" I asked Damon.

He walked straight across the living room and slid open pocket doors to the right of the fireplace and stepped inside. This room was a little different than the rest. The bedroom was almost as long as the entire house, but narrow. In the corner was an artist's easel covered by a white sheet. There were many canvases along the wall; all facing in to protect them from the strong light that I imagined must stream in through the windows during the day. Other than the artist's den in the corner of the bedroom, this house barely looked lived in.

"What's with all the canvases?"

"When I was very young, I used to paint and create charcoal drawings of people. I hadn't done it in a while and remembered how I found it to be quite relaxing and a good way to use my mind creatively. I decided to start doing it again, but have been moving a little slower this time; this girl I know has kept my mind very active lately."

I giggled. "Damon, why didn't you tell me about all this? I mean, it seems like a big secret."

"I feel about my home like you do about yours and, like I said earlier, this is a small place."

"Well, I think that I would rather come here than to Jekyll Island."

"I would have brought you here, but you were quite adamant about how you were turned off by wealth, or the appearance of wealth, so I was trying to keep things very simple for you."

"Okay, I understand where you get that; but it's not like this is your money."

"Would that really have made a difference with who I am?"

"At that time, it probably would have." I said sadly.

"What about now?"

"It would still probably make a difference."

"Believe it or not, Effie, I'm here trying to escape the same things. We have a lot in common."

"You're here trying to get away from money and a fast-paced lifestyle?"

"Not exactly; I want people to like me for me, not for what's around me."

"I guess I understand that; we will have to talk more later."

"Why? Are you ready to leave now?" Damon asked disappointedly.

"Hell, no! I'm ready to go swimming," I said as I turned and headed for the pool.

Damon started to ask about a change of clothes and swimwear, but before he could finish, my clothes were off and I was in the pool. Damon stood at the edge staring down at me. He was laughing.

"Nothing like a brazen girl to take the edge off," he yelled down to me. The water was warm, almost velvety smooth. Small drops splashed up into my face and I licked my lips. It wasn't as salty as the ocean; it was a bit milder, but still like swimming in the ocean. I dove under and swam to the other side and back again. Damon was still in the same spot watching me.

I yelled up to him, "Are you going to join me or let this perfectly lovely pool water go to waste?"

I was treading water as he started to take off his clothes. I continued treading water; tasting the water and feeling the currents swirl around my body as I kicked my legs to stay afloat.

I watched him slowly take his clothes off, silhouetted in the soft lights inset along the pool. This was the first time that I saw him head to toe, completely nude. He had to be the most stunning man I had ever seen, and he was standing right in front of me. He didn't stand for long, though; he dove in and swam to me. We frolicked in the water almost as if we were kids again.

We were splashing each other and trying to dunk one another. Soon we found ourselves wrapped in each other's arms. I was hot and cold all at the same time. He held me and we moved slowly through the water, kissing and clinging to each other. We neared the pool stairs and Damon picked me up in his arms and carried me up the shallow steps out of the pool and into his bedroom. I guess we wouldn't have to worry about wearing the photos on my quilt after all, I thought, as he laid me on his bed.

The next morning, I awoke to the smell of scrambled eggs, toast and coffee, along with the smell of the tide and the chatter of seagulls. I got out of bed and wrapped myself in the thick beach towel Damon had laid across the end of the bed for me, and then I walked into the kitchen. There was a note next to my plate.

I read it, smiled and put it down. I sat there swaddled in the beach towel and it was just fine with me. Damon came in the house with my clothes in his arms. They were washed, dried, folded and ready to be worn.

"Good morning. I thought you might like something to wear home, unless you're really comfortable in your towel, that is."

"Good morning to you, too. You're up early for someone who doesn't have to work till later. And, yes, I'm quite comfortable in my towel for now."

"I know how comfortable they can be," he eyed my chest longingly as he spoke. "But I also know that you do have to go to work and I am responsible for seeing that you arrive there on time, or close to it."

Damon handed me my clothes and a slip of paper with an address printed on it.

"Make sure you get that address to whoever will be delivering your boat. We will make the proper accommodations for its arrival next week." He smiled.

"I hope she loves it here as much as you seemed to last night," Damon whispered.

"We'll find out soon enough, won't we?" I looked at the address, feeling a vision coming on, but fighting it. I didn't know what it was about, but I knew I didn't want it ruining the moment.

CHAPTER TEN

Quiet Before the Storm

An old stone church with a magnificent steeple appeared before us now. I drove and Pea rode beside me, not saying one word the entire way. I could tell that she was thinking about a lot of things. Judging by the expression on her face, she was concerned. It was a beautiful Wednesday morning. The sun was out and the sky was filled with big billowy clouds. I often dreamed of what it would feel like to throw myself on them when I was a child. I could smell summer in the air, and it was almost May.

We followed a long gravel road until we came upon a college kid, who was directed people to parking spots. I was directed to a nice shady spot under a willow tree and was thankful for that due to the lack of a roof on my Jeep.

The sun was hot enough to fry an egg on our seats. I jumped out and waited for Pea. She was taking her time, but I didn't mind. My only job was to remain supportive and to keep my mouth shut. We walked up the steps and through the thick wooden doors. It was dark, lit only by candles, and I could smell the dampness of the rock walls on either side of us.

There were no more than twenty pews on each side of the center aisle; a plaque on the pillar to my left read,

"Built June 6, 1865." The people of Savannah knew how to build them and, more so, how to preserve them. My moment of admiration was interrupted by what caught my eye next.

There in the front, just two feet below the pulpit, sat a small wooden box on a stand. The box was absolutely beautiful and stained a deep red. Carvings of vines curled and twined around each corner. It wasn't the beauty of the box that stunned me, but the fact that it contained Helena's ashes.

We took our seats about four pews back and just off to the left. I looked over at Pea and could see her just staring at the urn. I could only wonder if she was thinking the same thing. How could they cremate her when her death was clearly a murder? My thoughts and any feelings I was having for Pea disappeared as, out of the corner of my right eye, I spotted Detective Fischer.

I could feel the hair on the back of my neck stand up. What reason did he have for being here? Then the unthinkable: he was greeted warmly by Helena's mother.

I didn't know whether to run and hide or just jump out and slap her in the face a few times, and tell her of my suspicions. On the same note, arriving early had served its purpose, as I thought it would. There is something comforting, even special, about being an observer.

No one expects anything of you and no one even pays that much attention to you. It's even better when no one knows you. I had already seen more than I wanted to, but I was anxious about what more was to come.

I sat quietly reading the service program, which had been set out on a table by the door next to the guest book. It was beautifully done and contained Helena's entire life, some photos, and a schedule of the events for the service. I stared at the photos for a while and then Pea looked over and said, "That thing doesn't do her any justice. This whole thing makes me sick. I'll be cordial and pleasant, but there's more going on here. Everyone seems to be avoiding the truth; someone took her life ... just took it."

"Pea," I said quietly, "What's going on here? I haven't heard anything from you until just now and, well, you sound very angry."

"I have been quiet long enough." I could feel the waves of angry energy wafting off her.

I leaned forward and in towards her just a little more. I lowered my voice, "Pea, don't get angry now. Keep it in a little longer or you might give us both away. This is definitely not the time or the place."

Pea looked down at me and her eyes filled with hot, angry tears as she squeezed out a choked, "Okay."

I reached over and squeezed her hand. I continued to hold it as we watched people enter the church. Their expressions varied greatly. I heard the two heavy doors close behind us and I turned my head to look back as the sound they made echoed throughout the room. The doors reminded me of the ones you see in the dungeons in old black-and-white movies, thick, foreboding, and dark.

As I looked toward the back I could see the backs of everyone else's head as they, too, turned to look at the doors. There was only one person who wasn't attracted to the sound of the doors closing. That one familiar face was of a man who remained standing in the rear looking forward. It was Sam.

I couldn't help but to wonder why he had come, but maybe he knew Helena. Maybe he was here for other reasons. My eyes met his and there were no smiles, just the most expressionless face I had seen all morning. I turned back around, as the Celebration of Life was about to begin.

It was a beautiful service with a lot of music and an interesting discussion of Helena's spirituality. I didn't know Helena, but I knew that her spirituality was deeper than the pastor celebrated. After the service, we all gathered our things and left the pews through a single door on the side of the church that poured out into a garden.

We followed a stone walkway through a garden filled with bright red, yellow and orange roses. Just beyond a vine-covered archway that exited the garden was a large field adorned with many exquisite graveyard tombstones.

It was quaint, private and there were several benches placed throughout. This was something that I liked. This is a place I would feel comfortable visiting. Our journey ended just beneath a tulip poplar, a tree native to Georgia and known as the "Brightest Tree in the Neighborhood." Pea leaned over to me and whispered, "This is the perfect final place of rest for Helena; she loved birds and was a vibrant person."

I nodded, looking up and remembering what I knew about tulip poplar. It's a tree for all seasons. It doesn't get any bigger than seventy feet and grows in most areas. In the spring, it is smothered in thousands of blooms and has a lovely fragrance that lasts all summer long.

The nectar attracts birds like the ruby-throated hummingbird, cardinals and finches. In the summer, the foliage is a beautiful green and in the fall, it changes to such a bright yellow that you practically need sunglasses to protect your eyes from the brilliant golden glow.

Pea's description was clear to me now and she was right; we needed to visit this fall. The pastor began his graveside service with the mention of the headstone. It kind of threw me off, but he definitely caught my attention. I was immediately drawn to the message. These were the pastor's words:

"Dear family and friends. Someone asked me this morning why there wasn't an end date on the gravestone. My response was simple: because it was the hyphen that was the most important part of the dates. The hyphen is the punctuation mark used to join two words. Just like two words, the birth date and date of death are merely the first and last markers in time.

"It's the time in the middle that most defines us because the hyphen is the time you spend on this earth. What we do with that time is up to us. Whether it's ninety years or merely fifteen years, it is all we have. Our lives represent the hyphen. So it is most important how we fill that gap between the two dates. It's not so much about when we were born and when we die, but how we lived."

I felt like I was the only one standing there for that one moment in time and that the pastor was talking right to me. As he began to talk about Helena's life and celebrating her hyphen, I began to think of my own life. I couldn't help but think that I may have wasted a part of my "hyphen." I think I felt as if he was talking to me because I was on the right path now. I was filling the time between my birth and death with something more, something vital.

Pea nudged me a bit, knowing that I had drifted off in my own mind, forgetting where I was. The graveside service had ended while I was lost in thought. People had begun to disperse. Pea and I decided to drive home and skip the luncheon.

I was actually looking forward to the drive. We followed the cobblestone sidewalk around the back of the church. The path brought us out into the narrow dirt road that we had come in on. Although it was quite dusty, the scenery on either side made up for it. Pea nudged me in the side again and I looked up to notice Sam waiting for us at the Jeep. I quickly looked all around to see who else might have noticed. I approached the Jeep hesitantly.

"Hello, Sam."

"Hello, ladies; it was a beautiful service, don't you think?"

"It most definitely was." Pea responded.

I piped in, "That's not really why you're here, though, is it Sam? You're not here to discuss the service. Are you keeping an eye on me?"

"You're half right Effie, but that's not why I came. I'm here to keep an eye on someone else."

"Do we know this person?" Pea asked.

"You know I can't tell you that, but what I can tell you is that I want the both of you to be very careful. Helena's death is far from being solved and I think we could be ass deep in a cover up."

"Sam, that doesn't sound good." I responded.

"Let's cut this short; we can talk another time, just watch your Ps and Qs—no pun intended."

Pea and I jumped in the Jeep and were well on our way down the winding road before either one of us said a word to each other. It was almost like we were both wondering who was going to say the first word, let alone what was the first word going to be.

Pea broke the ice, "Did you find what you were looking for the other night?"

"Sort of. I had a pretty good idea where to start looking when I left, but it was the ride home that made it click for me."

"What was different about the ride home?" Pea asked.

"Nothing."

"I don't get it?"

"I kept replaying the day in my head, over and over again, and then it just clicked."

"What was it then?"

"It was your greeting to Detective Fischer."

Pea smiled and asked, "Did you find what you were looking for then?"

"No, not exactly, but he was sloppy removing his information. He left a corner in the Rolodex."

Then Pea frowned. "That's not a lot of help then; we have nothing to show his connection."

"He doesn't know that," I interjected.

"That's a dangerous game you're playing, Effie."

"I know. It's also one that I'm not familiar with, but one that I already see is working."

Pea didn't say much more after that. We decided not to discuss it for at least another twenty-four hours. I really wanted a whole day to myself. I was as worried for myself as everyone was for me. For some reason though, I felt pretty safe. I had a couple of sets of eyes on me and one of those sets knew where I was most of the time.

I dropped Pea off at her car and took the long way home. I drove past a youth baseball game and heard all the cheers and laughter. I turned my Jeep around and headed back. I pulled into the small gravel parking lot, parking close to the exit and taking a seat in the stands. I didn't know who was playing, nor did I care; I just wanted to take my mind off of things for a while.

After the game, I grabbed a snow cone for the ride home. It was blue raspberry and had been my favorite when I was a kid. I parked the Jeep at my back door and went up to take a shower.

Luckily, no one was home and I was able to get in and out without any questions, let alone poking and prodding about where I'd been or what I'd been doing. I like Liz and

I knew that she was lonely, but I have never been the one to talk about others' business. I decided to finish my evening somewhere I hadn't been in a while. I could definitely use a change of environment.

The Seaside Grill was busy as usual, but there were still two seats available at the bar. I walked straight up to them and grabbed the stool at the end. Damon was taking a break and Dona was helping out. She approached me and placed a small cocktail napkin down in front of me.

"Hello, stranger, it's so nice to see you. What are drinking tonight?"

"I think I'm in the mood for a nice glass of Bordeaux."

Dona disappeared and I wondered where she went off to. I sat there for a moment, thinking of the day and what it all meant to me. Everything seemed very surreal. Too many things were happening too fast. Dona returned, opened a bottle and set it down next to me.

"This is a new brand that we just had imported in, and thought you might like to try it." I smiled and lifted the glass to my lips. It was definitely a nice, smooth, but bold, taste. Then Dona set down a plate filled with dipping oil, fresh baked bread and small pieces of melon wrapped in prosciutto. I knew this wasn't the same treatment everyone else received, but it didn't bother me at all. I shared some of the day's events with her. We chatted for a short while and soon she had me up to speed on her week as well.

"Hello," Damon whispered in my ear and then pecked me on the cheek. "This is a nice surprise."

He slid around the back of the bar with an ear-to-ear grin. I was so glad that he was happy to see me. He was always a sight for sore eyes. He left as quickly as he came, moving down to the other end of the bar, making sure that everyone was well taken care of before he came back to me. He tipped the bottle of wine just a slight bit to read the label, setting it firmly back on its base.

"Are you into it for the whole bottle?"

"I guess so. Why not?"

"How do you like it? This is one of our newest bottles."

"Actually, I like it a lot. I usually drink my reds in the winter, but I felt like a change."

"Are you going to stay for some dinner or are you just drinking tonight?"

"I think I might just have some appetizers here and there and stretch my night out."

Damon laughed and made his way back down to the other end of the bar. I really enjoyed watching him work because it seemed like he enjoyed his job. It's not very often that you find a bartender who takes a great deal of pride in their work. I wondered if he would ever let me look at his canvases.

I knew he just dabbled, but he seemed to be good at everything he touched, and I mean everything. He made his way back down to me and we talked briefly of the day. That all too familiar look of concern crept back on his face and I promised him that I would keep filling him in as the events continued to unravel.

Damon changed the subject and I was glad that he did. We discussed the arrangements made to receive the sailboat and the possibilities to put it to good use. Damon asked me to stay with him at his place, but I had to bow out gracefully. I really wanted to, but tonight was just not a good night. I knew it worried him that I was by myself, but I assured him that I knew the night was safe. He took the letdown well and we both agreed to let him follow me home.

We hung out until the last customer left and there were only a few employees left. Tony, the floor manager approached Damon and asked him if he needed to lock up. Damon told him to go home and he would take care of the rest. Damon sat down next to me and had a glass of wine himself. We chatted for a bit and he pointed at my purse hanging on the back of the chair.

"How about reading my cards for me tonight while we finish our wine?" He asked.

I turned and looked him straight in the eyes and asked, "Do you have anything to hide?" I could tell that my question caught him off guard.

A moment went by and then he said, "Let's see what the cards say." I have to admit that my curiosity had just peaked. I reached for my cards and placed them on the bar.

"Well then, Damon. Let us begin."

Because it was late, I set up for a simple three-card layout; one card representing the past, one card representing present day, the third card representing the future and a surprise card that sat above the three. Damon shuffled the cards and cut the deck to the left. I took the bottom card of the left cut pile and placed it at the top. I placed the cut pile on the right, on top of the left pile, and dealt out three cards. The three cards were chosen, and then each one was laid face down and side-by-side on the bar. I spoke to Damon sincerely at this point.

"I know I have a gift and I am somewhat glad that future telling is not part of it. I personally feel that if someone knows what will happen in the future they may try to change it. Some won't take the risks and others will run toward it haphazardly.

Reading the cards for me is fun. Although I have no visions of the future, I feel that my touch can guide me in the future. I am always afraid that someone will miss out on all the in-between stuff if they can see to the end." I paused for a minute.

"There's a song called, 'The Dance,' and in the song, a man sings about how he might have missed the dance if he had known that pain he would face in the end. Sometimes our lives are better left to chance. I just want you to know how I feel before we start."

Damon looked at me, smiled and placed his hand on mine.

"No matter what, Effie, I don't plan on missing the dance!" I hesitantly flipped the first card.

"The first card is the Ten of Wheels, which is also known as the wealth card. The usual time frame on a wheels card is measured in years. Because it is in the placement of the past, it basically means that you have achieved this, it is behind you and you have no concerns about it. This card also says that you have a prosperous family with inheritances, riches and real estate and you're carrying on the family tradition."

I laughed at this point, but Damon wasn't laughing. I told Damon not to be too upset; sometimes the cards weren't right. Then I quickly moved on to the second card.

I flipped the card and the Eight of Cups appeared.

"This is the seeking card, and the time frame on cups is days. This card is what represents the present day."

I described the card to Damon, "The covered wagon is leaving the field with eight cups left behind; there is no way of telling if this is temporarily leaving the possessions behind or not. What this basically means, Damon, is that you have become disillusioned with your life in some way and are leaving material success behind for new roads. You are abandoning a present situation or a disappointment in love. This card also says to follow your heart and do what you truly desire."

The third card was the Queen of Cups. The time frame was in days again. I sat for a moment and looked at the card for a long time. Damon interrupted my thoughts asking me if something was wrong. "No, not at all," I replied.

"This card is a little different. This person in this card will be a part of your future. Her description is fair-haired with hazel eyes, but if she has a visionary gift she may be dark-haired with dark eyes. She is a young woman, beautiful with expressive eyes and sensuous lips. She is very social, artistic and gifted. She is connected to Mother Earth, on a spiritual path possessing characteristics of truth and sincerity. She will be bringing you a visionary gift, poetry, imagination, success and pleasure."

Damon chuckled, "That's why you were so quiet; that card sounds a lot like you."

I just smiled at that point, not saying a word about his comment. Then I moved on to the card of surprise.

I flipped it. It was the Ace of Knives. This is the card of force and the time frame is in months. This was definitely an interesting card. I could see that Damon was anxious, so I finished the reading for him.

"This card says that things will be changing for the good, but not without having to endure one obstacle."

"What's the obstacle?" Damon asked.

"I can't tell you that, but it will come to you as a surprise."

"How do you know that it will have a good outcome?"

"The sword on the card that is piercing the oak leaf is at an angle; if it was straight up then it would mean disastrous. The oak leaf represents a tough obstacle that will require force; but the sword has pierced it, so you will be successful—not without force, though."

"That's pretty interesting. I liked it and someday I'd like a detailed reading."

I had to ask, "What did you like the best?"

"Your card!" Damon grinned.

"You seem awfully sure, Damon; make sure you try not to read too much into the cards. Obviously, they are not always right."

I gathered the cards carefully and put them away. I gathered them in such a way as to remember what order they were in. I would definitely consider writing this down at home to look over again. I had to admit that I didn't like the last card much; it kind of scared me. Damon was probably right about the other card, too. The description was "dead nuts," as my grandfather would say when something was right on the money.

Damon grabbed his keys off the bar and we walked out together. He locked up and walked me to my car. He gave me a long, warm kiss goodnight and it almost changed my mind about going home with him, but I needed to sleep in my own bed. He followed me home as promised and once I was safely inside, I watched him drive away until the taillights of his car disappeared.

CHAPTER ELEVEN

The Storm Begins

I approached the door to my loft, took my keys out and my heart fell to my stomach. My door was open. It wasn't open a lot, but enough for me to notice and enough for me to know that someone had been there. I stopped and backed away from the door very slowly. I made my way down the back steps and rummaged through my purse until I found the card I was looking for.

I called Sam. He picked up after only a couple of rings. I was impressed, considering how late it was. I explained the situation and he said he would be there in fifteen minutes. Meanwhile, he was going to send a police officer to stay with me until he arrived. I hung up the phone and sat nervously on the steps. It occurred to me that I hadn't given him my address, yet he already knew where I was staying.

A minute later a cruiser from the Brunswick Police Department pulled in the rear parking area. An officer got out of the car and walked as far as the sidewalk entrance, gave me a slight tip of his hat and asked if I was okay.

"I'm fine. I didn't go inside. I just called Sam and waited for you."

He nodded. "Sam wants me to wait until he gets here before we check the place out. We don't know if anyone is still inside, so why don't we wait inside my patrol car just to be safe." It was more of a direction than a question. He might be right, I thought. So I walked back to the car. He held the passenger door to while I got in, then stood beside the open door fiddling with the knobs on the radio at his side. We listened to the police chatter on the radio while we waited for Sam.

I have to admit, I felt a lot better with him there, but I also wondered if I shouldn't have been reporting this incident directly to the police in the first place. No, there was a reason for the way things were unfolding. I knew whom I could and couldn't trust.

A few more minutes passed, but it seemed like an hour until Sam showed up. The officer left my side and walked over to Sam as his car pulled up. I watched him as he had a brief conversation with the officer. I got out of the patrol car and walked over to meet him. The officer returned to his car, talking on his radio at the same time.

He didn't appear to be going anywhere anytime soon. I could tell that Sam didn't waste any time getting here because he had caught the bottom corner of his shirt in his fly and the tip of it was sticking out. I really couldn't help but laugh. I was sitting on the steps and he was standing in front of me, so of course it was in plain view.

"How on earth do you find humor at a time like this?" Sam said a bit gruffly. I held my hand over my mouth and just pointed. Sam turned around and readjusted himself, then turned back toward me.

"Is that better?" Sam said, a bit embarrassed. I stood up.

"Let us check it out first," he said, waving the officer over.

The officer and Sam both unholstered their guns.

"Who else is usually inside?" he asked.

"Liz and Ryan and whoever the guests are at the time," I said. "There's no one else staying in my suite, the attic," I explained, and told him about my private keypad. "The other guests have a separate entrance or come through an inside door."

"Okay, got it. Wait here until we come back."

I started to protest, but he held his hand up.

"We don't know who might still be in there. We'll just be a minute. I'll come back once we've cleared the place."

There wasn't a lot I could do, so I waited. Within ten minutes he was back outside, standing at the door and waving me in.

"There's no one inside, but I want you to tell me what's missing."

We both entered the house this time. Remarkably, we had not woken anyone up, and I didn't want to start now. We walked quietly until we reached my door to the attic. Sam had turned on the stairwell light his first time through.

Now he examined the door carefully, looking for signs of how the person had gotten in I supposed. I followed Sam closely as we entered my suite. Even though he had already searched the place, it felt like someone was still there, hiding. I shivered. I couldn't shake the feeling that someone had been in my room uninvited. We were now standing in my living room. To my amazement, not much looked out of place.

Sam checked out the entire attic again before he put his gun away. I started going through my chest, looking to see if the drawers had been disturbed. I could tell things were out of place, but I wasn't sure I would have noticed the slight disarray if I hadn't known someone had been there. I didn't have much to go through, so it didn't take long before I completed my search.

Sam said, "He was very careful not to make a mess." I didn't reply, but continued to look around for things out of place. I saw the corner of my bedspread had been lifted. It was left draped on the top of the bed. I walked over to the bed and looked underneath.

I sighed as I stood up. "He got what he was looking for, but he didn't get all of it."

Sam perked up now, almost like a dog that just caught a scent. "What do you mean?" He asked with one eyebrow raised in anticipation.

I began to describe the box of Helena's things from Candles and More. I explained that I'd taken them home and the reason why I just recently went through it all again. Now the whole box was gone. I had placed it under my bed today when I came home for a brief moment after the funeral. I had taken out the Rolodex, put it in a shopping bag and stored that under the seat in my Jeep. At least he didn't get that. At this point Sam was confused, so I had to fill him in on everything that had transpired over the past week.

Sam then asked, "Who is Reggie?"

"I may be wrong," I said, "But I think Reggie is linked to Helena's death. Reggie is Detective Fischer."

The news didn't seem to shock Sam. He began to pace a bit, rubbing his chin. Then Sam asked, "Why Reggie?"

"My guess is that he didn't want his name associated with Helena."

"Are you saying that he was involved with her?"

"I can't answer that, but he did come in to see her a few times for readings."

Sam asked, "How did you figure that out?"

"By chance, actually. Remember the day he came to question me? When he came in, Pea addressed him by that name. I figured out the rest."

"How much does Pea know?"

"About half."

"Does anyone else know any of this?"

"Yes, Damon knows all of it, except of what's happening now."

"Well, that's good. At least it's a little extra protection for you. I am going to leave that officer out back for a while. I trust him and he'll do it as a personal favor for me without telling anyone about what's going on. I don't want the department to know any of this in case you are right. That should give you enough time to make arrangements to spend some nights with someone else for a while. Just make sure you let me know where you are at all times."

"That won't be a problem. I think I may have another place to live on Friday."

"What do you mean?" Sam asked.

"I am receiving a rather nice sailboat on Friday, kind of an inheritance. It has living quarters and I have a place at a friend's house where it will be docked."

"Great; give me the details tomorrow and I will see to it that it remains unregistered for a while. I'll pull a few strings for you and then we will go from there. Now let's go down to your Jeep and take a peek at this famous Rolodex."

We made our way downstairs, where it soon became apparent our efforts to avoid waking anyone up had failed. Liz greeted us in the driveway. She didn't look angry, but there was no doubt she was very concerned.

"What happened?" Liz asked.

Sam was quick on his feet. "Effie lost her keys and didn't want to wake you so she called me, knowing that I was working; I came to help her out."

Liz yawned and, with a gesture of relief, turned and went back to her room. Thank goodness for Sam's capability to tell a lie on the spot, because that was something that I just was not any good at.

Sam stopped to examine the pre-coded keypad entry for my private entrance. I watched him as he poked around, both of us obviously wondering how the intruder got in the house.

Sam turned to me and asked, "Effie, was Liz gone at all today?"

"Yes, she was. She was gone when I came home earlier. She must have returned when I was gone. Why do you ask?"

"When she leaves like that during the day, how do the guests come and go?"

"Through the front door." I replied.

"There's no keypad?"

"There is, but it hasn't been working very well this week so she's left the door unlocked so the guests didn't have to wait on her to answer it every time. She asked the police to keep an eye out for a day or two. Oh no."

I just stood there feeling the blood drain from my face. The thought had just occurred to me that the intruder was in the house when I was there. This whole situation just went from bad to worse. My friends around me were now in danger.

I was in danger. Sam was right. I needed to make some arrangements, but ones that didn't involve anyone else. I was closer to Helena's murder than I wanted to be, but there was no turning back at this point. Sam interrupted my thoughts with kind of an odd question, coming from him. Sam asked, "Did you have any visions from your first meeting with Detective Fischer?"

"I didn't have any visions at first, but, then again, I really didn't come in any physical contact with him. After he finished berating me, he handed me his card. At first I had nothing, but that was most likely because I was focusing on his first name. That's when I first realized that the name Pea had called him was not the same as on the card. I didn't say anything, though. I kept that part quiet. When I had time to concentrate, the vision came to me. It was a bit strange and almost abstract.

"I saw a field that sloped upward. It formed a small hill in the background. It was a windy day, but sunny. There was a clothesline on the top of the hill and bed sheets were swaying in the wind. There were several bed sheets; mostly white, a few colored ones I think, and one was black. That was all I could see and I haven't made an attempt to try again, but I will."

"Are you kidding me?" Sam asked.

"What would you like from me, Sam? I mean you didn't really even believe me much at first and now you want me to be an expert?"

"I never said that I didn't believe you. I just wanted you to be careful whom you told that you get visions. I am very much a believer."

"Okay, fine. This is still pretty new to me. I have to figure out how to make it work for me. Sometimes I can go days without seeing anything at all."

"I'm sorry. I didn't mean to come across as pushy."

"It's okay. On the same note, this doesn't seem to be your typical PI work."

Sam and I didn't talk as we headed for my Jeep. I opened the driver's door and stuck my head under the steering wheel. I saw the flash of headlights as another car pulled up and I began to get nervous again. I grabbed the bag from under the seat and gave it a real quick tug. I lifted my head around the steering wheel slowly and pulled the bag out as I popped to my feet.

I was a bit dizzy but also proud of myself for actually hanging onto the now infamous Rolodex. I heard a car door close out on the street. Sam was standing at the very edge of the rear parking area.

The police officer was staying near me; only about ten steps away. I stood there at the Jeep and watched Sam as he greeted a familiar face. This time their conversation looked to be sincere. I waited patiently until both men appeared. Damon looked very unsettled and I was confused about why he had returned.

Sam spoke. "Effie, I know you're a very tough girl, but I would feel better if someone were to stay with you here, even though there will be an officer on watch. I took it upon myself to have Officer Daniels locate Damon for me; please don't take offence to my request."

I just smiled and agreed, with a slight nod of my head. I couldn't have been more pleased about the addition of my new protector, despite not being in mood for romance after this long day. I handed the bag to Sam and he removed the Rolodex. Damon left Sam's side, stood behind me and wrapped his arms around me. I couldn't tell if this was a comforting gesture or a possessive gesture. No matter. I liked it either way.

Sam took out the Rolodex and examined it thoroughly. I could see that he was concentrating on the area that I told him about, the area with the card missing but still containing the corner piece. Sam placed it back in the bag and was quiet for a minute. I could tell he was putting the pieces together, too. We all knew the situation and we all knew the danger.

Then Sam spoke up.

"Give me a call the minute your boat arrives in the morning. I will meet you there and will have a plan in place. For now, keep tight tonight. I'm pretty sure that nothing more is going to happen at this hour and our murderer thinks he has everything, so get some rest tonight."

I watched Sam walk to his car and Officer Daniels then took his place inside of his. A hundred things swirled through my head and, at the moment, not one of them was worth a damn. Damon grabbed my hand, not saying a word, and led me to the house.

We entered my room as quietly as we could and I watched as Damon cleared the bed and turned it down. It wasn't a big bed, but it was big enough for both of us. Damon undressed in front of me, leaving just his boxers on.

He sat just on the edge of the bed looking up at me. He took both my hands in his and pulled me close, leaning his head on my abdomen as if he was listening for the seashore from my navel.

He pulled me closer, wrapping his arms around my hips. I ran my fingers through his hair and let his locks intertwine between my fingers. My left hand fell to rest on his back and I continued to massage his head with my right hand until he relaxed. I lowered my head slightly and kissed him lightly on top of his head. Damon let go of me now, unbuckling my belt and lightly tugging my jeans to the floor.

He took hold of the bottom of my shirt and lifted it over my head, letting it fall to the floor as well. With a simple twist of two of his fingers, my bra now laid next to my shirt. He crawled into the bed and patted the space beside him a few times to give me the signal to climb in beside him. I slid in next to him with my backside nestled against him. I pulled the covers over us and he wrapped his arm around me, pulling me in closely.

Then the vision came.

I went from my bed into darkness. From darkness I slipped into a bright square room lit with candles, numerous candles. I was surrounded by round tables covered with white tablecloths. Chairs were around the tables and covered, too, by a white cloth.

A fog rises and I can't see my feet. I am walking all around, turning in circles, trying to figure out where I am. I must be nine years old. A hand takes mine and we begin to dance the way children do, but I can't see his face. Who am I dancing in circles with? His hair is gray and he is tall, but I just can't see. He disappears in the fog and I'm looking around in circles again, only this time I must be sixteen now. Another pair of hands takes mine and I am dancing with a boy my age; I can't see his face.

His hair is golden blonde and the light bounces off his figure. The fog rises now, it's at my waist and I am dipping my hands in it, attempting to push it off to the side. Then I am dancing again and I think I am at my age now. I am dancing a waltz with the tall gray-haired man from before and yet I still can't see his face. Why can't I see his face? I keep dancing and spinning and the feel of the old hands change. They feel familiar and warm. I look up through the fog and can catch a glimpse of the face. It's Damon. I am dancing with Damon. The entire room is now white.

Then sunlight flickered off the stained glass windows and bounced off the walls of the room. I could feel the warmth on my face and hear the birds harmonizing outside my windows. I slowly opened my eyes and found myself still safe and secure in Damon's arms. His breath at my neck continuously tickled me in a rhythmic pattern. His hands, still covering mine, reminded me of the dream I just had. I was trying to make sense of it all.

Who is the tall older man and where was I? I have always had dreams that I tried to figure out, but this one was different. It felt like I was actually there. Why was I dancing? Was I dead or alive, and why was it so misty? The questions I was asking myself were almost haunting. As I lay there thinking of it all, an ever so light peck at my neck a squeeze of my hands told me that someone else was awake now, too. A whispered "good morning" in my ear sure was nice for a change.

I tried to turn over. I thought to myself, "This bed didn't seem so small last night." I edged my way around and gave Damon a light, close-lipped kiss. I looked forward to the day off, even though it appeared I had a lot of work ahead of me.

"Damon, we are gonna have to try to sneak out of here." I said carefully.

"Are you worried about Liz seeing me here with you? Are you not allowed visitors?" he teased.

"It's not that. We woke her last night and gave her a story about me losing my keys. She was already suspicious. I think her seeing you wouldn't help that."

"I understand now. Well, let's take a shower, sneak out of here and get some breakfast along the way to my house. I need to get a change of clothes and my gun."

"Why do you need to get a gun? Do you have a gun?" I asked wearily.

Damon explained, "Yes, I have a gun and I think you need one too. I would feel better."

"I don't even know how to use one."

"Well then, let's add it to our to-do list for the morning; the boat is not due to arrive until noon."

"I'm just not sure, Damon. Can't I choose your arms every night?" I asked sheepishly.

"You have my arms every night, no choice in that, but you can't take them during the day."

"Sometime today, I have to tell Liz that I am moving out. I can't risk the safety of her family or guests. I just wouldn't feel right about it."

"Why don't you consider doing that tonight when she's not so busy? I'll come with you and this way it will look like nothing is wrong, okay?"

"That sounds reasonable. I like that plan. Now, let's shower."

"Together?" Damon asked sexily and then added, "After all, we need to conserve on water."

I laughed. "I think if we took a shower together there would be no conservation going on."

"It's nice to hear you laugh. We'll shower together, no kinky stuff. I promise."

We rolled out of bed, got cleaned up and I gathered everything that I thought I would need for the day. We began our descent to the bottom of the stairs and squeezed out the door to the attic. We tiptoed down the hall and very, very slowly made our way down the second set of stairs.

My stomach began to growl from the smell of hot maple syrup and hazelnut coffee. I think the growling was louder than our steps. Damon heard it, too, and placed his hand on my abdomen as we were in a holding pattern about half the way down the stairs. I heard Liz talking to the other guests and when I was sure she had gone back into the kitchen, we made our way down the rest of the stairs and slipped out the back door.

CHAPTER TWELVE

Awestruck

We were sitting on the front steps waiting for Damon's friend Rudy to arrive, and Damon was trying to give me a lesson on guns. I pretended to show a slight interest, but I wasn't in the mood for guns just then. What I really was excited about was seeing my boat. I was thinking about a hundred things all at once.

I had the picture of the sailboat, but it's never the same. I knew nothing about sailing a boat, and I was about to get my first lesson. The plan was to put the boat in the water, then sail it to Damon's dock and come back to the bed and breakfast later to collect my things. Rudy would give us a ride to the marina and then Damon would bring me back from his place, if all worked according to plan. I crossed my fingers.

Rudy pulled up in his Black Rubicon and gave a couple of honks of his horn. We walked to the Jeep and Rudy jumped out to greet us. He was a short young guy, with short dark hair, and dark eyes. He sported a well-trimmed goatee and wore a loose white t-shirt and khaki shorts that were entirely too long for his legs. He arrived barefoot, and I had to admit that I kind of liked that.

Damon had already told me that Rudy owned a couple of surf shops, one in Jacksonville, Florida, and one in Brunswick, and I could see now that it was probably the perfect business for him. They exchanged their special handshake and shared their man-hugs, and then Rudy said, "Yo dude, how it goes, man?"

I had to hide a grin as I thought, "Yup, he's a surfer all right."

Rudy looked me up and down and grinned at Damon.

"Is this your new sidekick?"

"Meet my girlfriend, Effie."

"Hey, Effie; hangin' high today?"

"Really nice to meet you, Rudy." I smiled and caught myself almost giving him the hang-ten sign.

Rudy shouted, "Ayight gang, mount up. Let's bound on outta ear."

Damon tried to get me to sit in the front but I convinced him that I was more comfortable in the back. I was, too. I could barely understand Rudy's short comments, let alone maintain a conversation for the next twenty minutes.

I climbed in the back and admired the electric guitar sitting on the seat next to me. I was a little shocked that it wasn't covered, but Rudy seemed like a "fly by the seat of your pants" type of guy. All of a sudden, everything stopped in my little world.

I just realized that Damon referred to me as his girlfriend. I was shocked that I didn't even catch it. I wondered if he was uncomfortable introducing me that way, but for right now, I just didn't care. I picked up my cell and phoned Sam.

"We'll be there in twenty minutes," I told him and enjoyed the remainder of the ride.

It was no time at all before we were pulling at the marina. Rudy pulled off to the side of the road near the entrance and dropped us off, waving good-bye as he pulled back onto the road.

I was looking for Sam, but he was nowhere in sight. Damon pointed to the end of the parking lot and said, "There she is, Effie; that looks like your boat." Damon and I walked over to the boat and walked around to the back. I wanted to see the back.

Damon said, "Lesson one: that is not the back, it's the stern."

There it was, my name written across the back—I mean on the stern—Franciska. Franciska was still on the trailer attached to the back of a truck, but the driver was not around. The boat looked much bigger in life than in the pictures.

"She is all of the thirty four feet," Damon said.

"I can't really tell, but it looks like she might need a little work."

"Yeah, not bad though. I know a couple of gals that can spiffy her up for you."

"Is that what they do?" I asked. "They restore boats?"

"Not really a restoration, more like refinishing. Their names are Brea and Autumn. They have spent most of their lives on boats."

"Can you call them for me, when I get settled?" I asked Damon.

"Sure can; this looks like it would be right up their alley. She has mahogany planking and solid white oak framing. The hull is a very faded white with a red boot top, green bottom and a sandstone deck. This sailboat was built very well, Effie. I haven't seen the cabin yet, but I can only imagine the craftsmanship is just as good. A little TLC and she will look fantastic, not as if she doesn't already."

Sam appeared from around the truck with two men. He introduced them to them to us. Ben, Sam said, was the driver from Yacht Exports. Yacht Exports delivers boats of all sizes anywhere in the continental United States. Ben shook my hand and asked me for my identification. I handed him my driver's license and he handed me a clipboard.

"Just sign here and it's all yours," he said.

I signed the forms and he handed me back my ID and a thick envelope of paperwork. I opened the envelope and looked at the papers. There was the boat title, a death certificate, a copy of the will and a letter addressed to me.

I stuck the letter away to be read later, when I was by myself. As I glanced through the papers, Sam introduced Walt, the second man he was with. Walt was the owner of the marina and a personal friend of Sam's. Walt shook my hand and assured me that he was going to take care of everything.

Sam asked me for the papers. I handed him the envelope and he quickly shifted through them, pointing out all the information that I was going to need to get insurance. "You'll need the size of the motor and its serial number, size of the boat, the kind of boat, the name of the boat, the hull number and the value of what it would cost to replace it," he said.

Then Sam turned to Damon and asked him to take me to McGinty-Gordon with the information. "They're waiting for you and will write out your policy for you in about an hour." Sam added. Sam handed Damon his keys and said, "Take my car; I know you didn't drive."

"What about the registration?" I asked.

"We're putting that on hold for right now." Sam said quietly. I looked at him. That was odd.

"Don't I need to have these things available on the boat?"

Walt replied, "I took care of that for you. We have some documents to keep on the boat; they're as close to authentic as you're going to get."

Sam interrupted, "Don't worry; it's only temporary, maybe a month at the most."

Sam and Walt exchanged looks, and then Walt started flipping through the forms on the clipboard.

"Sam and I will finish up a few things and wait for you to get back before we hoist the boat. I would like to do a quick inspection first anyhow," Walt said.

"So we're good to go?" Damon asked.

"Yep, go ahead," Sam nodded.

With that said, we were off. Damon drove and I sat next to him feeling like I was in a cloak-and-dagger flick. The insurance company was a short drive up the road, probably only three or four miles. Damon parked the car and we entered the brick-front building. It was getting warm, but not warm enough to turn on the air. Instead, the office had several fans going, that blew my hair back as I opened the front door.

It was a memorable feeling, taking me back to my childhood. The warm air in my face reminded me of when I was a kid riding in the back seat on a hot summer's day with the windows down, before air conditioning was a really big deal. Now, everywhere you go has air. "Even pop-up campers have air now," I thought to myself as I came to the counter.

A tall, slender man greeted us and called us back to his office. He shook our hands and introduced himself as David Gordon. We took a seat and I handed him all the paperwork he needed to get me the insurance on the boat.

It didn't take very long at all because he had begun the data entry before we even arrived. With my policy in hand, we were out the door and headed back to the marina in less than an hour. As we pulled in the driveway and parked the car, I saw that Walt had repositioned the boat so it could be lifted off the trailer and into the water. Sam walked out to meet us and Damon handed him his keys, thanking him.

We walked over to the slip. This was no ordinary slip. I had to admit that this was another whole new experience for me. I had seen people back their boats into a lake before, but I had never seen a crane system like this. I would say that it was more like a cradle than a crane, though. The slip was wall-to-wall concrete and appeared to be at least thirty feet wide.

On each side of the slip was a track that ran the entire length of the concrete dock, about the length of two tractor truck trailers back-to-back. The boat hoist itself looked like a square erector set on wheels. The wheels, two on each side, were the height of the men working the lift —and it took four men to operate it.

A large, blue steel beam shot straight up from each corner of the rig and connected to the other steel beams to form a perfect square at the top. Just below the top beams, running parallel to the dock and slip, were long steel rods with straps at each end. The straps reminded me of the tow straps that you often see in Michigan during the winter months.

Walt walked toward me with an ear-to-ear grin. "What do you think, Franciska?"

"I'm not really sure what to think; it's very bitter sweet."

"I only know part of your story, Franciska, but as far as the boat, I can say she is very well built and with a little elbow grease, she'll look like new in no time at all."

"She is pretty, the biggest gift I have ever received. If it wasn't originally my grandfather's, I would have sent her back where she came from."

"Do you not like to sail, or is it the water? What is it about her that scares you so much?"

"I love the water. I've only been sailing a few times, but that part actually excites me."

"I don't get it then."

"You're not supposed to, Walt. You barely know me. If you look at her, don't you see money?"

"Not at all, Franciska. A lot of our "boat people" don't have a pot to piss in; matter of fact, the boat is all they usually have to piss in, other than the open sea, of course."

"That's kind of funny," I laughed.

"Maybe so, but you really don't know how true it is. You have a beautiful and modest boat, my dear. Now, are you ready to watch her kiss the water?"

I nodded and Walt yelled to the crew, "Let her roll, boys!"

I watched the blue mechanical spider roll from the end of the concrete dock up to the back of the trailer. I watched intently as the men fed the straps under the bottom of the boat and attached the straps to massive hooks just below the long metal rod.

The rods on each side began to lift slightly until the straps were taut and then two of the men moved quickly along the boat, following a checklist to make sure they had secured everything that needed to be secured.

The two other men climbed up on the boat, one of them lifting his red hat to the operator and waving it. The rods began to lift upward, making a cranking, clicking sound like a cart climbing upward on a roller coaster, and Franciska began to slowly rise off her trailer.

She was about midway in the air when the straps were locked in place. The jacks were removed from the wheels and the mechanical spider began to carry my Franciska to the end of the slip, on her way to "kiss the water," as Walt said.

Damon's hands rested on my shoulders and he gave them a little squeeze. "What do you think of all this?"

"It's almost overwhelming." I watched the boat move as he rubbed my shoulders a quick time or two.

"Where did you run off to earlier?" I asked.

"When?"

"When they were getting the boat on the crane," I said.

"Oh, I had to talk to Sam about a few things."

"You weren't arguing again, were you?"

"No, we're setting our differences aside for a while. Sam just wants to make sure that you're kept safe until he figures out how to close this case without leaving any loose strings."

"I almost forgot about this whole mess."

"Look, Effie, I need you to promise me that you'll be extra careful. As much as I would like to send you away from all this, I would hate to lose you so soon after finding you. I know that's selfish of me and I'm sorry for that."

"Quit with all that, would you? I am in no mood to go anywhere. After all, I just got here."

At that moment, the giant wheels on the metal spider began rolling to the end of the dock, carrying Franciska effortlessly along. Then the whole unit came to a stop and I could faintly hear a checklist being confirmed by the two men on board. The cranking sound began again and I watched my boat being lowered into the water.

It moved so slowly that there was no splash at all. In fact, she merely kissed the water as promised, and then floated in place with minimal movement, almost as if she was holding her breath, although, I realized it was just me holding my breath.

I watched as all four men released her, then anchored her and went through their final checklist. The two men who were on board climbed the ladder on the side of the sea wall where Franciska was resting and spoke briefly with Walt at the end of the dock. Walt approached us one last time, clipboard in hand and a smile on his face.

"Well, miss, she's ready to go; please sign here. The estate took care of the fees, so she's all paid for. Any last minute questions?"

"No, sir." I shook Walt's hand. "Thanks for all your help; I guess my captain will take over from here."

"Damon, do you have any questions for me?" Walt asked.

"No, sir; I'm sure it's like riding a bike"

"Well then, you two kids have fun." Walt waved good-bye as he walked away.

Damon engulfed my hand with his and we walked down the right side of the slip until we reached the end, where the ladder to the boat was located. Damon climbed down first and stayed by the ladder until I reached the bottom. He told me to untie the ropes while he turned over the engine. She wasn't as loud as I thought she would be. Damon put her in reverse and we began to move slowly out of the slip. Once out of the slip, Damon turned her around and we were soon on our way out of the marina.

I sat quietly for a moment or two and then reached in my purse to pull out my letter. I knew it would be a couple of minutes until we were out of the marina, and I was almost alone, so no better time than now to read it. I slowly unfolded the letter, a slightly yellowed piece of parchment paper. The handwriting was neat and firm. I took a small breath and began to read it to myself.

"My Dearest Franciska, you have grown into a beautiful woman, but I still remember you as the little girl at her grandfather's heels with a fishing pole in her hand. Those were the days, and easier times, too. The sailboat was a long ongoing project for your grandfather and he had often dreamed of sailing with you. His dream was cut short and I vowed to finish what he started. I loved every minute I spent on her.

"If you are reading this now, then my time was cut short as well and I am now with my beloved Eleanor and your grandparents, looking down on you. I know your grandfather would have loved for you to have this boat so I have passed it on to you. It might need a little work, as I grew tired in the last few years. She is a beauty, just like you, and she was made with love. I hope and pray that she brings you years of enjoyment and enlightens all your days. Remember this: time is short. Don't live for tomorrow, live for today. My dearest Franciska, take care of yourself. With love, RW."

I discreetly wiped a tear off my face and slipped the letter back into my purse. We were headed north along the coastline now. Damon looked back at me and asked, "Ready to sail, Effie?" I nodded.

"Yes, captain; let's roll!"

"Effie, come over here. I want you to learn this." I rose to my feet and made my way to Damon.

"What are you getting ready to do?"

"We're going to raise the mainsail, so I'll explain as I do it. The first thing is, you have to have the bow in the direction of the wind. This is the halyard and it's attached to the head of the sail, which is called a bluff. Then you begin pulling until the sail reaches as high as you can get it."

I watched as Damon pulled the halyard, hand over hand. He had my full attention and it made me think of a day not so long ago that I stared as he muddled my first mojito. I couldn't miss the strength in his arms, and now that he was shirtless I could barely contain the sexual thoughts of him that were distracting me from my lesson on hoisting the mainsail.

The crisp white sail rose and the Romani Chakra on it caught my eye. I began to laugh out loud and Damon gave me a look as if he just may have been annoyed. "I am paying attention, Damon. I'll explain later."

"Okay, Effie; see how the sail is harder to raise now? This is where you use the winch to drive it the rest of the way up. Just three wraps around the drum, then into this small groove and cleat it off. Then put in the winch handle and crank it the rest of the way, until it has just the right amount of tension. Today is a light wind day, so we won't need nearly any of the tension. Then there will be more of a curve in the sail, just as now. Lastly, we brake the line and we're off!"

"What if it's very windy?"

"Then you get the sail as taut as you can." He glanced over at me. "Now, what exactly was so funny earlier?"

"It was the image of the wheel on the sail; it's the symbol of the Gypsy. My grandmother would have loved it."

"And I thought it was an image of an old wooden helm." Damon chuckled.

"There definitely are similarities, aren't there?"

Damon was at the wheel and I sat along the side, enjoying this phenomenal moment in my life. Franciska was like a dream. The small swells were no match for her and she slid through them like a knife through butter. My skin soaked in the sun at the same time as it welcomed the gentle prickly sensations from the salty air.

The cool waves flowed right through my body, pulling my hair back with it, and the salt air danced on top of my tongue. Being on the ocean at this very moment was the feeling I have been searching for, for so many years. It was a feeling of isolation, yet connected to something larger. I felt tremendous pleasure in the feeling of my existence there on the water.

The slight swaying and rocking relaxed me and nearly drove me to ecstasy.

"Effie, want to join me for a few minutes? We're almost there."

"Sure."

I joined Damon at the wheel. He gave me another quick lesson and then I took his place. I was now driving my own sailboat. "She is absolutely stunning," I thought to myself. Damon stood behind me, his arms wrapped around me and his hands resting just below my abdomen. I could feel his heartbeat and smell the coconut in the oil that glistened on his skin.

Just when you think things can't get any better than this, somehow life manages to do just that. Damon pointed to our destination and took over the helm. I watched as he lowered the sail and then effortlessly placed Franciska at the end of the dock. As soon as she was secure, Damon took me to the floor and showed me a whole new use for coconut oil.

CHAPTER THIRTEEN

Superstition

CHAPTER FOURTEEN

A Little TLC

The night came and went. It was the most restful night that I could remember having in a long time. I never knew that I would enjoy sleeping on a boat as much as I did. It was nice having Damon there, too. We fixed up the cabin as much as we could. Damon had brought pillows and blankets from the main house to make the bed comfortable.

We ordered out for Chinese from a dive down the road. Damon sketched in his pad all evening, while we shared two bottles of Chianti in the candlelight. I think he missed his calling because his drawings were gorgeous.

Maybe it was a "man thing" and he didn't want to call himself an artist. He had talent, though, and I hated to see him waste it as a bartender. Wait a minute. What was I thinking? That sounded kind of snobby. Nonetheless, we had a very nice night. Damon finally told me a little bit about his family back in Italy, and we talked and cuddled and laughed until the boat finally rocked us both to sleep.

Damon woke before me and was up on deck before I opened my eyes. I climbed through the hatch to meet a pair of feet at my face and Damon's hand held out for me. I took his hand and allowed him to help me up on deck.

"Good morning." He smiled. "How did you sleep?"

"I think I could get used to this. Good morning to you."

"How about omelets this morning?"

"Did I hear you talking to someone a few minutes ago?"

"Yes, I'm sorry I woke you. I called Brea and Autumn; they'll be here around noon to look over the boat."

"Damon, that's really nice of you, but I'm not so sure I can pay that bill."

"Don't worry about it. They owe me for some murals I painted for them. We only have to provide any supplies that they may need, like stains and such. She doesn't need that much work, Effie."

"Are you sure?"

"Look, honey, I'm sure. They will stay here on the boat until it's done and you could use some company and fresh faces too. Trust me on this one; you'll like them!"

"Okay then. Where am I going to sleep if they're staying on the boat?"

"Ummm, hello! With me, of course. Or are you sick of me already?" Damon made a sad face.

"I don't think that's even possible, you sly dog."

I slapped him in the shoulder, "Omelets! Omelets and a toothbrush; let's go!"

We ran down the dock, through the sand and into the sliding door of his pool house. I took a shower, brushed my teeth and entered the kitchen to find a Spanish omelet and tomato juice waiting and ready for me.

"Thank you, this is awesome. Is there anything you don't do?

"I don't do cats."

"No! I love cats, I miss my Peewee."

"I guess I'm just more of a dog person, plus I'm actually allergic to cats, especially the long-haired ones. So, who was Peewee? And tell me that name did not come from the movie, *Porky's*."

"Peewee was my last cat; he's gone now. He was the smallest of the litter and sickly too. We really didn't think he was going to make it, but I named him anyhow. He ended being the biggest cat I ever had and he was a gorgeous Russian Blue."

"And the name?"

"Yes, it came from *Porky's*." I laughed. "I can't believe you don't like cats. Maybe if you weren't allergic to them you'd learn to love them. Maybe you could at least learn to tolerate a cat at a distance Mr. Damon."

"Shit, I guess we can see who will be wearing the pants around here the next few days."

"I think now is a good time to get out of yours and take a shower. I'll get things cleaned up here."

Damon laughed all the way to the shower. I finished the incredible Spanish omelet and began to clean the dishes. I was about halfway through when I realized that Damon and I really don't know that much about one another. My mind wondered a bit. There has to be more to us than I like cats and he likes dogs. I wondered what his favorite color was, what kind of music he liked, hobbies, sports and so much more. Damon interrupted my thoughts again, wearing nothing more than a towel.

"You have got to stop that!" I begged.

"Stop what?" He smirked."

"You know what! Now go get dressed."

Damon turned to get dressed and purposely let his towel hit the floor. I had to admit; he looked just as nice from the backside too. I finished the remainder of the dishes and wiped down all the counters. It was kind of nice being here. Damon's place, although nothing more than a pool house, was bright, airy and cheerful. I could understand why he was happy where he was.

"Damon." I yelled to him. "I'm going out to the boat; meet me out there." I gently closed the door behind me and took my cell phone from my back pocket. I haven't talked to my mom in a while and thought I should give her a quick call. I tapped the bar on the screen that read "Mom" and the phone began to ring. Her voicemail came on. "Hi; you reached Marietta's phone. I'm not available to take your call right now. Please leave your name, number and a brief message and I'll get back to you as soon as I can."

"Hey, Mom, it's me, Effie. I just wanted to touch base with you. So much has happened in the last few days. I'm fine. Don't worry about me. I'll call again soon and we can catch up. Love you, Mom; hope all is well with you."

Well, that anticipation was short lived, I thought to myself. She never answers her phone and I'm not even sure why she has one. I don't even think she checks her messages. Once, I glanced at her phone and she had fifty-six messages.

I laughed to myself. Sometimes I do really miss her, but years of bad men in her life left me to question her values a bit. Not that I should judge my mother; after all I'm here, aren't I? I had to pinch myself. Sometimes it does feel like the last two weeks has been one long dream.

"Hey, you," Damon whispered, coming up behind me.

"Hey."

"Did I hear you say 'Mom'"?

"Yeah, I just left a message for her. I wanted to let her know that everything is all right."

"Effie, you should tell her what's going on, don't you think? Does she know anything about us?"

"Funny you should ask."

"Why?"

"Well, I was thinking about us, Damon. We have one hell of a connection, I admit that. There's physical attraction, no doubt about that! The sex is out of this world. However, we really don't know each other that well."

"What do you mean; we don't know each other that well?"

"Okay, you just found out about my love of cats. What is my favorite color?"

"Mmmmm, blue?"

"Bzzzzz! Wrong! It's green and it's the reason I love your eyes."

"Hmmm, okay. I know where you're going now. How about we use this weekend to catch up? My favorite color is blue, although I own a lot of green."

"When you wear green, it really brings out your eyes. A getting-to-know-each other weekend. Sounds good. I look forward to getting to know you, but don't leave out play time; I rather like that."

"So you said earlier. Out of this world, huh? It's good to know I'm doing things right."

I blushed a bit. I have to admit that I don't quite turn bright red anymore. I was getting more comfortable with Damon and all his little dropped comments every day. He actually cracked me up sometimes.

"We're not interrupting anything are we?" a soft voice came from beside us. I turned around to see two women standing behind us, hands full of bags and buckets.

Damon turned. "Hey there, I didn't expect you so early. How are the two of you?" He asked.

"We're good; Brea finished her job early, so we thought we'd get a jump-start on the day." Autumn announced.

"I am so glad that you found the place okay. I want you both to meet my girlfriend, Effie."

Brea leaned forward, set down her bag, and shook my hand. "It's so nice to meet you." Flashes came swirling in. Waves, sails, boats, cliffs, buildings, marinas and ocean vistas repeated themselves over and over again. Brea was a hair taller than me, with long sandy brown hair and light blonde sun-kissed streaks.

She was deeply tan, but that was to be expected. Although she had a thin frame, the definitions in her muscles proved to me that she was a hard worker. I felt great comfort in knowing that this was their first time here. I'm not the jealous type but I can't help but wonder how many ex-girlfriends might be lingering around.

Autumn shook my hand too. She was a little smaller, shorter and paler than her older sister, but had the same long, sandy brown hair. I received visions from her as well. Waves, boats, surfboards and ... and ... a Corona. "It's very nice to meet you both," I said and then laughed.

"What's so funny?" Autumn asked.

"Tell me if I am wrong. Both of you live for the ocean, without a doubt, and both of you enjoy boats of all kinds, but I'm guessing Brea is more responsible and business oriented and loves architecture and traveling. You, Autumn, love surfing and the night life, and ..." I hesitated only briefly, "A Corona is your choice of drink."

"How did you do that?" Autumn gasped.

"Yeah, I kind of would like to know too," Brea agreed.

"Well, I can read your energy. I can't explain it much and I'm learning more about it every day. Most of the images I see are very conservative in a way, but Autumn's energy was kind of fun and that's why I laughed."

"That's too cool," They both said at the same time.

"It can be, but it has drawbacks, too. Some people view it as a gift and others view it as a curse. I am still trying to figure it all out and I think you both just helped me to do just that."

Damon interjected, "Would you both like to see Francisca? I know you will truly appreciate her. She was built by the hands of two men over a period of years and the craftsmanship is unbelievable."

"Good idea Damon," I agreed and we all walked down to the boat. Brea and Autumn went ahead to check it all out and Damon and I stood on the dock and waited patiently. Brea had a clipboard and was making many notes. I could definitely tell they were sisters, almost like twins. They both had this natural beauty that I wish I had; the kind of beauty that doesn't require make-up. I could tell right away that I was in good hands and so was Francisca.

"I didn't mean to change the subject so fast on you back there," Damon said. "I thought that you might have been getting uncomfortable."

"Aww, you're so sweet, Damon. That was very thoughtful of you. They both have very strong energy and it was real easy to read them both. That's why I think I have figured out why I get visions from some people and not others. They are both very open and passionate, not hiding anything. So, I knew I was safe talking to them the way I did."

"How do you explain me then?"

"What do you mean?"

"Well, it just seems like you should be able to see more from me, but you can't."

"That is the drawback part of it all. If I am right about why I'm able to read some people, but not others, then either you're not as open as you claim to be, or there are things about you that you have locked the rest of the world out of."

"But you do get some visions from me, right?"

"I do, and I've figured all those out."

"Are you gonna let me in on it?"

"Okay. The colors that swirl all around people represent the primary colors on the color wheel, which is also representative in your passion for painting. The mix of straight and curved lines I haven't quite figured out, but my guess is there is something holding you back from doing what you enjoy doing. How did I do?"

"Not so great. You're way off base," he said stiffly.

I was surprised to hear it. I knew what I knew, but I wasn't going to push him. Some people, I was learning, said they were comfortable with my visions, but they really weren't. I made a mental note to be more cautious with him next time. Then I smiled.

"I know, so let's enjoy the day and not worry too much about what I see or don't see."

That was easier said than done, though. Even without any special abilities I could see that Damon was worried. Seeing him with that expression on his face worried me, too. Could he be hiding something? I didn't even want to think it for one minute. I could be wrong, though. I had been wrong many times before.

Brea and Autumn stepped down from the boat. Both of them looked very pleased. Brea took out her clipboard and read me the details.

"Damon is right," She said. "Your boat is well built. I'm going to give you a brief rundown of what were going to do to bring her back to life. Autumn will work on the cabin part of the boat. There are some minor repairs required for two of the cabinets and the sleeping area. She's also going to repaint and stain the entire interior. You will also need new cushions; do you have any requests as to colors?"

"Green."

"What about prints?"

"A solid color would be best; maybe an olive or pine green. If you can't keep it a solid color then no floral prints no matter what, please."

"Perfect!" Brea said. "I like your choice. I'll handle the deck and exterior part of the boat. A few minor repairs are needed there, too, but everything looks sound. A little sanding and a couple of coats of varnish and she'll be all set. I will keep the colors as they are and that will make this whole process go much smoother. Do you concur?"

"I concur. Concur? That's a term used in law; I like it."

"Ahhhh, yes." She blushed. "I used to date a lawyer. He used it a lot and it kind of grew on me," Brea said in a voice heavy with regret.

"Not a good ending, huh?"

"Not at all! But that's more than enough about him! So anyhow, I'll have one of the marina mechanics stop by today and check the rest of the functions of the boat. We should have her completed by Monday evening, or Tuesday at the latest. So, if we can start today, that would be great. We'll do the repairs, sanding and start the interior today. We have an account for the varnish, paint and repair supplies, and you can pay that when we're done, but we will need to have something up front for the cushions."

"No problem; I'll give you my credit card. By the way, Damon has to work tonight, so how about we get some pizza and beer, or anything else you might like?"

"That sounds like a good plan," Brea chirped, and then asked Autumn what she thought.

"Lemon drops tonight, babeee." Autumn laughed.

Damon laughed, too, and kindly asked that we behave ourselves because he wanted no cops at the house tonight. Then we all laughed.

The day went by fast. I spent the majority of it lying on the sand by the dock. I began reading a book I had wanted to read for a long time but hadn't found the time—Angel, by James Patterson. He used to be one of my favorite authors, but I felt his books lacked passion when he was writing about love, romance and sex.

One of the things that I liked best about his books, though, were his short chapters. When I used to be really busy, it was the only way I was able to read for fun. I could easily finish a chapter if it was only a couple of pages, and not lose my spot. If I had to reread a chapter to pick things back up again, then I wasn't spending an hour doing it. Today I had the luxury of reading as much as I wanted, and at my leisure.

The work had begun on the boat, and Autumn had returned from Jacksonville with my receipt and credit card in hand. The cushions were going to be done on Wednesday, which seemed remarkably fast. Damon gave me a kiss on my forehead when he left for work and all seemed to be going along pretty good right now. The girls were going to work until they couldn't see to work any more, which I knew was not going to be much longer, so I went inside to take a shower.

An hour later, Autumn and Brea showed up at the pool house, both covered in a white powder that made them look a little ghostly.

"How about a shower, ladies?" I asked trying hard not to laugh.

Brea chirped, "I'm first."

"Not if I can help it." Autumn yelled as she darted out the door.

I heard a large splash and knew right away what had just happened. Brea rolled her eyes and headed for the bathroom.

"You still win," I added as I followed her with a hand full of towels.

"She still has to take a shower, you know."

"Ugh, you don't know Autumn very well. That just might be good enough for her."

"I'll make her!" I laughed.

Autumn did eventually take a shower. I had to suggest that she wasn't allowed in my Jeep until she got cleaned up. The three of us drove to a small local pizzeria, ordered two large pizzas to go and drove them back to the house, mouths watering the whole way.

One of the pizzas was loaded with fresh veggies and extra cheese, and the other pizza was identical except for an extra double bacon topping. We each also got a Greek side salad and then stopped at the corner store for beer.

I enjoyed the dinner, light conversation and ice cold beer by the pool with Autumn and Brea. We cleaned up and saved some pizza for Damon in the fridge, or for us later on, whichever happened first.

Then I took out two decks of regular playing cards and shuffled. I explained the game, "65," briefly; it wasn't rocket science. I did make some changes, though. I added four jokers and whoever drew a joker could make a rule for the game. Shot glasses were set up and a bottle of Absolute vodka, lemons and a dish of sugar were ready to go. I dealt the three of us three cards each.

"The goal is to make three of a kind, threes are wild and you can either take the top discard or choose from the undealt pile." I had to explain again.

"Easy enough," Brea chirped.

"When does the drinking start?" Autumn asked.

"Well, we all have our beers now, but the shots come into play when we make rules."

Brea went out in the third round with three nines. Autumn and I added the points the cards left in our hand and I recorded it. The trick of the game is to have the least amount of points after the last hand. Then I explained the next deal. Four cards to each of us, fours are wild and you have to go out with a four of a kind or a run in the same suit.

"What's a run?" Autumn asked.

"It's like a straight flush in poker. An example would be four, five, six and seven, all in hearts."

"Okay, I got it now."

Brea drew the first card and got a joker. She was pretty excited to enact the "Viking" rule. The rule is that when Brea puts her two index fingers to the top of her head to pretend she has horns, everyone else has to pretend they're rowing a boat. The last to do the row action has to drink a shot. She slid the joker to the bottom of the pile and drew the next card. She threw her fingers in the air to make her horns and I began to row. Autumn caught on last and had to do a shot, but deep down I think she really wanted to. Brea went out again and the points began adding up quickly for Autumn and I.

We were up to the fifth deal now and I explained that now things were going to get a little tricky. Seven cards are dealt, sevens are wild and the goal was to create one set, two sets or one set and one run. Brea dealt and the second card I drew, I got a joker.

"I enact the thumb rule. When I place my thumb on the edge of the table, the last one to place their thumb on the edge of the table has to do a shot." This hand went fast and I was the lucky one this time.

We had played hands up to tens; three more rules added, including Autumn's " little man" rule and the laughter was now loud and contagious when Damon arrived. He took a chair, grabbed one of my beers and just stared at me.

His stare was more of a mix between a smirk and amazement, with a slight grin, not quite ear to ear. We made it to the last hand and Brea was the ultimate winner. We were all feeling pretty sorry for Autumn, as she was quite drunk.

Damon walked the girls to the boat while I cleaned up and went inside, waiting in bed for that gorgeous stud of mine, wearing nothing but an apron. By time Damon arrived however I was face down and fast asleep, but still able to hear myself snore in some weird sort of out-of-body way.

CHAPTER FIFTEEN

Feeling the Heat

Monday came early and I was ready to start work again. The weekend had given me a chance to clear my head and relax. I was feeling refreshed, but that soon vanished and the ache from deep down in my stomach grew as I inched toward Candles and More. Fire trucks, police and groups of rubberneckers made it quite difficult to get to the shop.

I pulled the Jeep over in the first available parking place, grabbed my things and walked through the crowds. I neared the yellow tape and could see clearly now. Pea's beautiful, eclectic shop had burned. I ducked under the tape and headed for the first available fireman. I needed to know what happened and I needed to know now.

My dash was abruptly stopped as a strong hand grasped my elbow and nearly yanked my arm out of socket.

"Just where do you think you're going, Ms. Varga?"

"Let go of me, Reggie," I screamed back.

He let go of my arm and stared at me in a confused sort of manner. Just then I realized that I made a fatal error. My throat became dry and the lump gathering in the center behind my Adams' apple was not going anywhere anytime soon. Our eyes were locked, and I could tell he knew that I knew. I just entered the point of no return. Our glare was soon interrupted.

"Effie!" Sam yelled from across the street.

I turned quickly and ran across the street to Sam. I nearly tripped as my high heel caught a cobblestone just in the right place. Sam reached out for my arms and steadied me upright.

"Sam, what happened here? Where is Pea? Was anyone hurt?" I asked repeatedly.

"No one is really sure what happened, although they suspect arson. The good detective over there is trying to blame it on the candles, but no one is really buying it. They have a professional inside now. No one was really hurt, but they did take Pea to the hospital for observation. She did inhale quite a bit of smoke when she tried to put the fire out."

"Why was she here so early?"

"Funny you asked. Pea got a call last night that someone was interested in one of the paintings, but needed to come by early. The police have her cell phone right now and are trying to trace the call, but it seems to have come from one of those disposable phones."

"You know what this means, don't you?" I asked quietly.

"Yes. Clearly we struck a nerve and poor Pea just reaped what we have sown. Don't worry, Effie; I think you're fine where you're at right now. Obviously you're out of a job, so Damon can keep an eye on you."

"Sam, I screwed up, though."

"What do you mean?"

"When asshole grabbed my arm back there I called him Reggie. He knows I know. He looked at me. He knows. He knows!"

"Shit, Effie. We're gonna have to come up with a new game plan."

"I'm sorry, Sam; it was an accident."

"It's okay; we'll figure something out."

"Sam."

"Yeah, what?"

"Can I look inside?"

"I'm sorry, Effie; they're still collecting evidence and it's not a safe site yet. Nothing looks like it can be salvaged, though."

"That's not it, Sam. I think I can help. Find a way to get me in there. I have to be able to read something from an item in there, any item, even if it's just one. Please, Sam, try?"

"Wait here, Effie. I'll go talk to the captain."

I stood patiently and quietly while I watched the conversation between Sam and the captain. I stretched my neck and tipped my head to the side, trying to hear their conversation. When that failed, I tried to read their lips, but that didn't work either. I could see the captain wasn't quite on board with Sam's request. I could tell that just by reading his facial gestures, but then something changed.

Sam was working over the captain good. His hands and his body worked together to tell him a story. But I noticed something else, too. Sam looked nice. His eyes glistened, and his hands and arms were strong. He wasn't quite the type I was normally interested in, but I saw him in a whole different light now.

They both smiled, chuckled and then shook hands. Sam walked toward me, put his arm around my waist and escorted me into the building, with the captain a few steps behind us. The captain asked everyone inside the building to leave and stood in the doorway watching intently.

I set my purse down on the floor and whispered in Sam's ear. "What did you say to get us in here?"

Sam laughed. "I told him you were a freelance psychic that has helped solve many cases—and that if you could prove to the captain you were reliable, you would be willing to help out with future cases on an as-needed basis."

"Sam! What were you thinking?"

"I was thinking you have no job as of right now and you're good, Effie. I think this is right up your alley."

"I'm not going to say a word right now and just go with it, but were gonna talk later."

"So get to it then."

I walked over to the front desk and laid both my hands on the glass top, which miraculously remained intact. I bowed my head slightly and closed my eyes. I saw nothing, though, nothing at all. I began to worry and my hands became clammy. Sam noticed the nervous shake and walked over to rub my back.

"Don't try too hard. Relax and let it come to you."

"Sam, I'm not used to people watching me and you know these things just pop in when they want. I can't control them."

"But you do, Effie; you just don't realize it. You block it when you want and let it happen when you want. Try to think back to when you get the visions. There is some common denominator. Think, Effie, think."

I closed my eyes and laid my hands back on the glass one more time. I dropped my shoulders and took a deep breath. I was thinking of myself this time. It was like I was looking down on the entire scene, similar to an out-of-body experience.

As I was looked down, I could see Pea wrapping my crystal ball. I could see customers entering and leaving. I could see Damon talking with Pea, too. I could not see anything that pertained to the fire, though. I looked up and nodded to Sam. Sam gave the captain a thumbs-up and I walked to the next area.

I neared the once-filled bookcases, but felt no need to work in the front area of the store. So, I made my way to the first room on the left in the hall. This was where Pea made her candles. I walked in the room slowly, stepping over the fallen beams. I edged my way to her special stool and laid my hands on it. Visions of Pea came flooding in. The painting hung next to her as she worked on a rather large candle. "She smelled the smoke first, Sam."

"Go on, Effie."

"Pea set her carving tools down and headed for the door, that's when she noticed the smoke billowing in from under the door."

"Can you see anything else?" Sam asked.

"Stop talking and let me concentrate."

I closed my eyes and began again. I watched Pea panic and rush to the door, only to find it screaming hot. She knew it was the only way out of the room. Pea rushed to the sink, opened the faucet completely and began to fill up canisters. She rushed to the door with a canister of water in her hand and took her chance to open the door.

That's where she burnt her hand. The flames were rushing through the door now, but Pea struggled to get them down. They were much too big for her canisters of water. She couldn't control the fire, so she got completely wet with the sprayer and laid as close to the floor as she could.

"Sam, she waited right here to die. She couldn't get out and just laid here on the floor."

I closed my eyes again and continued. My desire to find the truth had grown so large that the visions came flooding in now. I was able to control what I wanted to see for the first time. Water was rushing in now.

The firefighters were here. Pea lay on the floor screaming for help. Little by little the flames dissipated and a man dressed in yellow rushed through the door. He picked her up off the floor and carried her out. I explained everything I saw to Sam and if he wasn't a believer before, he was now.

"The fire didn't start here, let's move on." I whispered to Sam.

We made our way down the hall and to the room I once worked in. It was completely burnt. I stood in the middle and slowly turned in a complete circle to view the entire room. There wasn't much left to touch. Then my eyes caught something unfamiliar in the corner of the room on the floor. I walked over and Sam followed closely.

I bent down to pick it up a small jackknife I'd never seen before, when Sam bent down to grab my wrist before I could touch it. He accidentally hit my forehead with his chin. I stood up quickly, rubbing my head, and Sam grabbed my face with both of his hands asking me if I was okay.

Our eyes locked. His lips touched mine and his hands remained by my face. I drifted off in his kiss. It was soft and gentle. My heart raced and my body tingled. I didn't resist and found myself liking his movement, enjoying his heat and wanting more. I dropped my arms and grabbed him at the waist pulling him close.

I quickly pulled myself away.

"I'm sorry." Sam said

"I'm sorry, too. This can't happen, I can't do this. I love Damon."

"Effie, we just got caught in the moment; it didn't mean anything."

"But yes it did. You and I both wanted it, the desire was there and you can't deny that."

"Okay, but it was wrong of me to press it. I know you're with Damon. Why did you kiss me back?"

"I liked it; I wanted to know."

"Know what?"

"If I was just wondering about you, or truly desired you."

"Are you still wondering?"

"No."

"Well, what is it then; are you even gonna tell me?"

"I want you, Sam. I am attracted to you physically. I don't want a setting next to you at your dining room table, though."

"That's a strange analogy." Sam laughed. "I'll accept it though ... let's get back to work. Don't touch the knife. I need to put it in an evidence bag so I can check it for fingerprints."

Sam left the room to grab an evidence bag and while he was gone I couldn't help but to find my mind racing with excitement. My desire to have Sam engulfed my body and I couldn't shake it. My breathing was quick and my heart fluttered as I thought of what it would be like to be with him intimately.

"Effie!" Sam said. "Are you okay?"

"I'm fine. Why?"

"You look a million miles away."

"It's been a long morning and I really want to stop by the hospital and see Pea."

"Well, let's finish up then."

Sam picked up the small jackknife with his blue-glove covered hand and placed it into the evidence bag. He slid the zipper shut and handed the bag to me. "Now," he said. "You can try to get a vision from it."

I carefully took the bag from Sam and took a deep breath. Sam took a deep breath, too; I could hear it. Nothing. I tried again, this time walking to a different spot in the room where I felt alone. I now used both of my hands and cupped them around the bagged knife as if I were holding a baby chick. I slowly closed my eyes and concentrated to make it all happen, and it did.

It was pitch black and a man entered through the back door. He had on simple blue jeans and a black hoodie, with the hood covering a ball cap. The part that gave me the chills was that he used a key to get in. He wasn't large in build, more short and stocky. I could not see a face.

He came to this room and just to the left of the door started placing small, thin strips of waxy-looking paper in the floorboards, edging the entire room and then continuing out into the hallway. When he was done, he returned to this room, tipped over one of my small round metal tables near the curtains. He broke an oil lantern on the floor next to it.

He stood up and I could almost see him now. His pouty lips began to stretch out ever so slowly and soon they formed a very large smile. Then he tipped his head back slightly and began to laugh. At that moment, that very moment, horror filled my veins. I recognized the face. I watched my own vision for a minute more, seeing him set the fire and leave, and I just couldn't do it any longer—I was exhausted and my head began to hurt.

"Effie, are you okay?" Sam said as he lightly shook my shoulders. "You just look like you saw a ghost."

"I wish that's what it was."

"Quit holding back then and let me in."

I began to explain everything I saw, up to the horrible laugh. Then I told Sam the face that I saw.

"So, he did his own handiwork, huh? This makes things extremely hard and extremely dangerous. No wonder he could create such an elaborate set up."

"After his haunting laugh, he turned to leave and tripped on the very table that he knocked over; that's when the knife fell out of his pocket."

"There's something I don't get, though."

"What's that, Sam?"

"This was done in the middle of the night and the fire was in the early morning."

"He waited, that's why. When Pea came in and went to her candle room, he pushed the back door open just enough to fit his hand in and lit the wax paper with his lighter."

"So, he intended to kill Pea and make it look like an accident?"

"Probably."

"Anything after he lit the paper?"

"The fire took off like a stream, as if he made a trail with gasoline. The burning paper spread the fire down the hall, snaked around my room, continued out the door and ended right in front the crafting room."

"And?"

"I couldn't watch any more after that; isn't it enough?"

"Yes, but now we need the hard evidence."

"He keeps a key to the back door. My guess is that it used to be Helena's."

"I wonder if he's dumb enough to hang on to it?"

"Sam, he keeps it on his own ring of keys."

"You're kidding me?"

"Nope, right in plain sight."

"Well, then, let's hope that he forgets to take it off. I'm gonna get you to the hospital to see Pea."

On the way out the door, Sam handed the knife to the captain and whispered something in his ear. The captain nodded, his face not betraying any surprise or emotion. I learned later that Sam set up a time to talk to him in more detail, but made sure to mention that the captain was to be the only one to log the evidence.

"The fire scene and Helena's murder have a police connection," Sam said.

The captain looked up and asked, "How do you know it's not me?" I could read his lips from the distance.

Sam explained, "Because she could see that it wasn't you." The captain nodded his head and took the evidence. As Sam walked away, he told the captain, "One hour."

I got into my Jeep and Sam followed me to the hospital. I could see Reggie talking to the captain out of the corner of my eye as I pulled away. I could also see the captain shaking his head, no. "I bet that little fucker is trying to get the evidence," I said out loud to myself.

It didn't take long to get to the hospital from there, ten minutes at most. It seemed like an hour, though. I was parking the Jeep when my phone rang. I knew it was Damon by the ringtone, "Firework," by Katy Perry. I assigned it to Damon because he's so damn hot. It was about the only thing that made me smile this morning.

"Hello."

"Effie, are you okay?"

"Yes, let me guess—Sam called you?"

"Well he's concerned about you and I am too. Man oh man; you attract a lot of attention. Do you do this everywhere you go?"

"Very funny."

"I'm leaving now, headed to the hospital too; I want to see Pea."

"I'll see you shortly then. Sam is gonna stay until I get there."

I said good-bye, turned my phone to vibrate and headed into that big white building, dreading every minute. Sam was by my side and we didn't exchange one word. The mood seemed dense and unsettled. We made our way in, passed the desk and tapped number four on the elevator panel.

All I could smell was death. I know that the hospital smell is merely all the sanitizing cleaners, but I always associated it with death. The doors opened and we made our way to room 422. Pea looked pretty good, considering what had happened, and a firefighter was sitting next to her, holding her hand.

He stood up to greet us. "Hi, I'm Mike. Pea doesn't have anyone here so I offered to stay."

"I'm Effie; it's nice to meet you and thank you for saving her."

"I was just doing my job."

"Well it appears as if you went a couple of steps beyond your job. Call me Effie."

Sam shook Mike's hand and they exchanged some small talk. Apparently, they knew each other and had been fishing together a few times.

"I gotta get going now," Mike offered sadly. He looked at Pea and said, "I'll see you later, Paisley."

I chuckled. "Paisley? I haven't heard that in a while."

Pea interrupted my laugh, "You can call me Pea, Mike. Everyone else does."

"Pea it is." Mike said on the way out the door. "Sweet Pea."

I walked to the bed and gave Pea a kiss and a hug. We didn't have a great deal of time to talk, so I gave her a very brief rundown on the morning's events. She listened with a face that was pale and expressionless.

I tried to keep my distance because I didn't want to endure any more disturbing visions. Although I seemed to have a handle on it now, I wasn't taking any chances. I suggested that Pea take a much-needed vacation and this time she agreed with me.

"I'm working on something right now," Pea said.

"Good!" Sam and I all but screeched in unison.

Sam shot me a look and I shot one back. Pea stared at the both of us for a moment or two and asked, "There's something you're not telling me, isn't there?"

"No." I hesitated. "I covered everything."

"I'm not buying it; there is more. What happened in that building that you're keeping secret?"

"Really, Pea, nothing happened."

"What do you mean, nothing happened?" Damon asked doorway.

"Hey, there. Pea seems to think we're not telling her something from the crime scene today."

Damon interrupted, "Well, Pea, if there is something they're not telling you, I am sure it's for your own good."

Damon walked over to Sam and shook his hand. "Thanks for keeping her safe, man." He patted him on the back and sat down next to Pea.

"I'm gonna sneak out of here," Sam said. "I have a very important meeting with the captain."

Everyone said their good-byes and soon Damon and I also left Pea's room. We walked to the parking lot hand in hand. I got in my Jeep and Damon shut my door. He leaned on the door slightly and said, "I have something special for you back at the house. I'll follow you there." I smiled and gave him a soft, simple kiss and we were soon on our way.

CHAPTER SIXTEEN

Jib

Back at Damon's pool house, I pulled up a tri-fold lounger next to the saltwater pool and watched the sunlight dance off of the water. I closed my eyes and laid my head back, hoping for a short nap. I could hear the girls working on my sailboat, putting all the finishing touches together now. It distracted me a little, but it was a fun distraction.

I could hear them both singing off key as they went about their work, and I couldn't help but chuckle. It's amazing how much better you can hear when you close your eyes and really listen. Damon was in the kitchen throwing together some sandwiches and making fresh lemonade. I could hear the electric squeezer in action.

Soon everything was quiet and all I could hear was the wind and the waves. It was as if I leaned forward and turned the TV switch to "off." And then I heard the strangest little noise. It was like a cross between a squeak and a cry. I strained hard to hear it again, but all was quiet. I laid my head back again and felt the sun's rays pierce my skin.

Damon brought the food and lemonade out, setting them both on the table behind me. He reached up and pulled the cord that hung from the bell and gave it a couple of rings. I heard the girls yell that they would be right there. Damon came and sat on the side of my lounge.

"I have something for you." He said with anticipation.

"What do you have for me?"

"Wait here, but no peeking." He left, going back into the house.

A few minutes went by and I couldn't help but wonder what he was up to. Then he appeared from nowhere. "Are your eyes closed?" He whispered in my ear.

"Yes, Damon, hurry up. You're driving me crazy!"

Damon set a tan vented airline carrier on the lounge at my feet and I stared at the opening only to find another set of eyes staring back at me. They beamed a bright yellowish green, like a driveway reflector in the darkest of the night.

I leaned forward and unzipped the carrier as Damon watched with his breath held tight. The head poked through just a bit and I reached in with both my hands to pull the rest of him out. He was a gorgeous all black cat that quickly found his way into my arms, purring and nudging me slightly under my chin.

"I hope you like him! I got him from the animal shelter this morning. I thought you might like a little something to keep you company when I'm not here."

"I love him! But you said you hate cats!" I said, somewhat concerned that by making me happy he was giving up some of his own happiness.

"Hate is a strong word to use. I just said that I prefer dogs and that I'm allergic to cats. But this is an outdoor guy, so maybe I can handle him. Dona saw the ad in the paper and showed it to me. The owner died in a car accident and the cat used to sail with her. He's only a couple of years old, and I thought of you the minute I read the ad."

He wasn't too big, too small, too fat or too skinny. He was just the right size. His coat was medium length and very shiny. He appeared to be a Bombay. I held him close and sighed. "The ad was right; he needed a good home; thank you so very much!"

"How did you know the ad was right?" Damon asked.

"I just know. What is his name?" I asked, trying to quickly change the subject.

"Jib."

"Well, hello there, Mr. Jib; your owner named you appropriately for being a boat cat." I said to the cat as I giggled and scratched him under the chin.

I set Jib down and gave Damon a hug and a kiss. "Now you don't have to worry about a black cat crossing your path." I said happily.

"And why is that?"

"We have one of our own and that now makes us exempt" I laughed.

CHAPTER SEVENTEEN

Lessons

My phone rang. I had taken a much-needed nap. I looked at the number and didn't recognize it. Hesitantly I answered the call.

"Hello?"

"Hi, is this Franciska?" The woman's voice asked.

"It is. Who is this?"

"You might not remember me by name. My name is Kim and you read my cards for me at a rest stop."

"Oh, yes! I remember you and the reading. How are you doing?"

"I'm good; thanks for asking."

"Is there something wrong?"

"Oh, no, not at all. I was calling to thank you." Kim said excitedly.

"Thank me? I don't understand."

"You made the trip much easier for me and I was patient, like you suggested. Everything went really well and you'll be happy to know that I'm getting married. My fiancé and

I are moving to Wilmington, North Carolina, at the end of next month. Everything you said would happen is happening."

"That's great, Kim; but you don't have to thank me."

"Yes, I do. I was contemplating not going through with the trip when I saw you. You changed that for me. I'm not sure where you ended up on your journey, but I'd love to send you an invite to the wedding. Do you mind giving me your address?"

"I'm in Brunswick, Georgia. The address is tricky though. Keep my number and when you get close to sending the invites out, send me a quick text and I'll give you the address to send it to. I'm flattered and if I can make it to your wedding, I would be more than happy to come!"

"Thanks, Franciska. I'll let you go now. Take care and I hope you find what you're looking for."

"Call me Effie; and you take care, too."

I set my phone down at my side, laid my head back and closed my eyes. I enjoyed the warmth that my face was soaking in. I recapped the conversation in my mind and was feeling genuinely happy that I made some sort of a difference to someone, even if it had seemed so trivial at the time.

Thoughts of Sam soon took over. I couldn't help but to think of the intensity of the kiss we shared. It was different with Sam and I couldn't shake it from my head.

Why couldn't I shake it from my head? I asked myself. I was attracted to Damon. I loved everything about Damon. I was with Damon and yet thinking about Sam. The thoughts swirled around in my head only for a few moments longer and I was soon asleep, dreaming deeply.

The iPod in its cradle was playing a mix of Daughtry as I sat tensely at the table beneath the deck of my boat, listening to the weather station on the battery radio. From a gentle rocking and swaying, the boat began to rock and pitch as the intensity of the waves picked up. The wind began to whistle and howl, as if it was trying to call my name.

The pounding rain threatened my very existence, smashing against the outer hull and making me feel like I was trapped inside a drum as it pounded against the wood. The creaking of the cabin was eerie. The groans and creaks reminded me of rickety stairwells in horror movies from the eighties.

Even though the rocking eventually slowed a bit and the rain softened, it was dark, very dark, with the exception of the large vanilla-scented candle in the middle of the table. There was a lull, the eye of the storm passed over me. Then the rocking and hard rain started all over again. A loud thud echoed on the ceiling just above me and I could hear footsteps, the sound of heavy boots walking around the deck.

"Damon?" I called out. "Is that you?"

I heard nothing in return and the steps stopped. I held my breath, fearing the worst. As the boat began to rock violently again, the steps came closer to the cabin opening and were not as careful as they were earlier. They stopped just shy of the first step down. I didn't call out anymore, but quickly looked around for something I could use to defend myself if I had to. The wind howled again and I wanted to cover my ears with my hands and scream, "STOP!"

I was paralyzed though. I couldn't move and I couldn't talk as my heart pounded wildly. I could see the boots now. They were thick and black, like heavy military boots. Slowly, they descended and came to a crashing halt on the floor as the man jumped past the remaining three steps to the landing.

The sound of arguing from just on the other side of the ship's bulkhead woke me, and it was a good thing. The disagreement was between Damon and Sam, and that was not such a good thing. I wasn't quick to interrupt, because a small part of me wanted to hear what they were arguing about. I leaned forward and rested my chin on my hand.

"Look, Sam, I want her kept safe; can you promise that?" Damon questioned.

"You know I can't make promises like that. I can't be with her twenty-four hours a day; I don't have that ability, but you do."

"I can't do that right now, Sam."

"Can't or won't?" Sam shot back.

"It's complicated, Sam. You know that."

"She doesn't know, does she? You haven't told her everything about you?"

"I've tried. I can't just dump it all on her at once."

"Damon, if you don't tell her, she'll find out. She will see it."

"What exactly is that supposed to mean?" Damon asked angrily.

"My God, you don't know either. Shit, the two of you are fucking made for each other. Just tell her I stopped by and have her give me a call ... it's for her safety and she should know."

The arguing stopped and Sam left. I couldn't help but think how strange that confrontation was. It sounded as if none of us was telling the other person something that we should. I thought to myself for a moment and had to admit that I really hadn't been as honest as I should have been with Damon.

He didn't need to know about what happened between Sam and me, and I sure as hell hoped that Sam didn't expect me to tell him. Now I began to wonder about parts of the conversation that I may have missed.

I got up and walked up onto the deck. Damon was walking towards the pool house. I jumped off of the boat and ran to catch up with him as he entered the courtyard.

His hands were stuck way down in his pockets, almost pulling his shorts down, and his head hung low.

"Is everything okay?" I asked. "I heard you and Sam arguing."

"Yeah, Sam and I just have a few issues that need to be worked out."

"Damon, why was Sam here?"

"You should call him; he wants you to."

"I want to know what he told you."

"Well, the small jackknife that you discovered was run for prints. They're the prints of that detective that you both have been messing with. He was questioned by the captain."

"That's not fair. We have not been messing with him."

"I'm sorry, that came out wrong. Regardless, Effie, you're knee-deep in this mess and sinking fast."

"How do you figure?"

"I'm not really sure, but you're not telling me everything."

"I get visions, Damon. You know that. I see things happen. I see things that have happened. Reggie killed Helena and he's the one that started that fire. I saw it all when I went through the building."

"And?" His question hung in the air while I thought about how much to tell him.

"He knows that I know. I think there's more, though. I don't think this is his first rodeo."

"Well then, you should know that he has been temporarily suspended pending the investigation. He told the captain that he dropped his knife in the building before you entered; the police are trying to find someone to confirm his story."

"So, I'm not really safe then, am I?"

"No, and to make matters worse, no one seems to know where he is right now."

"That's why Sam was here then. I guess I should be worried."

"Is there another reason why Sam should have been here?" he asked.

"No. Not anything else that I know of. What should I do?"

"Well, the girls will be done with the boat tomorrow. We'll sleep there, and I'll take some time off work and stay with you."

"You can't do that; you'll be out money."

"First of all, your life is not worth me making a few extra dollars; besides I have some investments and it's only a few days. We will do a little sailing and just stay under the radar for a while. Besides, I think you have been spending too much time with Sam."

"Are you jealous?"

"No, I just think the two of you together equals trouble. Now, go change your clothes. Throw on some jeans, tennis shoes and a t-shirt."

"Where are we going?"

"You're gonna learn how to fire a gun."

We traveled about forty miles northwest of town and pulled into an old, boarded up Philips 66 gas station. We met up with Damon's friend, Jim, and followed his truck around back of the station and down an overgrown two-track.

We followed him closely for about a mile, and could hear the picker bushes scratch the sides of the Scout the entire way. The small dusty track dumped out into a clearing where the red clay ground was partially eroded from the recent rains. We parked off to the side of the clearing, got out of our trucks, grabbed our gear and headed to the rear of Jim's truck.

Jim was tall, slim and had short gray hair, worn cleanly and professionally cut. He must have been in his early fifties. I was envious immediately, as he was wearing running shorts and a tank top while I was sweating and sticking to my jeans and black shirt.

"Hey, Damon," Jim said.

"Hey, Jim, how's it going, man? Thanks for meeting us in such short notice. This is my girlfriend, Effie."

"Hello, Effie." Jim reached out his hand and shook mine. "So nice to meet you; are you feeling up to all this?"

"Nice to meet you, too; I'm feeling pretty good today."

"What's Effie short for?"

"Franciska."

"I knew this gal about twenty years ago, she was Greek and her name was Effie. I remember her telling me that everyone would ask her if her real name was Elizabeth; that's why I asked."

"Names can be interesting."

"Names aside, ready to have a little fun?"

"Not sure about the fun, but I'm ready."

"Never fired a gun before, huh?"

"Never. I was born with a fishing pole in my hand."

"Well then, let's get started."

We walked out about twenty yards. Jim set up a small table, setting his guns on top, and Damon set his two guns on the other side. I listened carefully as Jim described each gun on the table and went over the basic safety rules for using them. He then set up a simple target, called me over and began to describe the first gun I was going to fire.

"Can you shoot first?" I nervously asked.

"Sure, no problem."

I put my earplugs in and watched intensely as Jim unloaded the clip. He made it look so easy and graceful, if graceful is even the right word to describe it. He lowered the gun, put in a new clip and called me over. I walked to him slowly and carefully, and could see on his face that he knew how uneasy I was around guns. He grabbed my hand and gently placed the gun in it, showing me how to hold it properly.

"This is a .22 Beretta. It has a six-inch barrel, so you won't have the kick some of the others will have. It will be very smooth and the perfect gun for you to start with."

I held the gun for a moment. It was heavier than I expected—they always looked so light on TV, with the way people are always slinging them all over the place. It was cold, too. As instructed, I took my position and held it in my right hand, cupping my left hand just under the handle and using my wrist to steady my aim. I switched the safety off with my left thumb.

My hand started to shake a bit as I took aim at the target. I have to admit, I was holding my breath and then squeezed the trigger—I just fired my first gun, and it was okay! Two, three, four shots later and target practice became a bit easier. It was kind of cool watching the smoke roll out of the barrel after each shot. Several rounds later, I was finally getting comfortable.

Damon came over to me and had a very satisfied grin on his face. He took the .22 from me and gave me his 9 mm Smith and Wesson. It wasn't as heavy as the Beretta and had no safety; I knew it had a bit of a kick, so I was back to being nervous again. I handed the gun back to him and said, "You first!"

Damon took the gun, aimed and unloaded the clip into the target. He made it look easy, too. But I knew it was louder and could see the kick. This made it easier for me. Damon took the empty clip and loaded only five bullets, slamming the clip back in. He handed the gun back to me.

"Start with this."

I took the gun and placed my feet just right: left foot in front and right foot in the rear in what Jim called a "weaver stance." I aimed and squeezed the trigger. I squeezed it and nothing happened. My hands began to shake and I lowered the gun. Jim explained the difference in the triggers and firing, so I then took aim, squeezed harder and fired the gun. It had kick, but it wasn't as bad as I thought it would be. I soon realized that my control with this gun was not as good and I would need more practice. I fired the remaining four bullets.

Jim yelled over to me, "Let's break this up a bit. For fun, shoot this," and handed me a double-barrel shotgun. After a few minutes of instruction, I fired the shotgun.

"Good job!" Jim yelled out. "Now back to the nine-millimeter."

He walked out to the clearing and placed a Gatorade bottle filled with water on the ground in front of the target and said, "All right, Effie; hit the bottle!"

I took my place and held the nine-millimeter a little easier now. I took aim and fired. To my amazement, I took the bottle down on the first shot. I missed it on the second shot and the third shot hit the bottle again, popping it up in the air so it landed back upright and in place. The guys behind me roared with disbelief, and Damon yelled out, "That's my girl!" I was geeked, stoked, elated—all fired up!

I had the feel of the gun now and began to unload the clip, watching the smoke roll from the barrel and the shells dance out from the side. When I finished, I lowered the gun and removed my safety glasses and earplugs. Jim looked at Damon, "Damn, man; you didn't tell me you brought Annie-fucking-Oakley with you." We all laughed hysterically.

Damon and Jim shot some rounds and then I went through a few more clips. I liked this new sport; it made me feel empowered. I was still a little scared of guns, but felt comfortable firing one.

We said our goodbyes and headed back to the pool house, talking about my new experience. The whole way, Damon recapped the bottle incident over and over, mumbling that he wished he had recorded it.

I rolled the handful of smashed bullets from the bottle in my hand and smiled as I listened to Damon excitedly recount the afternoon's highlights.

By time we reached the pool house, the sun was just starting to fall. I wasn't hungry anymore and knew I had to call Sam. I had been putting it off, but the sunset is a great excuse to keep the conversation short. I grabbed my phone and called. Sam answered on the first ring. It sounded as if he had been waiting for my call, but I hoped not.

"Hello, Sam!" I chirped.

"Hey, Effie; you sound good. Did you and Damon get a chance to talk?"

"Yes, he told me about your conversation."

"Why do you sound so giddy then? The news I delivered is alarming, to say the least."

"I'm not going to let it get to me, Sam. I can't. Reggie is not going to do anything tonight; I would see it coming."

"Nice try, but I know visions of the future are not your thing. You're probably right, though. It depends on how rational he is right now. My guess is that he is very angry and more than likely wants revenge, which makes him extremely dangerous. The police department is going through his computer now, just as a precaution."

"Tomorrow, I'm moving my things onto the boat. The girls will be done with the finishing touches by mid-day. The two of us are going to sail for a day or two afterwards to stay low."

"The two of us ... meaning you and Damon?"

"Yes, he's taking some time off at work and is working out the details right now."

"I'll bet."

"Sam! What's with you?"

"Nothing. Forget it! That gives me a couple of days to work things out."

"Sam, it shouldn't have hap...."

"But it did and you can't deny that there is something there," Sam interrupted.

"I'm with Damon."

"What do you know about him?"

"Enough!" I shot back angrily.

"Really, Effie? Use your visions, or are you afraid to?"

There was silence and I didn't know what to say at that point. The sunset excuse had blown out the window five minutes ago. Sam broke the silence.

"I'll call you with an update the first minute I get one; meanwhile, our relationship is merely professional from this point on. Enjoy your evening."

He hung up and I didn't even have a chance to say good-bye. I stood there with thoughts of our kiss flooding in.

Sam was right. There is something there between us, something that I can't explain but surely can feel. I couldn't shake it and that bothered me.

I could see him, feel him, taste him and smell him as if he was standing in front of me. This is not a vision, but something deeper within. Thoughts of exploring Sam further excited me and once again I caught myself trying to imagine what making love to him would be like ... what is wrong with me? I thought to myself.

I grabbed a bottle of Chianti, two glasses and headed for the shoreline, giving Damon a wave so he would know where I was headed. I made my way through the gate, crossed over the berm and sat in the sand, not far from the dock.

I was staring at the beauty of the colors slipping down into the water when something brushed up against my back. It was Jib. He must have missed me already. You really are a boat cat, I thought to myself. I set the glasses and the bottle in the sand, picked Jib up and set him in my lap. He was butting me in the chin with his head and I knew that meant he was claiming ownership.

Damon showed up a few moments later with a large blue quilted blanket and laid it gently in the sand. I set Jib down on the blanket, grabbed the wine and glasses, and moved over to the blanket next to Damon.

"Are you okay?" he asked.

"I couldn't be better now that I'm with my two favorite men."

"I see that we have a joiner this evening. He really is quite an interesting cat."

"I love him already and thank you again!"

"By the way, you forgot this." Damon said as he held up the corkscrew.

I laughed. "I guess I did."

Damon grabbed the bottle and handed me the glasses. He slowly began to drill the corkscrew in. I always love it when he does that movement with his arm, and his veins and bicep pop. It just drives me crazy. The cork was soon out and he was pouring the red, full-bodied wine in my glass.

We tapped our glasses and Damon toasted to a new tomorrow. We sat and watched the sun continue to set, with Jib purring on one side of me and Damon on the other side, holding me close with his arm around me. The sound of waves and nearby seagulls was a relaxing voice after a day of noisy shooting lessons.

"Effie," Damon said.

"Yes."

"There's something I need to tell you."

"That sounds serious."

"Well, it is, I suppose."

"Can it wait till tomorrow, sweets? I can't take much more today and I'm really enjoying the moment. But if it really can't wait, I'm listening."

"No, you're right; and, yes, it can wait."

"Good; I'll remind you tomorrow."

"About tomorrow, I thought maybe we could do something fun after we get the boat loaded."

"What do you have in mind?" I asked

"I'm not sure, but I am gonna get a bunch of friends together … a nice big outing."

"Sounds good. We haven't really done that yet, have we?"

"Done what?"

"Gone out with other people."

"No, I guess not."

CHAPTER EIGHTEEN

One Helluva Ride

Brea tapped my shoulder as I stared at the brightly colored Ferris wheel spinning around.

"Sorry we're late. Autumn had to make a few stops along the way. So, how do you like the Glynn County Fair so far?"

"So far, so good. I do better on roller coasters than I do on rides that go around, though. I love fair food the most, and that's next."

"Who all's here?" Autumn asked eagerly.

"Well, Pea is here and she brought her firefighter friend, too. Damon went to get cotton candy, and Liz and Ryan are up on top of that dreaded wheel. The boat looks really good, by the way. You and Brea did a real nice job; she looks brand new."

"Thanks; we aim to please!" Brea and Autumn replied in unison.

"Where is that hot firefighter that I heard all about?" Brea asked.

"They went to the pig judging. We're supposed to meet them over there when this ride stops. His name is Mike."

"Hey, you two!" Damon said as he handed me my cotton candy. "I'm glad you two could enjoy a little playtime."

"Are you implying that we don't have any fun?" Brea asked. "I'll show you some fun."

Brea took about twenty or so steps to the right of us and stood there, staring at the sky. She pointed upward a couple of times, tilting her head a little to the left and then a little to the right. Autumn was soon at her side staring at the sky, too. Now understanding what they were up to, Damon and I joined them.

Thank goodness it was about five in the afternoon and the sun wasn't staring back at us. After a few minutes of staring at the sky, we all stopped and looked around. Sure enough, most of the patrons were now staring at the sky. We were all laughing when Liz and Ryan joined us and we giddily made our way to the pig corral.

We saw Pea and Mike standing next to a small section of metal bleachers and we made our way over to them, weaving and winding through all the people that had started to gather. I introduced Mike to Liz, Ryan, Brea and Autumn.

I did it quietly, too; all the while the auctioneer was calling out for the bids as a young boy led his pig around the corral. The auctioneer had a very southern accent. He called out for bids so fast that I couldn't understand a word he said. All I knew was that all these pigs were headed for the butcher and that kind of saddened me.

I pinched a piece of my blue and pink-colored cotton candy and slowly slid it into Damon's mouth. Then he pinched some of my cotton candy and slowly slid it in my mouth. I clamped my teeth on his two fingers and slowly slid my tongue all round them. I released his fingers slowly and sealed them with a kiss. I took another pinch of the sugary treat and lightly touched his lips with my thumb and then sealed them with my lips. We kissed long and hard, allowing the sugar to dance all around until it was dissolved in our heightened taste buds.

"Get a room!" Brea cried out.

"Hey! I had to find a way to keep my mind off of all the pig shit." I laughed.

"I have an idea; let's find a ride suitable for Effie," Damon interjected.

"There is no ride suitable for me here, unless Damon will let me take him for a spin?"

"A stud he is, for sure." Liz winked.

"That's it" Brea snapped. "Let's ride the stud, we can all take turns."

"Ummm, yeah. You can count me out. I don't want to be any part of that action," Ryan laughed.

"Hey, now." Damon said. "What's wrong with me?"

"No one is riding Damon but me," I laughed.

"Can we all get real for a minute? I meant the mechanical bull!" Brea said.

We all looked at each other and then started to laugh. The laughter was so loud that the auctioneer and the bidders both shot us dirty looks. Liz walked over to Pea and

Mike to let them know that we were all going to ride the mechanical bull and to meet us over there when they were done.

Our group quietly left the bidding area, and headed to the west end of the carnival, where we could just see the tip of a tall, blue tent. The sandy ground was thick but loose, and with each step we took, I could taste the dry chalk-like dust in my mouth.

Along the way I decided I needed a drink, and Damon ventured over to the concession stand to get me a Pepsi. Liz and Ryan went with him, leaving Brea, Autumn and I to watch the llamas at a nearby corral. We gently leaned on the wooden-railed fences, trying not to get a splinter. I turned my head just a bit to look for Damon and the gleaming face of a clown scared the shit out of me.

He was standing right behind me. I hate to admit it, but I do not like clowns. He smiled and winked while handing me a bright yellow balloon. I began to pass it to Brea, but was suddenly frozen in place. I had visions of sheets on a clothesline again. They were blowing in the breeze on a hill, the hill with one small tree at the top. I whirled to face my nemesis, but he had disappeared as quickly as he had appeared.

"Are you okay?" Autumn asked.

"Yeah, what's up with that? You look like you saw a ghost." Brea added.

"I'm okay; I'm just not a big clown fan."

"Oh, my God, you're one of those weirdoes that have a fear of clowns. What do they call that now? Colla ... coola .... clowera...."

"Coulrophobia, you ding-dong." Autumn laughed.

"Whatever."

"You two are nuts and I don't have a fear of clowns; I just don't like them."

While Brea and Autumn were feeding a few of the llamas, I did a quick scan of the area and kept reminding myself to be aware of my surroundings. Aware of my surroundings I was. I crossed the flow of traffic, passed the lemonade stand and took a seat on a bench next to the Tilt-a-Whirl. Next to me on the bench was a man wearing a baseball hat and reading a program of the carnival's events for the week.

"Hello, Sam. Are you following me?"

"No, I'm afraid not."

"Just as I thought, then."

"What is just as you thought?"

"The clown that gave me a yellow balloon presented me with that clothesline vision again."

"So you saw him."

"Yes, but by the time I realized it was him, he was gone."

"Effie, we need to talk." Sam said with heavy eyes.

I gazed into his beautiful blue eyes. They sparkled back at me and I could see right through them into his soul. He was real, sincere, and honest and, like before, I felt a connection unlike any other that I felt before, a natural or spiritual type of a connection. He placed his hand on my knee and I covered his hand with mine. His warmth jetted through my hand and filled my entire body as my heart fluttered. I asked myself, why do I feel so close to him?

"I'm sorry, Sam." I interrupted.

"For what?"

I shook my head.

"You said we needed to talk. About … ?"

He dropped his head in reply.

"It's more than that, Effie, and this is not the place to have that conversation. I feel so close to you and I'm very protective of you. I'd like to have some time with you."

"Sam, I … uhh … yeah," I stuttered out without even thinking. What was I doing? I couldn't even take my eyes from his. My body moved in closer, as if there was not another soul around. I wanted to kiss his lips, his neck, his ear or wherever he'd let me.

"Effie!" Damon yelled out. "We have been looking all over for you!"

"Hey, you found me. Sorry 'bout that."

Sam stood up and faced Damon; "I thought you were going to keep a close eye on her?"

"Look, Sam, I went to get her a Pepsi. She was with Autumn and Brea, or so I thought."

I jumped up and put my hand on Sam's shoulder. "I sort of snuck away, it's my fault—really."

"So, Sam, what are you doing here?" Damon asked bitterly.

"Following Reg."

"He's here?"

"He gave Effie a balloon," Sam explained further.

"Well, where is he now?" Damon asked.

"I'm not sure; I was distracted."

Damon grabbed my hand and pulled me over to him. "I have it from here, Sam. It's my turn to get distracted."

"Then keep an eye on your distraction this time."

Damon kept a pretty tight grip on my hand and swiftly walked away from Sam. I gave a quick look over my shoulder and could see the disappointment all over Sam's face, but I found enough strength to send him a wink and watched him crack a smile as we joined the rest of our group.

We were finally all together now and making our way to the large blue tent. As I walked between the Swings and the Zipper rides, they brought back memories of a younger me, who got sick on both rides. Brea and Autumn danced their way forward, two steps ahead of us, as we neared the entrance and I couldn't help but laugh, thinking how silly they looked, and yet I wanted to join them.

Then a tiny green tent off to my right caught my attention. A sign in front had a picture of an old gray-haired lady, gazing at a crystal ball. The sign read, "Fortune Teller, $10." I made a beeline for the green tent.

"I have to check this out," I yelled back to the gang, and I could hear Pea in the back saying, "Oh shit, here we go." I brushed the flap of the tent to the side and poked my head in. It was even smaller on the inside than it looked from the outside; it had room only for the typical round table draped with a black cloth, holding a crystal ball in the center.

I sat down in the chair and waited. Brea, Autumn and Damon came inside as the others waited by the entrance, crowding close enough to so they could hear what was going on. A short gal entered from behind the table. She was dark in coloring and was obviously wearing a wig to appear older than she was. The wig was long and gray, with streaks of black randomly placed throughout. "Want your fortune read?" She asked me. "Yes, please." And I slid her ten-dollar bill.

She grabbed both my hands, turning my palms up. Her hands were cold to the touch, but it felt good in the stifling heat of the small tent. Then she began to tell me my fortune. "Ahhh, I see you as a little girl playing with a little boy. You must have a childhood friend. You enjoyed Barbies and coloring as a kid. High school was lonely for you and you didn't go to college but regret not going. You haven't lived here long, but intend to do so. I see a man in your past; he is very dark and has caused you a lot of pain. You are clearly in good hands now. You are working at a retail store. Marriage is in your near future, and you are a mother to two children, one boy and one girl ..."

I drifted off, thinking of what it would be like to be a wife and have kids. I've always been so scared of that commitment, because I dreaded failure and divorce.

Men always have let me down and I believed they always would. I pictured being married to Damon, but what would I do as his partner? Then images of Sam filtered in my head. Why can't I get him out of my head? I asked myself. Why am I so drawn to him? It must be that we have a lot in common.

"EFFIE! Are you in there?" Damon nudged me.

"Yes, yes, yes … I'm here. What is it?"

"Your reading is done." Brea said. "Where the hell have you been?"

Autumn laughed, "Are you kidding me? Take a look at her. She was doing Damon in that little head of hers." And they all laughed.

"Are you done, really?" I asked the fortuneteller.

"Yes," she answered quietly.

"Good. Now it's my turn." I said sheepishly as I grabbed her wrists. "I see you as a small girl, with long, dirty, uncombed blonde hair. You're wearing tennis shoes with no laces, cut-off jean shorts and a stained white t-shirt.

"You're playing with a group of kids in the back of a tall, skinny, yellow house. Now you're two years older, a little more refined and eating dinner at a large square table with six other children; two are Hispanic, three are black and the last is a small white boy with thick glasses. You were orphaned at the age of four or five, and were in and out of foster homes.

"The last one you stayed at the longest ... maybe three years, and although it was a stable environment, you were in trouble a lot. You were arrested twice for shoplifting and once for possession of a controlled substance.

"You drank heavily and hung out with a gang, although you never became a true member. At eighteen, you left Atlanta and moved to Jacksonville with a man twice your age. He was abusive to you and you left a year later to travel with this carnival.

"You don't like it, but you feel that this will keep you away from those who have hurt you. You met someone from Savannah. He's a good man and owns some kind of a boating business. You like each other and he comes to each destination to meet with you when you're not working. He is tall, slim and has very light blond hair that is naturally wavy."

I stopped with my reading and stared at her. "Find your man, quit this gig—it's not you and, frankly, you're not good at it. Concentrate on the things you enjoy doing and then find a career that incorporates something you like to do. That is where you will be the most happy and successful."

"Take this." She said and handed me my ten dollars back.

"No, you keep it; you need it."

The tent was so quiet you could almost hear the astonishment. Brea and Autumn both had their mouths hanging open and Damon was as white as a ghost—

something I didn't think was possible with his beautiful olive skin. Outside I could hear Pea laughing hysterically. I got up from my chair, shook the young lady's hand and wished her the best of luck. As we left the tent, not much was said for at least a good minute. Then Autumn spoke up, "That was the best damn entertainment all night."

"I have to agree." Brea said. "How do you do that?"

"I'm not really sure; it's still pretty new to me and, for the most part, it comes and goes. I think stress kind of brings it out though. I have learned that I can block it and I am currently learning how to channel it and bring out the visions when I want to."

Damon leaned in to my ear and whispered, "We need to talk."

I smiled and nodded my head as we walked toward the large blue tent we still were working our way toward. The sun was starting to set now and the beads of sweat that were once glistening on my skin began to disappear. A light breeze had picked up a bit and I could smell the rain drawing near. The forecast was calling for a tropical storm and I kinda like storms. I was eager to feel this one.

We entered the large, big top tent. The inside was set up like a scene from an old western, with buildings lining both sides. There was a saloon where you could get drinks, a saddle shop, a building that sold miscellaneous western wear themed items and another building that sold arts and crafts.

Just down from those buildings was a blacksmith doing demonstrations and offering brandings to people. Tattoos were one thing, but brandings were out of my league. At the very end was a building where they were demonstrating glass blowing and selling the handmade glass pieces. In the middle of the tent, between the rows of building, were three corrals, each containing one fine mechanical bull in the middle. One corral was for kids, one for novice adults and another for more experienced adult riders.

"So, who's here to ride" I asked.

"Ryan and Damon," Liz answered with a wink.

"You two?" I pointed at them in amazement.

"Yes, us; what's wrong with that?" Ryan asked.

"Nothing is wrong with that; I'm just a bit surprised."

Damon laughed and the two of them walked over to buy their tickets. I had to admit, I did kind of think this was going to be interesting. Damon didn't surprise me so much, with him having such an athletic physique. Ryan, however, didn't look like the type that could ride a turtle, let alone a mechanical bull.

"Wait till you see this," Liz leaned in to say.

"What is so funny?"

"Those two; they always try to see who's the better rider; one is always trying to outdo the other."

"Ahhhh, so they've done this before."

"Oh, yeah." Pea yelled out. "Buckle your seatbelt, girl. If you hadn't have done Damon by now, you would have after tonight." The whole group laughed.

I just love how our sex life is such public knowledge, I thought to myself. I watched intently as the two of them played rock-paper-scissors like schoolboys to see who went first. I chuckled. Ryan won, paper covers rock.

Ryan jumped on the bull, prepared his grip and then gave the signal. The bull started to move slowly, but after a few seconds was spinning, turning and bucking. Ryan was pretty good. Liz screamed and whistled, and the others were clapping loudly. Ryan was going strong and finally was bucked off. "A minute eighteen" yelled out the operator.

"That's a good time!" Liz said to me.

"What do the times normally run?"

"An average ride runs between thirty seconds and a minute."

"Wow, that's even shorter than I thought it would be."

Our conversation was interrupted by Damon's shirt hitting my chest. Brea and Autumn whistled and laughed. Yes, believe it or not, Damon was shirtless and showing off that fine six-pack of his. This was exciting, watching him in a different light. Damon climbed on the bull, got situated and then gave the signal. He was amazing.

"He has someone to ride for this time," Liz whispered in my ear. Up and down, his body went with each of the bull's movements. To me, it looked like slow motion. Then he started to lean off to the side and I held my breath. Yup, he was off.

"A minute thirty-nine, and a fine ride," the operator yelled out as the crowd roared. Damon came straight for me, picked me up in the air and let me slowly slide down his body until my lips rested on his. I wrapped my legs round his waist and could feel his excitement, from either the ride or me; no matter, it was time to leave.

Damon and I said our good-byes and scooted out of the tent. We walked hand-in-hand out to the parking lot and jumped into his Scout. I was ready to go, very ready; the only trouble was, we weren't moving. Damon was staring straight ahead.

"What's up with you?" I asked

"Effie, I had no idea you could do what you did earlier, I mean to that extent. I have to admit, it kind of blew my mind. Why didn't you share that with me?"

"I didn't tell you everything because I didn't want you to think all the wrong things about me. A lot of people can't handle the metaphysical world. I even have a hard time with it myself."

"So, what do you see when you touch me?"

"Honestly, like I've told you before, just the three colors: red, blue and yellow. I see them in straight lines, curved lines, and thin and fat lines. When I saw that you dabbled with the brush, I just figured that's what my visions meant; I never figured out why those colors."

"They are the primary colors in painting; do you remember the color wheel from art class when you were younger? Is that the only thing you see?"

"Oh, yeah, I remember now; I was never a very good artist. I don't ever see anything else because I think I subconsciously block it out. I just don't want to know; I want you to tell me about you."

Damon started the Scout and we were soon on our way. He didn't say much for a while, and then reached over and grabbed my hand. "I love everything about you," he said, and smiled.

"Damon, not to sound paranoid, but is the car behind us following us?"

"I don't know, I haven't been paying attention; but I will now."

Damon sped up and made a few unnecessary rights. The car fell further behind, but still stayed behind us. Damon reached under his seat and pulled out his gun. I didn't say a word, but could see that he was worried.

Damon stayed on the road to his house and went past his drive for an additional mile, pulling into a short driveway and putting his Scout in reverse while waiting. The car went past us, never slowing down. Damon backed up and headed back to the entrance to his house. He pulled in the drive, parked and sighed.

"I'm sorry. I was wrong"

"No, I don't think you were."

"Are you mad?"

"Hell, no; I'm worried. Let's sleep on the boat tonight. We'll grab a few things now and get the rest in the morning."

Damon grabbed some bedding and a couple of pillows, a bottle of wine and two glasses. I was right behind him with a basket of candles, two flashlights and some cheese and crackers. We made our way to the boat and practically tripped over each other getting down into the cabin. I couldn't help but giggle like a schoolgirl.

Damon converted the bench into a bed and made it comfortable with the bedding, while I cut up the cheese and placed both the cheese and crackers on a plate. I set the candles out around the boat and lit each one with anticipation of what was soon to follow. Damon opened the bottle of Bordeaux, poured two wine glasses half-full and left the bottle on the small counter with the cork out.

"Is this is from France?" I asked.

"Yes, it's actually one of my favorites. I really don't discriminate."

I took a sip and then a few more. "This is very good."

Damon stood there smiling at me. His eyes were piercing mine and I was lost in his presence. I set my glass down and took a few steps closer. I looked at him, studying his face and knowing what was on his mind. I reached up to run my fingers through his soft, wavy hair. His musky scent filled me with extreme desire.

I kissed him ever so softly, softly enough to fully taste his lips. I was so taken back by the moment I had to stop and catch my breath. My heart raced, and I quickly pressed my lips on his again, not wanting to waste any more time. I could feel him grow hard against my body as the cabin got warm and my skin tingled with chills of anticipation.

I immediately became dizzy within the moment. Our kiss grew intense as he gently took my breasts in his hands and ever so lightly caressed my nipples to the point where they begged to be kissed. His fingers found their way under my shirt and unfastened my bra, then slipping it and my shirt off my shoulders and letting them fall to the floor. I slid my hands under his shirt, slowly lifting it up and over his head.

His lips found my breasts, kissing my nipples and nearly driving me over the edge. He followed the contour of my body as he slid both his hands in my jeans and gently guided them and my panties down to the floor. I could barely maintain the gentle motions of the moment as I raced to unbutton his pants, letting them drop next to mine.

We were both naked now as he eased me down onto the bed, kissing my breasts, my sides and tasting my wetness between my thighs. My head tingled as my velvet folds welcomed his mouth. He inched his way back up to my breasts and I reached down to massage his penis.

It trembled in my hand and I guided it inside me. Throwing my head back on the bed in pure delight, I pulled him down on me and my hips moved to meet his. Our motion matched that of the rocking of the boat. We moved fiercely together now, while sloppily kissing and trying to catch my breath in between.

The intensity grew hungrily from below and I couldn't hold back any longer; I screamed out in ecstasy, hands gripping the pillow under my head as if it were a lifeline. Just moments later, I welcomed his warmth as it entered my body, feeling the pulsation inside of me. He collapsed on top of me and we both fell asleep satisfied.

CHAPTER NINETEEN

Out with a Flare

I awoke the next morning to the boat rocking more than I was used to. Damon was not next to me, so I assumed he was back at the house making coffee. I threw my wrinkled clothes back on and climbed the steep steps out of the cabin onto the deck. It was misting out and the wind had picked up a bit, but nothing too drastic. Carefully, I jumped on the dock, and walked quickly toward the pool house to get out of the weather. I finally made it in the sliders and caught my breath. Sure enough, there was Damon, making my coffee.

"Good morning, sunshine," He said to me softly.

"Morning, sweets."

"Did you sleep well?"

"Really well; I could hardly believe how well."

"What do you think of this weather?"

"Honestly? It's making me a little nervous. We're not really going out in this, are we?"

"No, absolutely not. They upgraded the storm to a level one hurricane. We're just going to get the edge of it, but the winds will be strong enough, I assure you. I've started a list of things to do to the boat and we can still spend the day prepping it for our small trip. We can leave shortly after the storm passes."

"What do you want me to do?"

"I want you to drink your coffee, eat your breakfast and just sit there looking pretty."

"You're so fricken funny; like I really look good right now."

"Effie, you're just plain hot, whether you're wearing a burlap bag or a formal gown."

"You need another cup of coffee!" I laughed.

We finished breakfast and made our lists, but before we did any shopping we decided to stay and enjoy the morning in the comfort of four walls, a door and a bed. After all, it was dreary and raining; what else does one do when the weather is shitty?

By noon, we were finally up. I spent the next hour packing my clothes, toiletries and linens. Damon packed his as well. We loaded up the boat and I arranged everything neatly in its own place. When that was done, we both left to fill our lists. I went to the grocery store and Damon took care of all the mechanical needs.

We were back at the house by dinner and I had brought a pizza with me; of course that was not on my list but it seemed like a good night for it. The wind was picking up now, to the point where it was time to collect the pool furniture and tie it all down. Damon set the pizza in the oven on warm and we began our work around the pool. I collected chairs and Damon handled the tables, grill and umbrellas. Damon put the grill in the mechanical room and then joined me to fasten down all the chairs.

"Why didn't you take the gun I gave you?" Damon asked.

"I just figured I didn't need it."

"I would feel better if you have it on you when going out, at least for now. For all we know, that man could be out in the bushes right now."

"Think he was out in the bushes when we were screwing?"

"Well, if he was, the evidence has since washed away; and that's not funny, Effie."

"I'm sorry, just trying to lighten the mood."

"Visions of a man masturbating in the bushes to our lovemaking is an interesting direction ... I kind of like it"

We both laughed.

Damon left to grab some extra rope from the mechanical room. Laughter aside, I did feel like someone was continuously watching me. For the most part, I brushed it off because it reminded me of how I felt the time when a friend had lice; even though I didn't have them, I found myself itching for days. I was a young girl then but remembered it well.

A shadow caught my attention. I walked past the pool to the path down to the beach, and saw a dark figure walking a dog on the beach. He had on a raincoat and the hood was up, so I couldn't see his face. Those raincoats can make anyone look squatty, I told myself. I took a few steps back to the chairs and then turned to take a second look. He was gone. Who walks a dog on the beach in a storm, I asked myself. I called myself paranoid and headed back to the chairs.

"Is everything okay?" Damon asked

"Yes, I thought I saw someone. All this talk of the man in the bushes kind of made me paranoid."

"Good! Maybe it will make you more cautious."

"Okay, it's kind of silly for me to be paranoid of a man walking a dog on the beach, though."

"Huh? Are you serious?"

"Yeah, why?"

Damon dropped the rope and I watched him walk out to the beach, gun in hand. He walked about fifty feet in each direction and then returned.

"Is everything okay?" I asked.

"Yeah; you've made me paranoid, now. I saw the footsteps and, yes, someone was walking a dog. They went up to the house just a few doors down. My guess is the neighbor was taking his dog for a walk before the weather got worse."

"Okay, I feel better now." But I really didn't. I was reading Damon's face and I couldn't help but see worry written all over it. Maybe it's the situation as a whole, I thought to myself. That said, we finished securing all the pool furniture and headed into the house to enjoy some pizza and beer. Damon pulled the box out of the warm oven, opened it and laughed.

"You like a pizza with no meat?"

"Yeah, love it. I put Italian sausage on half, though."

"I see that; just didn't know that's how you liked your pizza."

"Well, there's a lot about me you don't know. We haven't exactly spent loads of time getting to really know one another."

"You're right and that's why I'm really looking forward to our mini voyage."

"Hey, I would have never guessed that you liked a light beer."

"Really? And what kind of beer did you think I would like?

"An ale or a stout?"

"Well, if that was the case, then you wouldn't get to enjoy all this." He said as he lifted his shirt and ran his hand up and down his abs.

"Oh, yeah, that's what's I'm enjoying," and rolled my eyes.

Damon sat back down and got quiet. I could tell that he was deep in thought about something.

"What is it?" I asked.

"I forgot to get the gas for the generator."

"No biggie; run down to the gas station and get it."

"Come with me."

"Are you kidding me? In this weather? I'm staying right here. You won't be gone that long anyhow."

"I suppose you're right," Damon agreed as he got up and disappeared into the bedroom. He returned moments later and set the gun on the counter. "Effie, I'm leaving this here. Please call me if anything at all seems off to you." He stepped outside, retrieved the red gas container from the pump room and poked his head in the door. "Back shortly, babe. The wind is really starting to pick up now"

"Love ya, honey. Drive safe."

"Love you, too."

I made my way to the small kitchen and began to clean up. I wish we had something sweet to eat, I thought to myself as one my funny cravings started to gnaw at me. I opened up the fridge and nothing jumped out at me. I checked out the freezer.

Ohhh, ice cream. I took out the container of coffee-flavored ice cream only to find a spoonful left. Ugh; why do people insist on filling up a bowl of ice cream and leaving a measly spoonful in the container?

I thought back to the time when I had a roommate that used to do that with cereal. It was aggravating thinking that you had a bowl of breakfast waiting for you, only to find a couple of spoonfuls left in the bottom of the bag. A banana split sounds good, especially on a night like this. I'll give Damon a quick jingle and have him bring some home. I reached in my pocket for my phone only to discover that I left it on the bed in the boat. Shit!

I grabbed the flashlight and put on my raingear. Edging my way through the door as the wind blew my rain hood off, I thought Damon was right, the wind and rain really had picked up. I made my way past the covered pool and through the gate, carefully inching my way down the path to the beach with the wind trying to push me backward.

I finally reached the dock and prayed not to be blown in the water, all over an ice cream craving. Finally the boat was in front of me, rocking almost as if it was keeping up with the beat of the latest dance mix. I fought slipping down the stair-like platform, but eventually won and made it on board.

All I could think was that if I was on this boat for much longer, I was going to get sick. She was really rocking. I opened the doors to the cabin and made my way down the narrow stairwell. I shined the flashlight around and saw my phone. I was right; it was right where I left it. I sat down on the bed and called Damon.

"Hey, honey, relax. Everything is okay. Can you please grab some vanilla ice cream? Thanks, sweets; see you soon."

As the boat rocked from side to side and the rain pounded on the deck, an eerie howl made its way through the cabin. This sucks, I thought to myself. The flashlight rolled off the bed and crashed to the floor, switching off.

"Fuck!" I shoved the phone in my rear pocket and scrambled on my hands and knees looking for the flashlight. I was about to give up when it rolled against my fingertips. Thud. I looked up, wondering what that was. Then my heart nearly stopped as I heard heavy footsteps on the deck. It wasn't Damon; I just got off the phone with him.

Fuck! The gun is on the counter. I scooted back as far as I could and remained crouched on the floor, knees pulled to my chest. I found myself holding my breath as the steps made their way closer to the stairs.

The last thud hit the floor as the heavy set of feet hit the floor of the cabin. He had barely used the steps and merely jumped to the bottom. It startled me so much I jerked my head back, hitting it on the cabinet behind me.

He started to laugh. I could make out the figure now, but it was still just a shadow. My heart raced and my gut wrenched. I felt as if a fever had just come over me. I had nowhere to go and no gun to protect me. Doesn't matter, I told myself. I will die fighting. Why didn't I see this coming? Why? I dreamt this. I could see the future!

The light flashed on and it shined right in my face. I dipped my head slightly as it pierced my eyes. I leaned to the side and it was just as I knew who it was.

"Hello there, Effie."

"Reggie."

"Expecting someone else?"

"Why, no, Reggie. You're always welcome; I leave a light on just for you."

"A smart ass, right to the end, huh?"

"Oh, no, Reggie. I say it with love and admiration."

"You may sound tough, but you don't look that way from where you're sitting."

"I always look this way when I'm refinishing the floors."

The boat was swaying and rocking so much I found I was more secure on the floor than Reggie was on his feet. He knew it too. He slid the large candle near him and lit it with the lighter that was next to it. The flame lit up the cabin more than I anticipated, and he was able to set the flashlight down; now he had a free hand to balance with while the other held the gun.

"Gee, Reggie, why didn't you call first? We would have set you a place at the dinner table. This is no way to act when you're late for dinner."

"Shut up, bitch; I've about had it with your mouth."

"Shoot me, then, and get it over with."

Reggie laughed a deep, ugly laugh that reminded me of the villains in cartoons. "That would be too easy. You'll meet your nosy whore friend soon enough, but this one's going to look like an accident. I'm gonna squeeze the air out of that pretty neck of yours and then dump you overboard. After all, you never really were that great of a swimmer from what I hear."

I looked around the cabin, thinking that now I had a fighting chance. He was planning to physically take me down and that would leave a lot of room for errors. My eyes glanced at the small cubby just under the bed that contained emergency items. Then I looked back at Reggie, who was feeling pretty sure of himself. He reached in his pocket and pulled out a condom, of all things.

"Oh, yeah," he said. "It's like that. No DNA. I'm gonna have a piece of the pie."

"You'll never get my dead weight out of this cabin, you short, fat boy fuck."

"What did you call me?!" His face suddenly contorted.

"Fat boy!"

That did it. I had pushed his last button and pushed it hard. He grabbed his condom and headed straight for me, grabbing my ankles and yanking them out from under me, jerking me so hard I hit my head against the cabinet door yet another time. With his knees on my feet, he pulled a rope from his jacket and tied both my wrists together and anchored them above my head, to the bar that held kitchen towels.

He was stronger than I anticipated. He unzipped his pants and slid them down to his knees; to my amazement, he was hard as a rock. He actually got off on this. I laughed hysterically.

"You call that a dick?" He stopped and pulled his pants up, and began to look around the cabin.

"Watchya looking for, Reggie? Something larger than that pathetic, shriveled dick of yours?" Even in the semi-darkness of the cabin I could see the anger growing as his face neared fire-engine-red status. Meanwhile, I knew how that damn towel bar came out and I was determined to get it loose. I worked madly as Reggie began to tear up the cabin. I felt the slight pop, as I was able to wiggle the bar from the wall of the cabinet. There was no time to waste, Reggie found what he was looking for—tape.

As he headed toward me, I ripped the remainder of the bar off, slid to the side by the bed and pulled out the small black box from the cubby. I popped it open with my hands still bound and fumbled with the flare gun a bit, trying to get it in my hands. He was now coming at me full force. I reached up and pulled the trigger.

The flare took Reggie's left ear off, knocking him down and making its way up through the cabin doorway to land, I prayed, where it would lodge in the beach sand and get Damon's attention when he returned. The howling of the storm was more prominent now and the boat was still rocking fiercely.

I took a deep breath and closed my eyes for a moment, only to open them to see Reggie on his feet, blood running down the side of his head. He came at me one last time just as two gunshots rang out, one finding a home in his back and the other in the back of his head. I was now covered in blood as his body fell dead right beside me.

Sam was still leaning in the opening, gun in hand. "Are you okay, Effie?"

"I'm fine, Sam. Get me away from him."

Sam came down the stairs, and put his gun away. He picked me up off the floor and carried me to the bed, where he gently untied my rope-burned wrists. He held me tight, stroking my hair with his free hand, and said, "I'm so sorry, Effie."

"What are you sorry for?"

"I should have had a closer eye on you. I would have died if something worse had happened. I don't know what it is about you, but I am drawn to you. I love you."

I looked into Sam's eyes, mine now welling with tears, then reached up and pulled his head to mine, kissing his soft lips.

"I'm so sorry, Sam. What was I thinking?"

"That's just it, Effie; you're mentally trying to escape the scene."

"I do want you, though."

"We'll entertain that thought another time. Let's just get through the rest of the night."

The sirens were loud and I could see the lights reflecting on the water as the boat still rocked, though the wind was lightening up a bit. The howling was still prevalent, though. I looked up at Sam and, after hugging me, he was now also covered in Reggie's blood. In the background of all the excitement, I could hear someone calling my name ever so faintly.

It was Damon, and the way he was calling it, I could hear the panic. His feet pounded down the dock and before I could blink, he made his way to the cabin. Sam was still holding me and gestured for Damon to take me now, so he could attend to the scene.

Damon slipped into his place and pulled me close, saying over and over again how he should never have left me. Sam turned to Damon and said, "It's not your fault. He would have eventually found her; he was determined." Then he left the cabin to meet the captain. I could hear many sets of voices in the background and couldn't understand what they were saying.

Soon the captain entered the cabin and told Sam to get me out of there.

"Any statements we need we can get at the hospital," he said.

"Wait!" I reached towards Reggie's body.

"What is it, Effie?" Sam asked.

"When he grabbed me I received a flood of images, but had to block them to concentrate. It was the faces of a lot of women I didn't recognize. Let me touch him before I leave, please?"

The captain nodded his head and I asked Damon to grab his sketchpad. I inched my way toward the still-scary lifeless body, and touched the ankle with my palm, closing my eyes slightly. I started to count as I saw each face flash in front of me, including the face of Helena. I was at nine and closed my eyes tighter, signaling Damon to get ready. He picked up the pencil and waited for my description.

"I see a tall, white house, old and the paint is peeling. It looks like a farmhouse that is all boarded up. Wait, not boarded; it has shutters and the shutters are closed. A small rusted weather vane still spins at the peak. The house has a wrap-around porch with the railings barely standing and the steps in front are broken.

"The second of four steps is completely gone. Just off in front is a well. It no longer works. The driveway to the road is made of dirt and not very long. I can see the mailbox now. It used to be white, too, but is very rusted now and only the first few letters of the name are on it: M, I, L. There are no numbers.

"I'm walking behind the house now and following a two-track through a small wooded area that runs right next to a pond. The two-track continues around the pond and to the bottom of a hill. I'm looking up at the hill and the scenery is now familiar to me. I've seen this before! One single tree is at the top and there's a clothesline with white sheets pinned to the lines; the sheets are blowing in the wind. One, two, three, four ... thirteen."

I stopped and got warily to my feet, looked at Sam and the captain, and swallowed hard. "Find this place and you will find thirteen bodies buried there. They all are young women, except for one, who is much older."

My skin grew cold and numbness took over my body; I collapsed to the floor of the boat. I grabbed my side in agony and we all realized suddenly that I, too, had been shot. Adrenaline is a funny thing; I didn't even feel it when it happened. All that blood on me wasn't just Reggie's. Some of it was mine. I grew colder at the realization of that, and my vision started to blur. I sagged back to the floor.

Sam yelled to Damon, "Get her to the ambulance, NOW!"

Damon tossed the sketch to the captain, picked me up off the floor and carried me out of the boat to the stretcher that was waiting for me on the dock. As they wheeled me to the ambulance, I could see all the officials entering my boat, including the forensic team and the coroner, who carried a black bag in his hand. I closed my eyes, unable to watch anymore.

My eyes opened slowly. The hospital room was white, cold and sterile. I have always hated the smell. I was in a small private room. My wrists were cleaned and bandaged, and my side hurt. I slowly reached to the area with my hand and Damon put his hand on top of mine.

He called the nurse in and she added some pain medication to my IV, which made me drowsy. Damon sat next to my side holding my hand. I drifted off again, waking just a few hours later. Damon told me that I had taken a gunshot to my liver. The bullet had gone through Reggie's body and into mine, lodging in the left lobe; I had required surgery.

"So, I'm going to live then?"

Damon laughed, "Yes, you're going to be just fine."

"How long have I been here?"

"A couple of days."

Damon explained the procedure and the doctor's instructions, and said I would have a full recovery. The nurse interrupted our conversation to take my vitals and check my sutures.

"The doctor will be in to see you this afternoon," The nurse announced with a smile.

A faint knock came to the door and a police officer poked his head in, then entered the room slowly.

"My name is Officer Michaels and I've been directed to get your statements. This is just a formality and then I'll be out of your hair."

"Okay" I said, somewhat groggily.

"Before I go any farther, I need to find out who owns property where the shooting took place."

"Oh, it's my boat."

"We know the boat is yours; we need to know about the actual property where it was docked.

"It's my property. I'm the owner," Damon said.

"What?" I questioned.

"I'm sorry, Effie. The house is mine; all of it."

CHAPTER TWENTY

Truth

My heart turned cold and my stomach ached. I had finished giving the officer my statement. Damon left my room and talked to him briefly outside in the hall, then they exchanged cards. I couldn't even think at this point. It was still early in the morning and I was completely exhausted, weak from surgery and unable to get that horrible night out of my head. I was now reeling from the blow Damon had just dealt me, leaving me to wonder, "Who the hell was just holding my hand?"

Damon entered the room. "Can we talk, now?"

"I take it there's more."

"Effie, I tried to tell you countless times. I kept saying that there was something that I needed to tell you. It was always brushed off for a later time. You almost acted as if you didn't want to know what I was about to tell you. I was waiting for our trip down the coastline to tell you."

"Is there more?" I asked again.

"Yes. Are you ready to hear it this time?"

"Well, it's not like I'm going anywhere at the moment."

"The house is mine. I bought it with what was left of the sales of my paintings. I used to paint when I lived in Italy. My family owns a vineyard in the Verona area. They were managing my sales, or so I thought. Their management fee was quite high, to my surprise.

"So, I took the rest of my money and made a plan to get away from it all. Between my family and some really bad relationships, I was tired of being used. The first thing I did was buy the restaurant. The original owner had cancer and couldn't handle the day-to-day tasks any longer. My sister, Dona, was here in Brunswick for the summer visiting a friend, and told me about the sweet deal.

"Shortly after that, I started an offshore company and the rest is history. I bought the house a few months later. For a while, I used the upstairs as a studio, but while I was painting one day I saw a better potential for the upstairs and decided the pool house was going to become my studio.

"Anyway, I eventually made Dona a part owner. She was dedicated, loyal and the only family that I have here. I made her promise to keep everything quiet, though. It was peaceful and tranquil, but I didn't like living in the main house by myself. I moved my other things into the pool house and found it to be quite comfortable as both a residence and a studio.

"So, let me get this straight. You are a successful painter, Dona is your sister, and you own the restaurant and the house. Is there more?"

"Yeah, that's right and, no, there's not any more."

"Do you still paint?"

"The paintings in Pea's shop were the last of them. I just picked up a brush again after I met you."

"How many people know all of this?"

"What?"

"How many people know everything about you? Let me reword it in a different way: who else knows all of this?"

"Pea, for starters."

"I figured that; after all, she had your paintings in her store. Who else?"

"Liz and Ryan, and Sam, too."

"Sam?" I said sharply. Then I began think back. Sam kept saying, over and over again, that I didn't really know Damon. Now I knew what he meant. The people that were closest to me all knew, except me. I wasn't really sure how that made me feel.

"Effie, I was planning to tell you. It just seemed like one thing happened after another, and some of the times we were together just didn't seem like the right times. The few people that did know, knew only because they had to. I really didn't want anyone to know."

"Why?"

"For the same reason you left Michigan. For the same reason you hesitated to tell me about your gift."

"I can understand it. I can relate. BUT ... I told you about leaving Michigan early on. The gift thing is not such a gift, is it? The reason I didn't tell you right away was because I didn't want you to think I was a quack."

"Effie, if I had told you the first time I set my eyes on you, would you have gone out with me?"

"Probably not."

"I rest my case."

"And I wouldn't be dealing with all this heartache right now, too."

"That's not fair, Effie."

Sam walked into the room. "What's not fair?" he asked. "Effie, you look so much better and I have news for you. Why does everyone look like someone died ... besides the asshole?"

"Well, Sam, apparently you kept Damon's big secret under your hat pretty damn good."

Sam turned to Damon. "See, I told you so. I said to tell her before it's too late."

"Oh, no! Wait just a damn minute. The two of you had a fucking conversation about telling me?" I asked with a raised voice.

Sam tried to talk. "Look, Effie ..."

"Nope, you just stop right there. I've heard enough. I don't want to discuss any of this any longer this morning with either of you. What did you come here to tell me, Sam?"

"The captain is not only impressed with you, but thrilled to have met you. He was talking about approaching you to be a consultant for the police department."

"That's interesting, but why is he thrilled with me?"

"You don't know?"

"No."

"We found the house. Apparently Reggie's mother's last name was Miller. Our crime scene team is still out there now. They went through the house all night and will probably be there most of the next few weeks, if not the next few months. They did find twelve small boxes, each of them containing personal items like jewelry, wallets and hair clippings.

"They found a box that has some of Helena's things, including her driver's license, a wallet and some photos. The box also contained a key ring, and one of the keys looks like it went to the back door of Candles and More. We'll know as soon as we can match it against your key, or one of Pea's, since the lock is gone now.

"Anyway, the FBI and the state police are on their way with a special team. They're going to look on the hill that you described. The cadaver dogs from the Park's Search and Rescue team are hitting on something big, so I wouldn't be at all surprised if we find thirteen graves after the investigation, thanks to you.

"It may take a few weeks and a lot of DNA tests, but, in time, I think all those families will finally have closure. Oh, we looked further into his family and his mother's records. Reggie is the result of a trick."

"What? What kind of trick?"

He blushed.

"I mean his mother was a prostitute and his father was one of her customers."

"Really?"

He nodded.

"Reggie, I mean Detective Fischer, didn't have a criminal record, but he did have a sealed juvenile record. Apparently he killed a dog, cut its throat—pretty vicious stuff. He had some breaking and entering and vandalism charges thrown at him when he was a kid. He was pretty violent and in trouble a lot until he was 18. He seemed to figure things out when he turned 18, or he learned how not to get caught. Either way, he's been angry and unbalanced for a long time."

"Who knew?" I shook my head.

"Apparently not too many people. Helena happened to be one of the unfortunate ones who figured things out. His mother used to be a fairly well known prostitute around town, but we haven't seen her in awhile. We weren't able to locate her, so we're thinking she may be the older woman in the first grave that you described. We also suspect that all the rest of the women, except for Helena, were prostitutes, too. We'll know more later. It's going to be an interesting next few weeks, though."

I stared at him for a moment, letting it all wash over me. It was all happening so fast.

"Helena found out. She discovered this and he killed her. She had a special gift, like me."

"It's amazing how you both worked in the same place and both of you have such a special gift. It's almost as if she called out for you."

"This special gift got Helena killed though."

"It may have killed her, but it probably saved many lives, too; Reggie wasn't going to stop. Effie, what are the odds of two people with similar psychic gifts ending up in the same place?"

"Pea would say that natural witches will always find one another."

"Is that what you think you are?"

"I have been wondering about that since the day she told me about herself. I don't think so. Even though I have many of the characteristics of the natural witch, I believe that I'm just a bit different. The metaphysical world is interesting. I don't know everything I want to know, but I do plan on taking the time to learn more. But for now, I just have the ability to see the unseen."

"Well, it doesn't matter to me what you decide to call it; it makes you who you are. It makes you special to all of us. People ask themselves on a daily basis, 'why am I here,' always looking for some answer to justify their existence. You don't have to ask, at least not in my eyes."

"I'm not sure what to say."

"Don't say anything; just get better. I'm going to leave and will check on you later; I'll also give you updates, if it's okay with Damon."

"No problem here." Damon said.

"Great; you kids play nice in the sandbox!"

"Sam!" I yelled out as he walked away.

"Yes."

"Thanks for saving my life … I'm still mad at you, though!"

"No thanks are needed; and don't be mad at me too long."

Damon walked Sam out and the two of them had a brief conversation, just out of earshot. Then he talked to the nurse for a bit before stepping back into the room.

"They're springing you late this afternoon, if your tests come back clean and you're feeling strong enough. They're still going to require you be under twenty-four more hours of around-the-clock supervision. Do you still want to go home with me?"

I gave a slight nod, "Yes." How long I'll stay is another question, I thought.

CHAPTER TWENTY-ONE

In the Air

I sealed the last box with wide, clear packing tape and labeled it as "Candles and More." Inside were the crystal ball, tarot cards, runes and miscellaneous tools for making candles. I set the box next to the others in the living room and sat down at the table to write Damon a letter.

He had left for work an hour ago, and my plane was scheduled to leave in just three hours. A carrier would be by to pick my boxes up in the morning, and I had made arrangements for my boat to be sailed to the marina and stored indefinitely.

I picked up the pen and took a deep breath before I put it to paper. My eyes filled with tears and the lines on the paper blurred. This was going to be harder than I thought, I said to myself.

Dear Damon,

Please forgive me for the cowardly good-bye. I have never been any good at leaving, and this is definitely no exception.

My time here, although short, has been the most eventful and memorable time in my life. I have learned to live, love and laugh again. I have come to discover a whole new part of my life that I thought I was ready to embrace, but instead has left me confused and filled with unanswered questions.

My time here also led me to heartbreak and feeling disillusioned. I put a great deal of trust in you and broke all my own rules in doing so. All I ever asked for in return was honesty. I do love you with all my heart, but I can't be with you right now. Your life is not the life I'm looking for, but instead what I was trying to escape from. I might have been able to adapt if I had known everything about you from the beginning. Adapt isn't quite the right word; accepted might be closer.

I need time. I need time away and time to think. I can't honestly say if I can ever come to terms with what has happened. I will promise you that I will take the time to think carefully about what you asked of me.

I thank you for the wonderful times, the intimate moments and for taking good care of me. You truly have a wonderful heart and great intentions, and I feel blessed that you shared a small part of your life with me.

Your generosity will never be forgotten. I will miss your smile, your laughter, your kisses and, most of all, I will miss you. You are a wonderful man who deserves a wonderful woman, and if you should find her, don't look back and worry about me; I will be all right. Please take care of Jib for me, but I will understand if you have to let him go to another home. He was one of the best gifts I had ever received, but at this time I am unable to take him with me. I have made all the necessary arrangements for all my possessions, including the boat, as I did not want to burden you.

Take good care of yourself; I wish you well.

All my love,

Effie

Tears streamed down my face and my nose began to run. I sniffled and ran to the bathroom for some tissues. I blew my nose a few times, and then pulled out about ten tissues for the road. I tucked the letter in an envelope, writing "Damon" on the front. I leaned it against the fruit bowl on the counter. I grabbed my carry-on and my purse, took one more look around and closed the door to the pool house behind me.

It was a long ride to Liz and Ryan's house, and I couldn't help but wonder if I was making the wrong decision. My heart wanted me to stay, but my head told me to go. My gut made me think that everything would work out in the end, but I had my doubts. Why can't I see what's supposed to happen to me, I thought to myself. This so-called gift that I have helps everyone else but me.

I pulled into the driveway and the cab was already waiting for me. Liz was talking to the driver; she more than likely knew him—Liz knew everyone. He popped his trunk open and I placed my carry-on inside. I came around to the front and handed Liz the keys to my Jeep.

"Take good care of her, and drive her at least once a week." I said sadly.

"You're making a big mistake, Effie."

"Maybe; but I need time away to decide for myself."

"Don't take too long. He loves you, ya know. His family is a complicated matter and, like you, he was trying to escape from that."

"He explained it all to me already. I know everything. I feel stupid that I didn't even recognize the fact that he's a very well-known painter. I've seen his paintings everywhere. They surrounded me at work and everyone knew but me."

"Superficial friends, girlfriends and shrewd managers caused him to be very protective. He wanted people to like him without knowing about his fame and money," Liz said. " Surely you can understand where he's coming from."

"I need time Liz. I have to find out, on my own, what I want for me. Having influences around me, all pushing me in one direction, won't help. This is the card of a friend of mine, who I've known since to law school. This is where I'll be. I want to see if I left law, or if I left bankruptcy law. I'm finally getting my chance to explore the criminal law arena, where I always wanted to be."

"In that case I'll say, see you later. No good-byes here."

We hugged, and I jumped in the cab and headed for the airport, but not without leaving a note for Liz to give to Sam, too. I hated to admit it, but he was a big part of my complicated feelings.

They called my zone to board the plane. I picked up my carry-on and headed to my gate, pausing briefly to look out the windows. A very young, blonde gal scanned my boarding pass and said, "Enjoy your flight." I headed down the long corridor, my stomach feeling empty and beginning to ache.

It was a silent ache, not the rumble of hunger. My heart quivered, and my skin grew clammy as I took my seat against the window, just over the wing. There were people all around me, but I couldn't hear a word. It was almost as if their mouths were moving and nothing was coming out.

The stewardess went through her normal song and dance, but it all seemed like a blur to me. The plane taxied out and I stared out the window endlessly, as that familiar lump in my throat began to grow. I tried to swallow, but it hurt. I raised my left hand and rested it on the glass as if I was trying to hold on to what I was leaving. Don't do it, I kept telling myself; but it was too late.

My eyes glazed over and filled with tears. I slid down my sunglasses and held my breath, but that failed, too, and tears streamed down my cheeks. Why did I feel so bad and why did this hurt so much; if this was right, then why did it feel so wrong, I wondered dismally.

I leaned my head back and closed my eyes tight, but only found myself reminiscing even more; so I opened my eyes and just simply stared out the window until they slowly began to dry up.

Leaving this time was different than any other time before. I felt like I was leaving a piece of me behind. The fact was, I was in love with two men and leaving them both.

CHAPTER TWENTY-TWO

Painted Memory

Summer ended, fall came and went, and we were headed into winter, which was the season that I disliked the most. Los Angeles did keep me from dreading it quite so bad this time around, and one saving grace was that Christmas was my favorite holiday. I practically ran from the courthouse, thrilled over our recent victory.

We had just put Dennis Dillard, rapist of seven children, away for life. I worked merely as an assistant on the case, but took as much pride in the outcome as if I were the lead attorney. I headed down the steps, wishing my heels would let me take them two at a time. I was looking forward to cracking a bottle of champagne this evening with some of my colleagues. I had my eyes on an idling taxi, but before I made it to the door, I heard someone calling my name.

"Effie!"

"Pea? Oh, my God! What in the world are you doing here?" I gave her a big hug.

"I'm here on business."

"Well great; let's get together."

"That's actually why I'm here. I have an invitation for you to a private showing tonight."

"Tonight?"

"Yes. It's the last night and it's invitation only. I am managing writers and artists of all media now, so I travel a lot, promoting their works. I would like you to come see what I do now."

"Sure, I'll be there." I agreed, and took the envelope. "Oh, yeah; I know where this place is. It's very high class. I'll see you at seven."

I grabbed another cab and headed for my apartment. Along the way, I canceled my current obligations and ordered a Thai platter to be delivered from a little dive from around the corner. I didn't have much time to eat, get ready and make it to the gallery by seven.

The cab dropped me off. I tipped him generously, and promised to do so again if he would return to pick me up at six thirty to take me to the showing.

I climbed the five flights of stairs up to my small two-room apartment. I put my briefcase on the table and made a beeline for my closet to pick out something in black. I opened the closet door and laughed. All I owned at this point was black.

The doorbell rang and my mouth watered, just like a Thai-loving version of Pavlov's dog. I tipped the young man and sat down at the table to eat my chicken satay with peanut sauce.

Seeing Pea had blown me away. I was thrilled to see her back on her feet after the fire, too. Gee, was it six o'clock already? I glanced at the clock. No time for a walk down memory lane, but I couldn't help but think of Damon and Sam, and wonder how they were doing. My heart started to ache. Both of their faces and personalities were still fresh in my mind. I could smell Damon as though he was standing in front of me, it was so vivid.

I shook my head and finished getting dressed. I grabbed my handbag and headed down the stairs. The driver was early, waiting for me.

"Four fifty one South Main, please," I said to the driver. We were soon on our way, and I was refreshing my makeup as we bobbed in and out of the L.A. traffic.

I arrived ten minutes early and tipped the driver generously a second time. I stood at the bottom of the steps of the gallery and took out my invitation. I studied it carefully. "Bert Green Fine Art Gallery invites you to a private showing of the "Romantic Collection" by the national-known artist, Damiano 'Attila' Bertinelli, featuring "Reminiscence," Best of Show winner from the Best of America 2010 Exhibition. The entire collection consists of seventeen oil and linen portraits."

I drifted off and never even finished reading the invitation. This has to be Damon. My heart started to race as I wondered if he was here. What would I say? I paced a few moments and thought about leaving. No, I have to do this, I told myself. I thought of all the paintings that were destroyed by the fire at Candles and More, all signed Attila.

I entered the large, glass double doors and was greeted by a tall, gray-haired man, who wore his hair long and pulled back into a ponytail. He was wearing a nicely tailored black tuxedo. I handed him my invitation and accepted a glass of champagne from a waitress nearby. The gallery was like others I had been to—large, cold, sterile and white.

I walked down the halls, looking at each and every painting in amazement. Some were similar to the painting that used to hand at Candles and More, city scenes reflecting on the water. Then, as I moved along the corridor, the paintings became surreally familiar—the beach where Damon and I first kissed; the picnic area on our first date; the restaurant; and the boat, my Franciska, rocked gently on the ocean. I could almost smell the salty air and feel the rocking motion that used to lull me to sleep.

I moved further down and there was a large section of wall that held only one painting, was titled "Reminiscence." It was surrounded by a handful of people. I inched my way closer and could see all the awards it had received, but couldn't yet see the painting.

I waited patiently until three people stepped out, leaving me room to move close enough to view the painting. I took several steps forward and was suddenly standing in the front of the painting. I looked up and lost my breath. Hot tears filled my eyes quickly, almost making it impossible to see.

I leaned forward and ran my fingers ever so softly across the painting before standing back up. I was trying to catch my breath and wipe away the tears. They came faster than I could wipe them away. That was me in that painting.

That was me, after Damon and I made love and I lay on the dock, wearing only a sheet. I knew he had sketched me at the time, but I had no idea he would paint me, too.

I remembered how contented I felt as I stroked the water with my fingers. I strained to look a little harder at the painting. There was my letter to Damon, floating in the water not too far from my fingers. Other than my eyes burning in their sockets, I felt completely empty.

Pea rested her hand on my right shoulder and I placed both my hands on top of hers.

"Are you okay, Effie?"

"That's me in that painting."

"Yes, it is; and he still loves you."

A crowd had formed now, learning that I was the subject of the painting that had won so many national awards. It was too much attention, and I felt really warm. I needed to leave.

"Is he here?" I asked Pea.

"No, he didn't want to interfere with whatever you might have been thinking. He also knows nothing of what you're doing; that's why I'm here. Are you okay?"

"What do you think?"

"Honestly, I think it's time for you to go back home."

I kissed her on the cheek and gave her a hug. "I need to tie up a few loose ends, but I'll be on the first flight tomorrow."

I didn't tie up all the loose ends I promised myself. There was just no time. I did keep my promise to Pea, though. I was on the first flight the next day. I know I was in the air for hours, but it seemed like minutes I sat in numbness, going back over the events of the last week. The "fasten seat belt" sign came on and the plane began to descend.

The plane may have landed, but my emotions were on the rise. While I waited for the plane to taxi to the gate, I began to feel like a schoolgirl being kissed for the first time. I looked out the window at the tarmac and turned on my cell phone. I sent a text that read, "Landed," and received one right back: "Here waiting for you."

— The End—

Revenge: Book Two in the "Lost Souls" series. Effie is back in Brunswick, Georgia, to help solve a series of serial murders with her psychic gift. Her ability to see visions when she first moved to Brunswick grew stronger as she was there; but it's nothing compared to how strong it is after she leaves and returns. The one thing linking all the murders together is the vision of something near and dear to her—her sailboat, the Franciska. Damon and Sam are back to help her turn her visions into clues, in the race against time and an all-out effort to stop the next murder. Read Chapter One of "Revenge" here and buy the book through Amazon, Barnes & Noble or any online retailer. Available in paperback and digital ereaders.

REVENGE

CHAPTER ONE

Home Coming

Hartsfield Jackson Atlanta International Airport was larger than life, and with the holiday bustle, the intensity increased ten-fold. I sat on the plane and waited as everyone else strolled, walked or hustled down the aisle.

Some were scrambling to get their carry-ons unloaded from the overhead bins, as they had connections to make. This was my final destination, so I took my time, letting those in a hurry rush on by. Who really wanted to tangle with an angry mob during the holidays, anyhow?

I stood up, or tried to, as you can never crawl out from a window seat without wrenching your back. I grabbed my carry-on from the rack above and made my way to the front of the plane. I edged my head in toward the cockpit on the way out. I always like to get a good look at the captain of a plane.

You can look, but rule number one, no pilots or bartenders, I reminded myself. After catching a glimpse of a uniformed pilot old enough to be my father, I headed out the door humming. Sometimes it was easier than others to keep from breaking my rule.

The corridor to the waiting area was long and a bit chilly. Atlanta was colder than I had expected. I made my way out into the nightmare thinking, "Soon I'll be out of here." I never really cared for crowds much. Airports and shopping malls were the two least favorite places I wanted to find myself. I wasn't nervous, like I thought I'd be.

This was going to be a safe arrival for me, with no complications to greet me. Liz had no problems escaping from her bed and breakfast to drive up to get me, and I looked forward to seeing my Jeep. I took the moving walkways to speed up my exit and finally made it to the arrivals area. I made my way through the large glass doors and stepped outside. I looked up and down the streets several times for Liz's familiar smile. Then my heart sank, and the lump in my throat grew like the Grinch's heart did in the end of that Christmas movie. She wasn't here.

"Effie." A deep voice called to me.

"Damon." I should have guessed. This was too damn simple, I said under my breath.

"You look great; how was your flight?" he said, reaching out to hug me.

"As long as they usually are when you're going coast to coast. You look good, too. Where's Liz? I just texted her phone and received a text back."

"She actually wasn't gonna call me, but Ryan got called out on business and she was scrambling; you know how she gets. She didn't want you to know I was coming for you."

"Nice! Secrets among everyone. I see things haven't changed a bit." Damon smiled tightly, but didn't go for the bait. I could feel the tension rising, and bit my tongue. Be nice, I said.

"Actually, things have changed, and all for the better, I think," he said. He shifted my carry-on to his other hand and started walking towards the baggage claim area.

"You do have luggage?" he asked.

I nodded. I traveled light, one case. Damon grabbed it and we headed for the parking lot. I was glad for the chance to stretch my legs after the long flight. It was cold outside and the coat I had on wasn't nearly warm enough. Stop one, I thought, a shopping center. Damon seemed to enjoy the cold. He turned to look at me and smile, and his teeth seemed even whiter and his smile larger than the first time I met him.

Then there we were at my Jeep, and Damon put my carry-on and suitcase in the back. I hesitated, wanting to drive, but not wanting to fight the unfamiliar Atlanta traffic with Damon sitting in the passenger seat.

"I'll drive until we're out of the city if you'd like," he offered.

"Deal." I stepped back as Damon opened the passenger side door for me. As I stepped into the Jeep, I heard my name again.

"Effie! Wait!"

Damon and I turned our heads towards the sound of the familiar voice. Sam was running across the parking lot and was nearly out of breath when he reached us.

"Well, how nice; did Liz call you too? Nothing like a family-fucking-reunion." I snarled. I hadn't even had my feet on Georgia soil for ten minutes and I was already in a shit storm.

"Nice to see you, too," Sam said. "I just flew out to hell and back looking for you."

"Where exactly is hell? I know of a town named Hell in Michigan."

"Are you serious? I went to L.A., only to find out you were on a flight here."

"Sam, why are you looking for me?"

"I need your help!"

"Help for what? You don't have my phone number?"

Sam blushed, and stammered. "I do, and I did call. I guess it didn't go through because you were in flight. I thought you just weren't returning my calls," he said, shrugging.

"Anyway, I've been called in from DC to work a huge murder case here in Atlanta. There have been a total of six bodies in the last month, but only three murder scenes. I really don't want to give you a whole lot of details right now, but there is a reason that they're calling this a federal crime. Can you touch something for me? I need your gift. I'm sorry it's so abrupt, but this all happened so fast and we're stumped. We have no suspects."

"Federal?"

"Yes, I'll explain more later; can you do this please?"

I looked over at Damon, managing to look patient and dumbfounded look at the same time. I couldn't quite explain it, but could definitely feel it.

Damon interjected, "There are no more secrets; go ahead."

"Sam, I haven't done this since I left."

"Can you please just try," Sam begged.

"Okay."

Sam reached in his pocket, pulled out a pair of latex gloves and I slipped them on. Then he pulled out a plastic evidence bag. He handed it to me. Inside was a zip-tie, soiled with blood.

"Evidence bag. You can't open it, but I'm hoping you can get something in spite of the baggie," he apologized.

"I have before," I said. "Remember Reggie's pocket knife?"

"Ah, how could I forget?" he smiled.

I took the evidence bag, held it tight and shut my eyes. At first, it was very cloudy, but then the vision came through soft and bright. This is odd, I thought to myself. A blackened, almost charbroiled, pentagram came to my sight, then the image of a pair of wedding bands and ... I took a breath and almost fainted; it was my sailboat.

"Effie!" Sam called out.

Damon reached around from behind me, catching me around my waist and steadying me. "Are you okay?"

I caught my breath and explained my visions to Sam. "I'm not sure what this all means, but here it is. I see a pentagram; it's dark and charred, and then get a vision of wedding bands. At first, they're interlocked and then they're broken."

"How did that scare you?"

"That didn't."

"Then what did?"

"I saw the back of my sailboat."

"Are you sure it's yours?" Damon asked.

"It said Franciska across the back," I said.

We all stood still for a moment and no one said a word. Even Sam was stunned; he wasn't sure what to say. I could hardly believe that I was standing outside an airport in Atlanta with Sam on one side and Damon on the other. What were the odds of that happening, let alone a vision of my very own sailboat being linked to what Sam was calling a series of brutal murders?

"Sam, what does this mean?"

"Well, I think we have a serial killer here in Atlanta. We have a total of six bodies, but only three crime scenes. Each scene consists of a male and female, both of whom are married, but not to each other. They are completely nude, with both wrists sliced from wrist to elbow. They're zip-tied to one another by their wrists and their feet.

"Each body has a pentagram branded into the chest. The government thinks this is a hate crime of some kind and they called me in to investigate. When I saw the scenes and the pentagrams, I thought that maybe you could help me. But your boat, Effie? Why your boat?"

"Sam, I don't know why, and I'm a bit intrigued as well as kinda horrified. But this is supposed to be my vacation, and I feel completely bombarded at the moment. I will help you as much as I can in the next two weeks, but for today and tonight, I just want to go home and rest. Can you call me tomorrow?"

"Home, huh?"

"Tomayto/tomahto, Sam. I'm tired and this is NOT quite the greeting I expected. Can you do that much for me? Oh, and nice to see you're doing well; I wondered what you were up to."

"Okay, Effie; I'll call you tomorrow. You drive safe now."

Sam walked away and Damon still had that same look on his face. Then he spoke. "That was very intense, Effie. You have a talent that is almost indescribable."

I shrugged, "Maybe you should drive all the way back. Suddenly I'm really, really tired."

"Sure, no problem. Do you want to talk about this?"

"Not really."

We got into the Jeep and were soon out on Interstate 95. Because it was an early Sunday morning, the traffic wasn't that bad, after all. It was very quiet for the longest time, as if we weren't quite sure what words to say next. I have to admit, I was completely unprepared for this.

"Well, I guess I don't have to ask if you've seen Sam anymore."

"You were wondering?"

"Yeah, we all were. He left a few weeks after you, and no one had seen or heard from him!"

"Sooo, were you thinking Sam was out in L.A. with me?

"No, absolutely not; why would you insinuate I was thinking that?"

"I wasn't; it's just that you mentioned he left two weeks after me."

"Yeah, but what would that have to do with anything?

Shut the fuck up, I told myself. Damon doesn't know that anything ever went on between me and Sam. Don't give him any ideas.

"Nothing, I suppose I'm just tired and you know how I get when I'm around loads of people."

I felt awkward, like we had just met.

"Can we change the subject for a bit? After all, this is a long ride to the hotel."

"What hotel?" Damon asked.

"The one I'm staying in. That one!"

"Bzzzt, sorry. I have my pool house all set up for you; Liz cancelled your reservations."

"That match-making bitch."

"She meant well; besides, I'm staying in the main house now. Unfortunately, everyone now knows it's mine. Dona redecorated the pool house; I'm sure you'll love it."

"I suppose; just as long as you don't think that your painting wooed me and I'm about to drop my pants."

"Why, Effie, you have gotten a bit more brazen since you've been gone."

"Yeah, well a murder will do that to you."

Silence took over again as I began to recall the events that took place on my lovely boat. A boat made of love from my grandfather's hands. A boat where Damon and I made love, and a boat that almost took my life.

"How is she?"

"Who?"

"My boat!" I squeaked.

"You can see for yourself. I made all the arrangements to have her docked at the house, and Autumn and Brea cleaned her up nice for you. They missed you! Autumn said something about how you kicked her ass doing shots, and she's been practicing while you've been gone."

"Really? That's hilarious. What made her think I was coming back?"

"Effie, we all knew you were coming back; we had visions!"

Damon and I started to laugh. It was almost like old times. I felt a lot more relaxed now, and had to admit that I felt comfortable about returning to the pool house and having my boat a stone's throw away. I wondered what extravagant thing that Dona had done to the pool house; she was that way, after all.

"How is Dona?" I asked.

"Great. The lady who owned the boutique passed away and left it to her. Hard to believe she had no children. Dona has invested all her time into it and loves it. She's seldom at the restaurant."

"Does that bitch, Cali, still work there?"

Damon laughed. "Yeah; she has been after my ass since you left, thanks a lot!"

"You're welcome." I glanced sideways at Damon. He was handsomer than I remembered, if that was possible. He was focused on the road, giving me a chance to study his profile. He took his hand off the wheel and reached over for mine. I grasped it, interlocking fingers with his and giving his hand a squeeze.

It was a bad move. The vision I had when I held the evidence bag with the zip-tie returned. Only now, in addition to my beloved Franciska, Damon was also in the vision, standing with his back to me while large dark clouds gathered on the horizon and then swept in, covering the boat and ending the vision.

About Rose Marie

I've always loved reading, romance, mystery and crime solving. Funny how all that came together to allow me to write a book about–romance, mystery and crime solving.

The mother of four, three kids and a husband, I also work full-time, surf part-time (not really, but it sounded good, didnt it?) and cheer my family on from the sidelines of football, soccer and life. But I took time out this past year to write a book, my first. It's something I've wanted to do forever. And now I have.

www.ingramcontent.com/pod-product-compliance
Lightning Source LLC
Chambersburg PA
CBHW070649180626
46817CB00006B/2289